# MOONDOG

# MOONDOG

## Henry Garfield

St. Martin's Press • New York

Design by Junie Lee

ISBN 0-312-11857-0

First Edition: March 1995
10 9 8 7 6 5 4 3 2 1

*to Polaris Michelle Garfield*
*and Rigel Stuart Garfield,*
*the lights of my life*

The author wishes to thank his agent, Barbara Markowitz, for taking on an embryonic project and providing assistance beyond anything he had a right to expect. The board members of the Normal Heights Community Development Corporation of San Diego generously provided use of their computer equipment. Thanks to all those too numerous to name who read early drafts of this work and offered constructive criticism and information. Special thanks to Kate Garfield, the author's sister, and David Lemmo, the author's friend, whose unwavering enthusiasm for the project meant more than they can know.

# Author's Note

The setting for this story is the mountain and high desert region surrounding the unincorporated town of Julian, California, in San Diego County. Names of actual geographic locations have not been changed; the physical picture of the area described on these pages is presented as essentially accurate. In places, it has been altered in small ways to fit the narrative.

*Moondog* is a work of fiction. The events in this tale are fictional events. The characters in this story are made up and spring wholly from the author's imagination. Names are either fabricated or used fictitiously. Any resemblance of any character herein to any actual person, living or dead, is coincidental.

The story takes place in 1989. Though care has been taken to preserve the 29-day synodic month—the period between full Moons—the dates of the lunar cycle for that year do not correspond to the dates in the story. The author begs the reader's indulgence for this small inaccuracy.

# MOONDOG

# Chapter One

THE HORROR BEGAN several months before Halloween—in early July, just past the Fourth, on the night of the lunar eclipse. Everyone went up to the top of Mount Laguna, by the old NASA tracking station, because that was the best vantage point from which to see the blood-red Moon, fully dipped in the Earth's shadow, rise out of the murk over the Imperial Valley.

Carloads of skywatchers streamed up Interstate 8 from San Diego; some had telescopes and got there in the late afternoon, hours before moonrise, to grab an optimum spot. Most of the Julian people came because it was close, and offered the best viewing spot in the area. On the west coast the Moon would rise in mid-eclipse, an event rare enough to draw even those normally uninterested in celestial phenomena. At just over six thousand feet, Mount Laguna is not the highest mountain in San Diego County, but it is the most accessible, and looks directly out over the desert to the east, parts of which lie below sea level. The road that runs along its crest is called the Sunrise Highway, but on this evening it was the Moon the crowd had come to see.

A group of fifteen or so intrepid adventurers made the trip—twenty-one miles more or less south and two thousand feet up—by bicycle. The Laguna and Cuyamaca mountains are bicycling paradise for anyone who likes up-and-down terrain and the pleasurable sting of crisp, thin air in the lungs. Mount Laguna, eclipse or no, is one of the area's most popular destinations, and Stafford Emerson, proprietor of the Julian Bicycle Emporium, led a small group of enthusiasts up there regularly.

The little store at the high point on the road, adjacent to the tiny Mount Laguna post office and less than a mile from the peak itself, did a brisk business that evening, much of it from its beer cooler. At the wind-whipped summit, from which one could watch the sun set into the ocean fifty miles to the west, an atmosphere of revelry prevailed as dusk approached. It was party time, and no one would later remember hearing or seeing anything dangerously out of the ordinary.

The couple had been arguing, witnesses would say, though not especially violently. As the fully eclipsed Moon rose out of the haze above the desert into the company of the brighter stars coming out against the deep blue background, the young woman had gone into some sort of ritual chant, a song to the spirit of the Moon she had maybe learned in some college class on pagan religions; embarrassed and annoyed, the young man had told her to shut up. When she didn't, he relocated to a nearby rock where he could enjoy the eclipse in relative quiet. But that wasn't what they had been arguing about. Lost in the grandeur of the event or in her mantra or *something,* she had sat down squarely on top of a beavertail cactus, and he had made the mistake of laughing at her.

Stung both by the spines and her boyfriend's insensitivity, she lashed out at him, and although he tried to apologize, laughter kept bubbling up and getting in the way. Even after he realized that she really was angry and in pain and quite insistent that it was NOT FUNNY AT ALL, and after he managed to stop laughing and began to apologize in earnest, realizing that the future of this evening and perhaps many evenings to come depended on his skill at contrition, she was still mad. So mad that she stomped wordlessly off into the night, away from the eclipsed Moon and the crowd gathered there to watch it, and into the darkness of the Cleveland National Forest.

She'll be back, he said to himself. He opened another beer, and settled down to watch the eclipse. When she didn't return right away, he figured that she had probably found a secluded spot and was now bent over, her jeans around her knees, trying to remove some of the spines that had penetrated her fair skin in such an inconvenient place. Despite himself, he chuckled at the image.

The total phase of the eclipse ended about an hour after moonrise. The edge of the darkened Moon popped suddenly out of the Earth's shadow into full illumination. People cheered; a few of them howled. Some would say later that a few of the howls were pretty good, and yes, people screamed, but it seemed to be all in keeping with the festive mood atop the mountain.

Did any of the screams sound, well, alarming? they were asked. Not at the time, apparently. Hell, it was a party.

The illuminated part of the Moon grew steadily larger, the party went on, and only when some of the amateur astronomers began packing up their telescopes and people began to move their cars and bicycles for the descent did the young man begin to worry seriously about the whereabouts of his date.

By the time the red shadow of the Earth fell completely from the face of its cosmic companion, only a few cars remained on the mountaintop, and the young man, whose name was John Reese and who worked at Julian Elementary School as a bus driver and custodian, was frantic. No one had seen her. He drove to the little store, which was now closed, and from one of the pay phones outside managed to reach a dispatcher at the sheriff's department in San Diego. The dispatcher woke up one of the local deputies, and by the small hours of the night two sheriff's patrols had been joined by crews from the U.S. Forest Service, the California Department of Forestry, and the Mount Laguna, Julian, Pine Valley, and Cuyamaca fire departments, their high-powered flashlights probing the darkness between the tall, thick trunks of the pine trees.

It was midmorning before they found the young woman's body and the sheriff's homicide detail was called in.

At first the detectives thought the unfortunate girl might have been attacked by a mountain lion. But such attacks were extremely rare, and a Forest Service ranger pointed out that the wounds, though apparently inflicted by sharp objects akin to teeth and claws, were inconsistent with a mauling. The attacker—whoever or whatever it was—had gone unerringly for the woman's jugular, killing her in the most direct and purposeful fashion.

They talked to many people over the next few days, people who had been on the mountain that night and people who had not, but the officers really had no leads. A thorough search of the area revealed no weapon, no torn clothes, no signs of a squatter's encampment. After more than a week of unrelieved frustration, the sheriff's department held a press conference and admitted that in the absence of witnesses the case was probably unsolvable.

Her name was Brandy Allen. She was a local girl who had graduated at the top of her class from Julian High School two years before, had starred in school plays and on the girl's basketball team and was now studying psychology at San Diego State. She had been homecoming queen and Miss Julian in her senior year, and of late had been seen on weekends behind the old-fashioned fountain at the Julian Drug Store, her blond hair bound in a thick braid that nearly reached her waist, with a smile for the tourists who braved the crunch for a sundae or a malt. She was smart and pretty and polite, didn't do drugs and didn't sleep around, and everyone knew she was going to be somebody. The town of four thousand souls united in outrage that one of their shining lights had been so brutally taken from them, and had there been a suspect there might also have been an old-fashioned lynching. Julian, after all, has a tradition of such things. Her murder was still the talk of the town a month later, at the time of the next full Moon.

# Chapter Two

MUCH OF THIS story was related to me, during and after the fact, by a man who became my friend—and that in itself was remarkable, for Cyrus "Moondog" Nygerski had few friends. I suppose we were drawn together because we were both misfits, we were both loners, and we were both, for a time and probably because of our solitary, outlaw images, suspects in the wave of murders that swept over the Julian area during the late summer and early fall of 1989. Yet records at the Warner Honor Camp and the employee roster at Bucky's Barbecue clearly show that I could not have arrived in Julian until three days after the lunar eclipse, which I watched through a crowded east-facing window in the darkened wooden barracks. The bastards wouldn't even let us go outside to watch it. I guess their reason was pretty obvious—it would have been a great escape opportunity.

Nygerski did not tell me where he was that night. No one kept track of Moondog's whereabouts, and that was just the way he liked it.

I was not to meet this singular individual, however, until I'd been in Julian for several weeks. The first person I met after hitchhiking the twenty-odd miles to town was Arnold Cousins, my new boss.

He was alone in the place when I entered, standing behind the high counter with his back to me. I let the screen door slam loudly behind me to announce my presence. He turned around and scowled. I stared right back at him. I was used to unfriendly faces.

"We don't open till eleven," he said.

"Are you Mr. Cousins?" I asked, pleasantly enough, I thought.

"Yeah. Who're you?"

I laid the small duffel bag that contained all my worldly possessions on one of the checkerboard-cloth-covered tables and advanced toward the counter. "My name's Joe Acton. Ted sent me. Said you had a job."

Cousins set down the beer glass and the towel he had been wiping it with, and looked me over. He was fairly tall, with short-cropped brown hair and a muscular build shown to great advantage through a tight-fitting black T-shirt. I suppose he thought he looked intimidating—but I had just spent most of a year being intimidated by professionals. I just stood there, looking back at him, waiting for him to speak.

"Ted called yesterday," he said. "About you. Said you were a good worker." He paused, presumably for effect. "I hope you are, 'cause a lot of these fuckers from that honor camp don't last too goddamn long."

"I'll earn what you pay me," I said, and flashed him a smile, which he did not return.

"You bet your ass you will," he said. "Or you'll be outta here so fast it'll make your head spin. There's always more where you came from."

I gritted my teeth behind my placid expression and said nothing. It was a job, after all, and I was lucky to get it, for I had no real skills in the legitimate world. I had to start somewhere, and it might as well be in Julian.

I had spent the past four or five years being an asshole—doing burglaries of unoccupied homes up and down the California coast and living off the money I got from selling the stereos, jewelry, televisions, and silverware I stole to patrons of professional thieves who got two or three times as much money for the stuff from law-abiding citizens at swap meets. I never meant to hurt anyone—I'm terrified of physical pain myself, and avoid it whenever possible—and I certainly never meant to get caught, but this overamped kid I was doing a job with in Oceanside took a baseball bat to the head of a homeowner who surprised us by being home, then testified against me and the other two guys in exchange for leniency. I ended up at Warner, lucky that it wasn't the slam, with a crew boss right out of *Cool Hand Luke,* a couple of even meaner co-convicts, and a heartfelt desire to go straight once I got out.

What jobs I'd had during my life of crime—and I mean straight jobs, not dealing dope or playing midnight auto—had been strictly for show and hadn't lasted long. The freedom of being an outlaw had given me a piss-poor attitude toward authority. I'd show up late, work as hard as I felt like, and bail at the first hint of a reprimand. Working was too much of a drag on my freedom.

It was the freedom I loved most about being a criminal—the absolute sense that no one, unless he had a gun, could tell me what to do and make it stick. The hours and the pay were great. I rented a nice place in Cardiff-by-the-Sea, with a humongous deck overlooking the ocean, which I shared with two other guys in the same line of work. Since our jobs were usually at night, we went surfing or sailing or driving around whenever we wanted. There were girls, and trips to Baja, and there was always grass, and crystal and occasionally coke. Money was never a problem. I pitied the poor suckers who lived all around me, who slaved away in coats and ties from nine to five and battled the freeway traffic for an hour in the morning and an hour at night. Of course, when I had my freedom taken away for the better part of a year, and five years' probation tacked on top of that, my attitude changed.

"Come on back in the kitchen," Cousins said. "That's where you'll be workin'."

In the kitchen, where everything was coated with a layer of grease and the smell of cooked meat would linger until the place burned down or was bombed, my boss explained my duties, which consisted of cooking ribs and scrubbing pots. "Can you start tonight?" he asked me.

Of course I could. You could see from one end of the town to the other, and I didn't know anybody in it. I sure as hell didn't have anything better to do.

"You got a place to stay?"

I shook my head. "I just got out of the honor camp this morning."

"I know a place," he said. "Rent's cheap—I'll take it out of your checks till it's paid. Come on." He started toward the door, then stopped, and looked at me hard.

"You ain't into drugs, are you?"

"No. Well, I drink beer from time to time."

"Shit, I don't care about beer. I don't care if you smoke a little weed, even—after work, that is. I just don't wanna find out that you're into that crystal meth shit. Lot of guys from out there at Warner, that's the first thing they do when they get out. Get themselves a noseful of poison."

"I never touch the stuff," I said.

"Good. 'Cause I believe in giving a guy a chance, you know? People make mistakes, they do their time, they deserve another shot. I've hired guys out of Warner who've done real well here. Hired a lot of losers, too."

I said nothing.

"You know why you got this job?" he continued. "You got the job because the last fuck I hired was dealing crystal right out the back door of my kitchen." He stared at me for emphasis. "He's now watching pigeons from a ninth-floor window in downtown San Diego. You get my drift?"

I nodded. I'd spent a few nights in that jail myself, before they moved me out to Warner. But my boss didn't have to worry—crystal wasn't my drug of choice. I'm kind of naturally wired, anyway, and all the stuff really does for me is make me not eat. A lot of people like it, though, especially in Julian, I was to find out. Some locals call it "Crystal Mountain" because of all the labs hidden out in the woods, and all the tweakers who call the place home. But I was in Julian to make a fresh start, and I vowed to leave the stuff alone.

I want to say just one more thing before I get on with the story, and that's this: I never stole to support any kind of drug habit. That's bullshit put out by politicians trying to get elected, that drugs cause crime. I got into burglary because it was easier than working for a living and because I couldn't get fired, not because I needed money for dope. There are plenty of yuppies driving Porsches and working in high-rises who are worse substance abusers than anyone I ever met in my walk of life.

But, like I say, that life is behind me now. The place my boss found for me to live turned out to be a one-room cabin in a little cluster of no-questions-asked bungalows called Sleepy Hollow, less than a mile from town. We were met at the gate to the main house by a short, big-breasted woman of Hispanic descent, whose mouth muscles seemed incapable of producing a smile. Behind her, in the yard, two young boys in camouflage uniforms ran back and forth, shooting each other with plastic machine guns.

The woman, whose name was Cindy, explained that she and her husband Derek ran the place for an absentee owner "down the hill" in exchange for reduced rent. The owner came up on weekends, collected the rents from them, and (supposedly) did all the repairs himself.

I let Cousins do most of the talking; he was, after all, fronting me the money for rent and deposit and signing the application as my only reference. Besides, the woman was all but ignoring me, except to throw me sidelong, suspicious glances while my boss answered her questions.

I filled out the rental application at the desk in the large living room, which faced out a picture window toward the fenced yard and the highway. As I was finishing up, having glossed over my checkered past as best I could, the door opened and a squat, thickset man in a California Department of Forestry uniform entered.

His dark hair was slicked back from his forehead. He wore tinted glasses, and one cheek bulged with a plug of chewing tobacco. The man nodded in recognition to my boss, cast a quick, dark look in my direction, and turned to his wife.

"Honey, call Haley for me, willya? That bitch in number five is moaning about her stove again." He removed his glasses, and stuck them in a shirt pocket.

Cindy's shoulders sagged. "He's not gonna be happy," she said.

"Just call him, okay? Have him bring a new one up this weekend, or whatever. I'm sick of listening to her." He turned his attention back to my boss. "Hi, Arnie," he said. "What've you brought me this time?"

"This here's Joe Acton, Derek. He's working for me, starting tonight. Joe, this is Derek. He'll collect your rent and take care of any problems."

"Within reason," Derek growled. We shook hands; his grip was firm, but the look in his steely eyes was anything but friendly. "Don't believe I've seen you before," he said to me.

"I'm new in town."

"That so?" His eyes didn't move from mine.

"Yeah," I said uncomfortably, as he continued to stare.

"What brings you to Julian?" It wasn't a casual question.

"You know. Work." Weakly, I tried a smile. It was lost on him.

"Plenty of jobs in the city."

"Maybe," I said evenly, "but this was the first one offered to me."

He didn't like me, that much was plain. And I was to encounter this attitude of suspicion and distrust wherever I went in Julian during the coming weeks. It wasn't until my second day at work, where the head chef wouldn't talk to me and the waitresses wouldn't return my smiles, that I learned of the death of Brandy Allen, and that my chilly reception was more than a pronounced case of small-town xenophobia.

There were something like twelve cabins at Sleepy Hollow, unevenly scattered around a wooded glen filled with stacks of fence sections, paint cans, and dead appliances. My dwelling had no screens, badly needed a coat of paint, and the bathroom in the back was at least a foot lower than the kitchenette up front. I was to discover that most of the cabins were in similar condition. The place was the gateway to Julian for those of marginal means, and some tenants had apparently lived there for years. Rent was cheap; maintenance was mostly an illusion. It was a haven for hangers-on to the rickety economic ladder of rural California—people like me, a whisker away from homelessness, one misstep from the joint. For me, it became home, and a front-row seat for the drama that had already begun to unfold.

# Chapter Three

THE WHITE 1953 Ford pickup truck belonging to Cyrus "Moondog" Nygerski kicked up sheets of rainwater as it negotiated the curves a mile or so west of Julian's small business district. Its driver, a man of indeterminate age whose lined face lay half-hidden behind a black handlebar mustache, tapped his fingers on the steering wheel and hummed along with a tune on the tape player by Crosby, Stills, Nash, and Young. The name of the song was "Country Girl, I Think You're Pretty."

Nygerski was on his way back from Jacumba, an impoverished little town on the Mexican border east of Tecate, where he sometimes did some work, and the road was wet because a line of summer thunderstorms had that afternoon paraded over the mountains. All along the route he'd followed the clouds—colossal, billowy towers with flat, blackened bottoms—and he'd driven through several three-minute deluges that would provide psychological if not much physical relief from the area's drought, now in its fourth year. He'd taken the route over the top of Mount Laguna, rather than down through Cuyamaca Park, because although it was three miles longer and almost half a mile higher it offered by far the better view of the march of the thunderheads as they rose up from the desert to drop their loads. It was the first time it had rained in months.

Now it was night, and he was glad. He always liked to come through Julian under cover of darkness. Although Nygerski had lived in nearby Mesa Grande for nearly four years, and his byline regularly appeared in the *Julian Nugget*, very few people in the area knew him well enough to connect the face to the name, and fewer still had been out to his place, which was several miles from pavement and had no street address. He was known to a handful of other outlaw types out in the desert, on both sides of the border, and he had a few friends in L.A. and one or two he still kept in touch with back in Boston, but he preferred not to have his past follow him to the area where he had chosen to live, in his own way and on his own terms. Thus he traveled incognito, in the shadows of public life, a stranger to all but a carefully selected few.

The rain had stopped, and the clouds, stretched thin by the wind, were scurrying away from the tops of the mountains. A fuzzed Moon, two days short of full, strained to shine through. Moondog, less than half an hour from home and thinking about the one cold beer he'd left in his refrigerator most of a week ago, caught glimpses of his namesake from time to time in his rearview mirror, or out one of the side windows as he wheeled smoothly around the curves.

But home was not in his immediate future on this night, for as he rounded a particularly sharp descending curve, fate intervened. There was a car there on the gravel shoulder, a white Volvo with its hazard lights flashing, and a woman wearing some sort of jumpsuit standing beside it. She waved at him, and he stopped.

The air still felt moist, and the wind whipped at his shirt as he got out. He touched his hat, a tacky Stetson with glittering plastic studs he'd once won at the Del Mar Fair, to make sure it didn't blow away. "It just died," the woman said. "It hates it when it's wet."

"Does it turn over at all?"

"Yeah. It just won't start."

"Let me try." Moondog opened the door and slid behind the wheel. Both the car and the woman smelled of tobacco. He turned the key; the engine revved but didn't fire. He pressed the gas pedal to the floor and held it there. There was a little more promise in the noise, and a couple times it almost caught and held, but after about thirty seconds it began to sputter and cough, and he gave up.

"It does this every time it rains," the woman said from outside the window. "It hasn't rained for so long, I haven't bothered to get it fixed."

Moondog got out. "Hang on a second," he said. As the woman watched, he got a can of WD-40 from his truck, popped the hood of the Volvo, removed the filter cap, and sprayed the stuff in and around the carburetor.

"What's wrong with it?" she asked him.

He looked up, and caught her eyes directly for the first time. The effect was startling. They were cat's eyes, yellow-brown and glinty despite the darkness, and Moondog realized that her eyes, and not her clothes, were responsible for the feline impression he'd had at the first sight of her. The woman was really quite pretty, notwithstanding the ridiculous way she was dressed—in tight leopard-skin-pattern pants that ended just below the knees, and a matching, long-sleeved top. Something a teenager would wear, he thought, though her face was closer to thirty than twenty. It was framed by light brown hair that fell to her shoulders in thick curls; she had high cheekbones and thin lips that seemed to curl slightly upward at the corners. She

1 5

clutched her elbows to her sides, cold in the wind.

"Sounds like you're not getting enough gas to the engine," he said. "Put the gas pedal all the way to the floor and try it."

She got into the car and did what he said. The car revved, caught, sputtered, caught again, sputtered again.

"Wait," he called. "Okay, try it now." He stuck his finger into the choke, holding it open. "Keep trying until I tell you to stop."

This time it caught and held.

He put the hood down and she smiled at him gratefully, her narrow shoulders sagging with relief. "Nothing to it," he said, holding up the can of WD-40. "Here, keep this. And take it in for a tune-up when you get the chance."

"Thanks so much," she said, still behind the wheel. "By the way, my name's Patsy Kittredge."

"Pleased to meet you."

"Do you have a name?" she asked, after a moment of awkward silence. "Or do I remember you forever as the Stranger in the Night?"

"It's Cyrus," he said, and hesitated a moment before adding, "but my friends call me Moondog."

Her cat eyes widened. "You're the Moondog who writes those weird columns in the paper?"

"I beg your pardon?" he said, in mock anger.

"Well, I don't mean weird, exactly. Let's just say . . . distinctive."

"Okay," Moondog agreed. "Let's say that."

"It *is* you! You're real."

"I'm standing here, aren't I?"

"Well, I mean, I never thought you were," she said, embarrassed. "I mean, I thought . . . I guess I thought you were a pseudonym. I mean, who has a name like Cyrus Moondog Nygerski?"

"Me."

"How come I've never met you before?"

"I kind of don't get out much. I'm not very social."

She smiled again—a nice smile, catlike, like everything else about her. "Neither am I," she said. "Although I'm trying to find a few new friends. Listen, the least I can do is offer you a beer or something. I live right down this road here. You want to come over for a few minutes?"

Much later that same evening, they lay in bed together underneath the high ceiling of the bedroom in her small, cozy cabin a mile from the main highway. She lived in the woods on a narrow road utterly unlit by streetlights, owing to the proximity of the Mount Palomar Observatory. The trees overhanging the roof dripped irregularly, the drops echoing softly in the wood. In the canyon beyond the main windows, the light of the gibbous Moon played on gray-white boulders and the near black of evergreen trees that marched shoulder-to-shoulder down toward the canyon floor until they disappeared into the darkness.

Moondog ran a hand gently over her body, admiring it in the light from the candle she had placed on the table beside the bed. Her lines were good, if subtle; she had small, well-formed breasts, a flat stomach unstretched by childbirth, and narrow, canoe-like hips. He admired her place, too; its wooden interior was filled with bookshelves (he'd checked out the titles earlier, while she was in the bathroom), and a stone fireplace built into one wall added to the earthiness. There was a real cat, all black, with eyes like hers, which ducked behind a piece of furniture every time he looked at it. The living room was dominated by a framed portrait of Janis Joplin, whom Moondog had once met, but he did not tell Patsy this. He was not the sort to give away details of his past, not for free, anyway, and without being asked.

"Do you really believe all those things you write?" she murmured. "Or are you just putting everybody on?"

"What things?" he said languidly. Their lovemaking had been unhurried and mutually satisfying; conversation was dessert. They had talked earlier, and for hours—mostly about her—and the last Grateful Dead tape Moondog had selected was still playing softly on the stereo.

"Well, like you said, all drugs should be legalized and sold over the counter, in stores. And advertised too, like beer, with bimbos and everything."

"Absolutely," he said. "What's the difference between cigarettes and crack? Both kill you. You should have the freedom to choose your poisons."

"And what about the column where you said all the RVs in America should be gathered together and blown up?"

"Wouldn't that be something? I've always been amazed at how money can't buy taste. I'd like to blow them up myself."

She laughed, and curled a finger through his dark hair, which was almost as long as hers, but straighter. He smiled back at her, the thick mustache twitching ticklishly, the faint network of crow's feet around his dark eyes deepening. He had an angular face, with hollow cheeks and a somewhat pointed chin. His chest was nearly hairless, and he was skinny and agile-looking, like the media image of the male rock star. Perhaps part of his immediate attraction to Patsy was that they possessed similar body types.

"You know," she said, "I know your editor. At the *Nugget*."

"Gunn? Nice enough guy."

"Yeah. He wants to fuck me, I think."

"Oh. Well, what's holding you back?"

"Come on." She drew the sheet around herself, and put her hand over his, which was on her left breast. "For one thing, he's married."

"And that bothers you?"

"Not necessarily. But with him it does. It's hard to say. He's just . . . not my type, I guess. He tries way too hard to impress me. Besides, it'd be all over town in an hour. He already told one of my students he loved me."

"Students? You're a teacher?"

"Mm-hmm. At the high school."

"Bet half the boys in your classes want to fuck you, too."

"Oh, stop." But he felt her tense against him, and knew there was some truth in what he said.

"So," she asked him, "how did you get the name 'Moon-dog'?"

"Not telling," he said. And he twirled his tongue in her ear and moved his hand down toward the warm spot between her thighs. She sighed pleasurably, and did not ask him again.

He left before morning, with enough darkness remaining for the drive home. She slept soundly as he dressed, but when he stroked her hair she awakened, and he kissed her good-bye. "What do I call you?" she muttered sleepily. "Cyrus or Moon-dog?"

"You can't call me," he said. "I haven't got a phone."

She smiled, her eyes closed. "See you again, lover?"

"I'll drop by sometime," he said.

# Chapter Four

JULIAN WAS FOUNDED on gold lust. At least two dozen mines operated in the area during the years between the first strike, in 1869, and the turn of the century, by which time most of the fun was over. In its heyday, Julian was a raucous, bawdy frontier town, every bit as lawless and violent and drunken and sexually uninhibited as the more famous settlements of the Mother Lode country up north, which preceded it by two decades and thus secured their place in legend. Casual death from the barrel of a gun or from the neck of a bottle of overstrong spirits was routine, and the town, despite or perhaps because of the subsequent self-conscious bottling of its own history, has never quite lost this streak of violence.

I learned what I know of the area's history through conversations with Moondog and others, and visits to the Julian Library, itself a conspicuous monument to the past. The building was an old schoolhouse that had been renovated and transported to the business district, where it perched on a hillside looking down at the shops on Main Street and across to a higher hillside where

Julian's dead were buried in San Diego County's second-oldest cemetery. Barely big enough to house the collected works of Shakespeare, Steinbeck, and Seuss, the inside of the library was half given over to a permanent exhibit on the mining days. The town's storied past had generated a fair number of books, some of them low-quality paperbacks put together for the quickie tourist buck, but others rather informative. Julian in the 1870s had a population rivaling San Diego's (which is to say both had a few thousand people), and at one time the town was considered as a site for the county seat. It had saloons, whorehouses, an outmanned and outgunned police force, and even a jail. The jail is still there. Something of a curiosity, it sits on a side street near the library, a dark, dank, concrete hole with a missing door and one small window. Tourists peek in on most weekends, and sometimes kids play there, but only on Halloween is it ever really used.

One of the mines is still operating, too—at $4.50 per person for a half-hour tour. Three blocks behind Main Street, at the edge of the town site proper, a dirt road winds its way through the trees to a parking lot beside the opening of the shaft. Nowadays the mine's owners take money from curious visitors rather than out of the hills. Oh, there's still gold in the ground, but after 1900 it was no longer profitable to get most of it out, though a few historians dispute this. Nonetheless, the mines began closing, one after another, and the town turned to growing fruit trees and later to picking the fruits of weekend day trippers from San Diego and Los Angeles looking to soak up a few hours of what they imagined to be a simpler life.

Today, Julian is dominated by restaurants, apple-pie bakeries, and stores with names like The Golddigger, Yesteryears, and Stagecoach Crossing. The town, whose population has not significantly increased in a century, has struggled hard to maintain its Old West look despite its commercial intentions, and succeeded in 1976 in getting its antiquated architectural guidelines written into county law. Thus you will see no golden arches, no cubist storefronts, no building motif or sign that is not in some way a throwback to the mining days, when mules stood tied to posts outside saloons, and men were shot dead in the streets.

I knew nothing of this on my first night in Sleepy Hollow, more than three weeks before Moondog would meet Patsy Kittredge in the rare summer rain, and less than one week after Brandy Allen died. But it relates, in a way, to why I slept so badly. I got off work about eleven, two hours after the restaurant closed, and walked down the hill toward home, dead tired. The Moon, nearing last quarter, had just risen over the tall pines on the ridge above the town, and cast eerie shadows ahead of me as I placed one foot in front of the other, letting gravity do the work. The stars were glimmering pinpoints in the clear, dry air, and though the power of the Moon had abated, the town was still frightened; there was no one else out walking, nor did any cars pass.

My little cabin had a bed, a stove, a refrigerator, a bar that served as a kitchen table, and not much more. I'd added a digital clock radio, an overstuffed chair rescued from storage at the restaurant, a small bedside table, and a backpack full of clothes. I opened a beer, took a shower in the closet-sized bathroom, and was under the covers with the light out before the beer was even empty. It wasn't until then that I noticed the sound.

It was metallic, and aggravatingly regular, as if someone were pounding the world's largest or most stubborn railroad spike. Chink, chink, chink—I lay there for at least an hour, tired though I was, unable to shut out the sound and fall asleep. Either somebody had a set of cast-iron wind chimes, or a new and obnoxious kind of clock, or some piece of metal out in the appliance graveyard was repeatedly banging into another. I couldn't imagine why anyone would be up at that hour making that noise deliberately.

Finally I got up and turned on the radio, to an oldies station, and dozed off sometime between the beginning and the end of "Closer to Home," by Grand Funk Railroad. When I opened my eyes again, the clock said 4:11, and the station was playing static. I switched it off, and discovered that the tapping had ceased.

It started up again sometime around seven, which is when it woke me from a deep snooze. Sunlight streamed into the cabin's unshaded windows. Since additional sleep seemed out of the question, I got up, stumbled over to the stove, and put on some water for instant coffee, which, aside from beer and a quart of milk, was the only thing resembling food I had in the house. I'd be eating my meals at the restaurant until I got paid.

I'm one of those people who's nonfunctional in the morning until that first cup of coffee hits the brain. Been that way since I was fourteen. I sat on the bed, staring stupidly into the sunlight, listening to the tapping sound, regular as a heartbeat, wondering what the fuck it was. Midway through the second cup, curiosity got the better of morning sleepiness, and I ventured outside to check it out.

It seemed to be coming from near one of the lower cabins. Sleepy Hollow lay on the inside of a descending bend in the highway. Most of the cabins, like the one in which I lived, were well back from the road, but the lower three teetered atop a steep embankment, choked by weeds, beneath which the highway wound on its way to Santa Ysabel, Ramona, and the urban flatlands. Around the nearest of these three cabins, the tenants had thrown up a chain-link fence, enclosing a small yard without a blade of grass anywhere in it. The surface—where it could be seen through the accumulated piles of scrap boards, rocks, and metal pans of varying shapes and sizes—was packed mud. A tall wooden structure, which looked as if it could collapse at any moment, took up one corner of the yard. Perhaps it was supposed to be art—I couldn't tell.

A toddler, about a year old and in need of a bath, stood on the doorstep, staring at me as I approached. He was wearing a diaper and nothing else. His small hands clutched a blue plastic hammer. In the middle of all this junk knelt a man with a real hammer, which he brought down with rhythmic regularity on a succession of rocks from the pile in front of him. Chink, chink, chink.

His back was to me, and the little boy did not tell him I was coming, but only continued to stare. The man was tall and whip-thin, wearing only a pair of blue jeans that hung low on his pointed hips. The rocks were the size of baked potatoes; it would take him two or three blows to smash one, and then he'd toss aside the pieces and reach for another, without missing a beat with the hammer. I stood a few feet to the side and watched him work for a minute or two. He showed no signs of slowing down or speeding up; like a wolf on the trail, he seemed capable of keeping up the same methodical pace for hours.

"What are you doing?" I finally asked.

The man turned around. Light brown curls bobbed just above his eyebrows. His beard, which he had apparently been working on for some time, was wispy and unfull despite its length. Streaks of dirt mixed with sweat ran down his hairless, concave chest. He grinned at me with full lips, but there was no humor in the eyes, which were distant and too bright, like those of a fanatic. I could tell in an instant he was a crystal head, a tweaker. You learn to recognize the look.

"Breaking up rocks," he said, as if it were the most natural thing in the world.

"What for?"

The hammer stopped. "To see if there's any gold in 'em."

"And this?" I asked, pointing to the rickety wooden assemblage.

"Sluice," he said, still wearing that damnable grin.

Now I understood why the yard was muddy. The guy was actually trying to run his own backyard gold-mining operation. And he stayed up three quarters of the night doing it. What a wacko, I thought. A character in a Stephen King novel. How long before he goes berserk and kills his whole family?

"You gotten rich yet?" I asked him.

"Not yet," he said. He raised the hammer and—chink, chink, chink—broke another rock.

"Look," I said, and the hammer stopped again. "You kept me up half the night with your pounding. I just moved in here. The guy said it was supposed to be quiet after ten."

For the first time his face took on what I would call an expression—one of genuine surprise. "Was I bothering you?" he asked.

"Yeah."

Just then a woman appeared in the doorway of the cabin, behind the boy. She was barefoot, like the man, and wore a short, summery dress with no sleeves. "Tom," she called, "are you gonna go to the store? We're out of milk."

She looked about sixteen; her face was pale and her eyes had the same faraway look. Jesus, I thought, they were both tweaked. The poor kid was probably lucky if they remembered to feed him and change his diaper once a day.

"Sorry," the man said to me, as he put down his hammer. "I'll try not to keep you awake."

And he did try, I'll give him that. I know from experience it's hard to keep still when that shit's in your system, but he must've

25

done something else with his nervous energy for a while, because I didn't hear his restless, relentless nocturnal hammering for more than a week.

During that time, when I wasn't working, I began to feel out my new surroundings. It was good to be free again, at least in a physical sense; I knew perfectly well that my liberty was being subsidized, at first, by my new employer. I had twenty-five bucks when I left Warner's, and my first two paychecks would go directly to the manager for rent and deposit. My boss had secured my loyalty for the first month by seeing to it that if I didn't show up for work, I didn't eat.

I didn't see much of Derek, whose work sometimes took him away for days at a time. There was a big fire that summer in the Sierra Nevadas, and a lot of the Julian firefighters went up to battle it. He'd been sent as far away as Yellowstone to fight fires, though usually the combustible mix of people, sagebrush, and Santa Ana winds kept the CDF within state boundaries. When he was off on a mission, the management of the Hollow would be left to his wife.

A lot of us at the Hollow lived well away from the economic mainstream, without bank accounts, and paid each month's rent in cash. Since the first often rolled around during the week, and the owner waited until the weekend to collect the rents, it didn't take a genius to figure out that during a span of a few days at the beginning of the month, there was something like three thousand dollars in cash sitting somewhere in the main house. Three grand would buy you a quick ticket out of Sleepy Hollow, or a lot of crystal, depending on your aim in life, and I have to admit that the first time I was in Derek and Cindy's home I glanced around for clues to where they stashed the money. I'm sure some of my fellow tenants entertained the same thought. They were perhaps discouraged by the knowledge that Derek was the sort of guy who would have no qualms whatsoever about blowing away an intruder in the night, and that his kids were into guns, too.

Two cabins occupied the small hill above the main house, and this circular area was the Hollow's social center. A double-ended driveway looped around behind them, and different cars came and went fairly consistently at all hours of the day and night. Many of the visitors came to see Blind Ben, who lived in the cabin farther from the road. Ben, of course, could not see them, but he had a huge assortment of friends, some of whom stayed for days and weeks at a time. He played the guitar—rollicking, foot-stomping stuff, half of which he wrote himself—and on busy tourist weekends he'd sit on a bench in front of the Chevron station on Main Street, banging away and singing, his guitar case open in front of him to collect the coins and dollar bills tossed in by passersby. He had wild hair that snaked and kinked its way eventually to his shoulders, and an enormous bush of a beard—he couldn't see to shave, after all—and looked every bit the ragged street minstrel. I guessed he was about forty, give or take five years or so. Many of his friends were musical, or tried to be; jam sessions that rang out across the complex from his tiny cabin were fairly common. One long-term visitor donated a drum set and, one night, wired on crystal, treated us all to a three-hour rendition of ''Inna Gadda Da Vida,'' with copious improvisation. That particular performance ended abruptly at about two in the morning, when Derek went up there and promised to shove both drumsticks up the guy's butt if he didn't stop immediately.

Sometimes the guests took over the asylum, for Ben, despite or perhaps because of his blindness, was an avid hiker, and knew the mountains around Julian better than most sighted people. For him it did not matter whether it was day or night; armed with only a canteen, a backpack, and a metal walking stick with which to feel for trail markers and the sides of the road, he would embark on days-long forays into the wilderness. Once, in winter, he had been rescued from the woods near the top of Cuyamaca Peak; the snow, he said when he recovered from hypothermia, had covered his familiar markers and he had wandered off the trail and gotten lost. Since then he'd been more careful, but the close brush with death had not dampened his enthusiasm for the outdoors.

The inside of Blind Ben's cabin was, as one might expect, a hole. Although an occasional girlfriend would show an interest in cleaning, no one could have kept up with the refuse left by a pretty much constant stream of visitors. The carpet was a mosaic of cigarette burns and stains from spilled drinks, which was okay, because it could seldom be seen under the ankle-deep layer of newspapers, empty beer bottles, bags of chips, overflowing ashtrays, cassette tape cases, and musical equipment. But the outside of the place was almost pristine. It was kept that way by Stu, who lived in the neighboring cabin and who, for the pleasure of it, took care of the lawn and the landscaping within the perimeter of the circular driveway. He tended an impressive collection of flowers and dwarf trees, and had even installed a gopher-proof old bathtub in which he was raising tomatoes and bell peppers. He'd also constructed a horseshoe court, in front of his cabin facing the main house and the rest of the complex, at which there was a nightly game.

Jim, a quiet sort who rented the cabin at the very end of the row where I lived, and who left early each morning in a brand-new Jeep Renegade and a park ranger uniform for duty on Palomar Mountain, was Stu's primary opponent at pitching the shoes. When it was warm enough, they doffed their shirts to reveal a pair of beer bellies that would have been the envy of many Australians. Stu's live-in girlfriend, Tanya, a blond, five-foot-tall wisp of a girl who kept six cats in a dwelling barely big enough for two adult human beings, collected the cans they tossed to the side and supplied them with fresh ones. Sometimes Tom Keeler, the dude with the backyard gold operation, joined the game, and often visitors from outside the complex showed up as well.

Among the most frequent visitors was a guy named Sven, who hobbled around on metal crutches, or with the aid of one of a collection of homemade walking sticks. He had dark hair, parted in the middle and curled behind his ears, and the kind of blue eyes that seemed to look right through a person, to hold one's gaze against one's will, as a powerful flashlight will do to a deer at night. He could almost hypnotize a person with a stare, and his smile was ghastly. His apparent poverty was a great loss to the profession of orthodontics, for many of his yellowing teeth were in the wrong places in his mouth and pointed forward, giving him an overbite that could have kept a corrective dentist in business for years. A closer look revealed that the two teeth that should have been next to his front top teeth were missing, allowing the canines to move up into a more prominent position. The effect was wolflike and frightening.

Sven's left leg ended just below the knee; he hobbled because his prosthesis fitted him poorly, and he couldn't afford a new one. The canes he made seemed to be his chief hobby; they were usually adorned with feathers, beads, leather thongs, and colorful bandannas. I once watched him cut a piece of manzanita in the woods behind Blind Ben's house, and over the next few days he sanded and polished it with loving care while sitting on Tanya's stoop, methodically drinking the beers she brought from inside. This went on while Stu was away at work, and I wondered if Sven wasn't getting more from Tanya than beer. But when Stu returned, it was old-home week, the game would start up, and Sven would often hang around until late at night, before hobbling off to wherever he lived.

The cabin next to mine was occupied by a huge, armored

tank of a woman named Darlene, who was forever battling Derek (whom she could have rolled easily) about why her stove didn't work right or the fact that the owner hadn't replaced her screens. A Mexican family of about four adults and six kids, most of whom worked at one of the apple orchards, crammed into the cabin on the other side of hers. In the cabin below the gold mine, at the back of the complex, three party girls just out of high school entertained a series of boyfriends. Another cabin near me was occupied by a reclusive old alcoholic named Bill, who got out once a day in his old Cadillac with Montana license plates, to drive the half-mile to town and back.

The owner of the Hollow lived in San Diego and only appeared on the weekends. His name was Bill Haley and he showed up every Saturday morning in his El Camino to paint the picket fences or water trees or put up some ridiculous piece of plastic art—anything, it seemed, but to give the decrepit buildings the attention they so desperately needed. In the back of the car he carried tools, a case of beer, and his dog named Bear. But in truth Haley was the bear; he was huge, slow-moving, and ill-tempered. Only Darlene ever confronted him, and he told her that if she didn't like the condition of her home, she was perfectly free to move out.

For three weeks everything was fine in my life. I worked off the first month's rent, met my neighbors, and began to learn my way around Julian. I didn't have any money, but my meals were free, and one of the guys usually bought me a beer or two when our shift ended. I took walks in the morning, up the path through the woods to town, and on into the hillside graveyard from which one could see the whole village. The days were hot and relentlessly sunny—just the way I like them—and the nights were clear and cool. I read the *Julian Nugget* and thought idly about contributing an article or two sometime, though I've never considered myself much of a writer. I didn't have a girlfriend, but I figured that, too, would come if I gave it time. Time—that was what I had now, time that was my own, with no curfew and no crew boss and no more counting down the days to freedom. I delighted in the simple pleasures of walking through the woods, or sitting on my small front porch sipping coffee, because they had been denied me at the honor camp. For the first time in who knows how long, I *relaxed*.

Then it rained, and a few days later the Moon was full. And relaxation ended.

# Chapter Five

Patsy Kittredge woke early, alone, and brewed a pot of coffee. Taking a cup and a cigarette out onto the deck, she sat down to soak in the view offered by the morning sunlight on the tree-studded canyon that fell away toward the coast, fifty miles distant, and mentally prepared an agenda for the day.

The Sun warmed her bare feet as she stretched to rest them on the railing. By ten o'clock the temperature in the mountains would reach the nineties, as it had for the last several weeks running, and thunderheads would begin to build over the desert. In all probability they would stay there, idly threatening, or pass to the south and briefly soak Pine Valley or the hills in Mexico. To the west, the gray, razor-straight wall of the marine layer blocked the view of the distant ocean she would have otherwise enjoyed; she was familiar enough with the summer weather patterns in San Diego to know that later in the day the clouds would drift out to sea and the temperature at the shore would be quite tolerable.

There was a message on her answering machine from Erik

Gunn. She had been awake last night when he called, but she hadn't answered. He was calling to say hi, he said, but she knew that it was more than that. He was probably at home alone, his wife off somewhere with somebody else, and would have likely, if she had given him a chance, asked her to come over, or to have lunch with him the next day, or something. Once they had had a simple, casual friendship, which had been fine with her. But now he clearly wanted more, and besides not feeling that way about him, she wanted no part of the small-town innuendo and gossip she knew so well from her upbringing in New England. Though he lacked the self-confidence to truly harass her, she was finding his attention more and more annoying.

Fuck that, she thought, as she drained her cup of coffee and got up to get another. In another week she would have to start preparing class schedules and attending meetings, dressing for success and smoking in designated areas only. For a few more days at least, she was on vacation, and it was too nice out and Southern California was too vast and varied for her to hang around Julian. She would take care of business, and then head off to someplace more interesting.

Among the people she had to see that day was Steve Dakota, Julian's new and boyishly handsome superintendent of schools, who was in his office bright and early, in part to impress early-rising parents, in part because August was the month before school started, and, being new at the job, he wanted to get the jump on his staff.

Though formal preparations for fall classes would not start until the following week, Patsy was already thinking ahead to September. She had been invited to a conference of women educators in Santa Barbara, a sort of feminist think tank for those in positions to influence the politics of the next generation. It would mean missing two days of school and would require the superintendent's signature and a small capital outlay from the school board. She intended to secure his signature and mail in her acceptance before heading down the hill.

Steve Dakota had arrived in Julian in June, brimming with the aggressive optimism that is the mark of the newly and fortuitously promoted. He was forty-two but could have passed for twenty-eight. Patsy's opinion of him was one of faint contempt. Though she had only been at the school for three years, he was the fourth superintendent under which she'd worked. One guy had come down with a rare and debilitating disease, another had quit three months into his tenure to take a better job, and the third had proved to be an alcoholic. The revolving door at the top of the school hierarchy was the subject of jokes, disgust, and an increased number of interdistrict transfer requests from parents. The superintendents had all been men, which Patsy thought privately was part of the problem.

Her impression of Steve Dakota was that he would have made a pretty decent basketball coach. He had the height; indeed, he had told several of the male teachers that he had played some hoop in high school, and that his dreams of athletic glory had ended only when he wrecked an ankle in a car accident. Patsy wondered how much of the story was true. She had seen him run the bases in a year-end softball game between faculty and students, when he had scored from first on a double, and his ankle didn't seem to bother him at all. She knew he rode regularly with the group at the Julian Bicycle Emporium, a sport in which he used his long legs to great advantage, but there was something strange and awkward about him, like an adolescent who grows too fast, which made her doubt that he had ever been as much of a jock as he let on. He also had the annoying habit of not looking into a person's eyes during conversation.

Whatever his athletic accomplishments, however, he had a sports mentality. He had been introduced to the faculty a week before graduation, and at the ceremony itself he had delivered a speech replete with metaphors like "touching all the bases" and "going the distance." He would be great for leading the surge at pep rallies and getting the school colors shown around town, and the high school for sure needed a cheerleader—but after several conversations with him she had concluded that probably every teacher at the school was smarter than he was. Talking to him about educational ideas was a waste of time; his eyes either glazed over or descended toward a spot below her collarbone. But so far the town loved him and, given his youth, and the school board's weariness at confronting crowds of parents who accused them of letting the school drift aimlessly in a current of drugs, sex, and disrepair, he might last as long as the Reagan-Bush Republican empire. She supposed she was stuck with him.

"Hi, Patsy," he said, as she entered the school lobby. He was the only one there; even the secretaries took time off in the summer. "Beautiful morning, isn't it?" His cheeriness struck her as artificial. He was cheerful about everything, which for her was another turnoff. Nonetheless, she flashed him her best smile as she handed him the form requiring his signature.

"It certainly is," she said. "A good day for the beach."

"And a better day for the mountains," he rejoined. "What's this?"

She explained the mostly self-explanatory form to him while he examined the freckles near the top button of her shirt. "The deadline for acceptance is August fifteenth," she said. "But I've got until September fourth to pay, which means you can get it approved at the next board meeting."

He took the pen she proffered and signed the form atop the secretary's desk. She noticed that he held the pen awkwardly; though his fingers were thin, for some reason they seemed poorly coordinated. They were too long, she concluded, out of proportion to his hands and wrists. Like a teenager who has undergone a sudden growth spurt, he seemed unsure of where his body ended and objects he touched began.

He handed back the form, but not without a caveat. "We're going to have to watch these things, Patsy, and make sure they relate pretty specifically to the curriculum. I understand that you want to go to this—that it's, ah, an interest of yours—but the board's told me to really watch the purse strings this year."

She could have told him that part of the conference, one of the lectures in fact, would focus on women in literature, and that she would likely gather reference material she could use in class. But since he'd already signed the form, there was no point in being drawn into a debate. Besides, he had the school board in his pocket, and they both knew it. The members of the board were so ecstatic at finally having someone who wasn't going to die or retire or immediately move on to a higher-paying job, that he could almost have bought a new car with district funds without their censure. They paid him sixty grand a year, and for that sum they expected him to tell them what to do. As Erik Gunn, the newspaper editor and her most ardent admirer in town, could have told her, school boards and other like groups existed for the purpose of *not* making decisions. The more members, the more blame there was to hot-potato around when something went wrong, and any administrator with an agenda and the will to stick to it could mold them like putty.

Erik Gunn saw Patsy Kittredge that day, too. He was putting a stack of the new issue of the *Julian Nugget* into one of the racks on Main Street as she drove by. He looked up as she waved at him, and he waved back. As usual, he felt his heart flutter between his chest and his throat; as usual, she felt nothing.

It would not be a good day for Gunn, whose height, prematurely balding head, and presence, with notebook in hand, at virtually every public gathering made him something of a local landmark. Anytime a major story broke on a Friday, that was bad, because Friday was the only day his weekly paper came out, and he would have to wait a week before getting his version on the streets, long after the dailies from the city and the television stations had had their cracks at it.

Gunn had edited the local newspaper for two years, which was about the longest continuous length of time anyone had edited any newspaper in town. The town was not well-read. Nor did it have a reputation for attracting honest businesspeople or encouraging outsiders. One newspaper had sold "lifetime" subscriptions and published three issues; another had folded after three months, its owners disappearing in the middle of the night with several restaurants' two-year advertising payments. Gunn had come by his job by convincing the mostly absentee publisher that she was better off putting her paper in his hands than trying to run it herself from an office that was seldom open.

And with Gunn, the paper at least had visibility. He was a familiar face, someone whom people stopped on the street or came to see at the office, bearing the latest tidings of what they considered important. But he discovered that there was a downside to this. In the eyes of the townspeople, his identity became so enmeshed with his job that it became difficult for people to really confide in him, for fear that they were talking to the newspaper rather than the man. Even his wife wouldn't share gossip with him, and close friendships proved almost impossible. An affair was probably out of the question.

Wally Leach saw Patsy Kittredge seconds after Erik Gunn did. Wally Leach saw most people in Julian on most days and knew almost all of the locals by name, though Moondog Nygerski, with his uncanny skill at slipping in and out of town before anybody noticed, had somehow managed to keep his identity from him. Eric Gunn, by contrast, could not go to the store for a sandwich without being subjected to a diatribe on the contents of that week's newspaper, gossip on his wife, or a dissertation on the origin of the Universe, and most other townspeople could expect similar treatment.

Leach served a triple role in the community. He was the town crier, the town drunk, and the town gossip all rolled into one. Some people liked him, most tolerated him, and others crossed the street to avoid him when they saw him at his customary post outside the town hall. His story was a sad one. Near the top of his class academically at Julian High School more than two decades ago, he had been the team's star football player, and had gone off to college to study philosophy and continue his athletic career, his future full of promise. An injury in his sophomore year ruined his knees and left him with a prodigious limp he would never lose. It got him out of Vietnam but also out of sports and into drugs, an arena in which he competed no less enthusiastically than he had on the gridiron. He tried everything, in every conceivable combination and quantity, and damn near killed himself before settling on good old alcohol. He had always been big, but his weight ballooned with inactivity, and the added hundred pounds only worsened his lameness. Now past forty, he lived with his parents, hobbled around with the aid of a metal crutch, picked up occasional work painting signs for local businesses, and spent most days sitting on the low brick wall in front of the town hall, a bottle stashed behind him, talking loudly to anyone who would listen. On weekends, when the tourists were in town, he would don a sandwich board provided him by one of the local pie shops and get paid for being a fixture; on other days he was just there, because he had nowhere else to go.

The president of the chamber of commerce, who owned the Chevron station across the main intersection from the town hall, had once tried to have him permanently barred from the corner, on grounds of public drunkenness. Wally had taken to hailing him across the street, in a voice that simultaneously boomed and grated and seemed to echo between the hillsides and carry over the entire town. "El Presidente!" Wally would shout, when he spotted Danny Taylor by the gas pumps. "When're you gonna stop poisoning the water?" Then he would click his heels together, as best he could with sneakers and nearly nonfunctional legs, and give him the fascist salute. Everyone on Main Street could watch this, and other similar greetings, on a daily basis.

When Taylor got a new girlfriend, things grew progressively worse. "There she is, the First Lady of Julian!" he'd shout, when she was the better part of a block away. "How's it going, Mrs. Chevron?"

Once or twice the local sheriff's deputies did actually drive him home, but he was always back the next day, cheerful and gregarious, and sober until midafternoon. The cops finally decided, like most everyone else, that the best way to deal with Wally Leach was to ignore him. They required only that he keep his bottle out of sight and not interfere with people going into or out of the building. Since Wally was a sedentary figure, whose abuse was strictly verbal, they pretty much left him alone.

And he was, whether the chamber of commerce liked it or not, something of a tourist attraction. He had a good mind, and could hold forth lucidly on a wide range of topics, including the shortcomings of the Big Bang theory of creation and the latest advances in molecular biology. But he was also something of a show-off, delighting in using twenty-dollar words to deliver fifty-cent messages. Never at a loss for something to say, he was forever getting on TV whenever the stations came up from San Diego, sounding off about the water situation, the poor apple crop, and, most recently, the death of Brandy Allen. He was the most accessible interviewee on Main Street, instant local color,

39

and it was a long drive back to the city for the news crews, who had lunch to think about, pies to purchase, and deadlines to meet.

"Hey Pa-a-a-atsy!" he yelled, when he saw her car roll to a stop in front of him. "I got some new books for you!"

Patsy Kittredge, too, had once thought him colorful. She discovered his interest in philosophy, he hers in literature, and he'd started giving her old, mostly useless volumes he'd found in thrift shops somewhere. But the gifts were more often than not accompanied by requests to buy booze—his mother had gone to all three stores and asked them not to sell to him—and the routine had grown tiresome.

"Wally, I'm late," she said, smiling to take the sting out of the rejection. "I'm in a hurry." And she pulled through the intersection and parked in front of the market on the other side.

Kay Sables, working the counter at the Corner Market, saw Patsy approach and smiled. During the school year, Patsy came into the store nearly every weekday around three o'clock and bought a pack of Camels, and sometimes a bottle of wine or a six-pack of light beer, and sometimes food, though Kay's motherly appraisal of Patsy's figure and buying habits told her the girl wasn't eating enough. She had a son and a daughter at the high school, both of whom earned Cs in Patsy's classes, and genuinely liked her.

Today it was only the Camels. "How's your summer going?" she asked brightly, as she rang up the purchase.

"It's going okay," Patsy replied. "I'm still getting over the shock of one of my former students being murdered." Brandy Allen had been a senior during Patsy's first year in Julian.

"I hear you," Kay said somberly. "My kids aren't over it, either. I still can't believe it."

"I hope they catch the guy soon," Patsy said. "Have you heard anything?"

Kay shook her head. "Nope. Frank Blaisdell told me they think it might have been someone just passing through the area. A group of wetbacks, maybe, or a transient. He says they've got no suspects at all."

"What a tragedy."

"I'll say. It's all anyone talks about when they come in here. She was a beautiful girl."

"It's a crazy world we live in, isn't it?" Patsy said, as she tucked the pack of cigarettes into her purse.

Kay sighed. "Indeed it is." She passed a hand in front of her eyes, and looked out the window. "But life goes on. And it's a beautiful day. Are you doing something good with it?"

"Going to San Diego for the weekend," Patsy said. "Every so often I have to get out of this little town and head for the big city."

"I hear you," Kay said again. "Gonna hit the beach?"

"Hope so."

"Well, soak up some rays for me. Have fun."

"Thanks. 'Bye."

But Patsy Kittredge was not sure that afternoon whether she would, in fact, spend the entire weekend on the coast. She had someone to see there, it was true, but she was not thinking of him as she aimed the car down the winding road toward Ramona. She was thinking instead about the stranger she had taken into her bed two nights earlier, and wondering when he would pass her way again.

# Chapter Six

ON THURSDAY NIGHT I got paid, the first paycheck that was mine to spend. On Friday, after opening a savings account at the tiny Home Federal branch in Julian, I hitchhiked down to Ramona to pick up some supplies, including an ounce of grass from a guy I'd met at the honor camp. Patsy Kittredge was on the road that day, too, at about the same time, but our paths never crossed. I think I would have remembered even a chance encounter, for hers was a face not easily forgotten.

I got hung up in Ramona. The dude from the honor camp, the guy with the grass, was late. I was supposed to be to work at five; at five-fifteen I called my boss collect and told him it looked as though I wasn't going to make it for a while. He was pissed; here he'd just given me my first real paycheck and it looked like I was skipping out on him the very next day. But he didn't offer to come down and get me, either. And he didn't fire me. In fact, he said—between a lot of swearing—that he'd call somebody else, and that I might as well take the whole night off and work Sunday, which was supposed to be my day of rest. I thanked him for being so understanding. His reply to that was a grunt; I could hear the phone jangle when he slammed it down.

My friend finally showed at around six. We did our deal, smoked a bomber joint on the playground of a school a block or two off the main drag, and went into a bar to catch up on old times over a couple of beers. He'd already quit the job they got him when they released him from the honor camp; dealing dope, he said, was more profitable. He wanted to know what the scene was in Julian. I told him I hadn't made it my business to find out, and didn't plan to. I'd been there three weeks, and already considered the little town my sanctuary. Whatever forays outside the law I might find necessary, I would do them somewhere else.

By the time I saw him off on the last bus to Escondido and wished him luck in his new career, it was starting to get dark. I walked to the east end of town, past the last traffic light, and stuck out my thumb to the cool of the evening.

Though the distance is only twenty-two miles, it took a while to get home. Traffic was sparse, and most of it was going the other way. But as I stood there by the abandoned Hi-Way Food Mart, with its broken-out windows and spray-paint art, a big, fat full Moon rose over the mountains that were my destination, and soon the rock-studded, hilly landscape was awash in moonlight. It was an absolutely gorgeous night. I retreated into the trees to roll another joint, and as I stood there puffing on it and soaking in my surroundings, I felt, really, for the first time since my arrest, the sense of freedom that I still cherish above everything else. Unburdened of my schedule, I didn't really care whether I got a ride or not. I was simply happy to be alive, in that place and moment, and to have the time and ability to appreciate it.

Two rides eventually brought me to Santa Ysabel, less a town than a crossroads, six miles from Sleepy Hollow. As soon as the car sped off up the road to Warner Springs, it was almost unbearably quiet. There wasn't a whole lot to Santa Ysabel, a long, three-thousand-foot-high valley where state highways 78 and 79 converged. Around the intersection were a gas station, a couple of stores, a post office, and the massive, low-slung hulk of Dresher's Bakery, which is famous throughout Southern California for its many varieties of fresh-baked bread. A few paces up Highway 79 a future shopping complex was under construction, and its skeletal timbers cast shadows in the moonlight on the grazing pasture directly behind it. The few houses in Santa Ysabel lay back from the highway behind a row of trees, out of sight from where I stood, and not a sound came from any of them.

The whole place lay bathed in light—from the Moon in the sky, the five or six yellow streetlights at the intersection, and the outside lights of the bakery, switched on to blast away potential burglars and vandals. I could see more than a mile back the way I'd come across the valley, and since there were no approaching headlights in that distance I ambled over to the front of the bakery, fished a quarter from my jeans, and took a copy of that week's *Julian Nugget* from the apple-red machine. Inside, on page two—the editorial page—I saw for the first time the name Cyrus "Moondog" Nygerski.

There was plenty of light by which to read. I suppose it was the headline, and not the strange name, that first caught my attention, but it was Moondog's prose that held it. I scanned the front page, which contained an uninformative story on the continuing Brandy Allen investigation, a report on the water situation (not good), and an interview with the fire chief about the dry conditions. I didn't read past the first paragraph of any of them.

Ant Immigration Strains Defenses, read the first headline I saw when I turned the page. I barely noticed the crappy editorial cartoon above it, or the editorial advising people not to water their lawns. But I took note of the byline—his was not, after all, a common name—and once I started reading the column, I didn't stop until I got to the end.

The warm weather has brought the ants out again, and the borders of my home are no longer secure.

Last week I woke to find that a huge colony of them had invaded the kitchen from their home outside the window. A steady stream of the little buggers poured through the wall through a hole I couldn't see, let alone repair. They were after the cat's food, the gooey stuff that comes in a can, and several hundred of them were already immersed in it. Meanwhile, a separate stream, not content with that free lunch, had branched off toward the cupboard, with designs on my potatoes and onions.

I had to do something quickly. After all, the ants had no legal right to be in my territory. But there were so many of them! Figuring deportation to be the best bet, at least in the short run, I grabbed the vacuum cleaner, sucked up as many of the ants as I could, and dumped the receptacle outside.

I knew this wasn't a permanent solution. There is more food on my side of the wall than on theirs, after all, and once I dumped them outside, I knew there was nothing to stop them from trying to enter again.

Since I wanted to get some work done, and didn't have time to spend all day deporting ants, I decided on a follow-up strategy: Foreign Aid. I placed an open can of old and tired cat food, not as good as fresh but better than what the ants were used to, on the ground near their anthill. My thinking was that if they could get it at home they needn't come into my house for it. I hoped they wouldn't get spoiled by free handouts, or turn on me if I suggested they start feeding themselves again, but I decided to chance it, at least for a while.

As a last line of defense, I took what was left of last year's can of Raid and sprayed it around the areas where the ants were most likely to get in. Border Security. I knew it wouldn't work for long, but my budget was limited, and they had numbers and determination on their side.

Mexicans, I realized, about halfway through. He's talking about Mexicans. I read on:

I realize that the ants are motivated only by the desire to survive and the yearning for a better life— pangs which stir the heart of any intelligent species. But this is my kitchen we're talking about here, and I bought the food with my hard-earned American dollars.

So I've decided to take a hard line. I pay the bills around here, and if I don't want to feed a bunch of uninvited ants out of my own pocket, I don't have to. But they keep coming back, and yesterday one had the audacity to bite me. I went out and bought two big cans of Raid, and the next ant I see in my house is gonna get it. I may even dig a ditch outside the kitchen and fill it with the stuff.

I have nothing against one ant in my house, or two, or even a dozen. But when the sheer force of their numbers, coupled with their parasitic ways, disrupts my life and costs me money, something has to be done. If it isn't they'll eat me out of house and home.

The credit, in bold type, read as follows:

**Cyrus "Moondog" Nygerski once crossed the border illegally at Jacumba, looking for an escape from poverty and despair. Finding things little better on the other side, he soon returned to the United States.**

Now, I've lived in Southern California for a good part of my life, and I've seen the attitude a lot of white folks have toward illegal immigration. Here was that attitude parodied with Jonathan Swift-like savagery. I was impressed. I hadn't expected to pick up the local rag and find a wit-in-residence. And reading the column would set me on a course in collision with the terrible events that were, indeed at that very moment, unfolding in the Julian area.

Two or three cars had whizzed through Santa Ysabel as I stood there, on the front porch of Dresher's Bakery, reading Nygerski's column. Somewhere off in the night a coyote howled. I folded up the newspaper, stuffed it into my back pocket, and walked out to the highway. Three more cars, at widely spaced intervals, passed my outstretched thumb before I caught the ride I needed, with a group of teenagers in an old rattletrap Pinto, out for a night of drinking and joyriding—bait, I thought, for any cop on a lonely country road with a thick sheaf of unwritten tickets.

There were four of them; they stuffed me into the backseat and gave me a beer, which I only half finished before they dumped me off at Sleepy Hollow and careened onward into the tempestuous springtime of their lives. I could not have said whether or not the car in which I rode passed another vehicle, pulled over onto the shoulder with its driver's-side door askew and its hood partially open, its headlights staring vacantly into the night, its paint job visibly ruined even in moonlight. Whether the car was there by the time I passed I do not know. I said so, when asked; I said it repeatedly. It did not stop my questioners from asking again, for I was new in town, and it was clear that they did not believe me.

# Chapter Seven

FRANK BLAISDELL SAW the car on his way down the hill, but didn't think enough of it to stop or call in. Just someone pulled momentarily to the side, he thought, to take a piss or look at a map or fish a new cassette tape from the glove compartment. Besides, in another half hour it would be eleven—a quick spin out to Lake Henshaw and back, a nice quiet ride that he was sure would prove uneventful, should finish up his shift.

Frank Blaisdell was a local boy, a month shy of his thirtieth birthday, the youngest sheriff's deputy at the Julian substation. He'd landed the Julian job, which he looked upon as an incredible stroke of good fortune, after two years at the Vista jail in San Diego's explosively growing North County. On the infrequent occasions when he had to drive someone down the hill for booking, his former co-workers ribbed him about the dangerous life he must be living in the mountains, where a leftover pocket of the Manson Family or a fugitive serial killer could turn up at any time. Since the death of Brandy Allen, which had happened on one of Blaisdell's days off, the jokes hadn't seemed so funny.

Still, Frank would not have traded his rural life in the community in which he grew up for anything, especially not the mind-numbing routine of the jail, whose unceasing parade of poor, mostly drug-addled lowlifes without much of a chance to be anything else always made him feel unclean. Life was good. He was paid decently enough that he and his wife, a teacher at the elementary school, could afford their modest home in one of the town's better outlying sections; their daughter Kara was three, and growing up far from the random street crime that police families in other parts of the county lived with, at least in their thoughts, on a daily basis. The little girl saw both sets of grandparents frequently, attended a church-sponsored preschool, and in about six months would welcome into the world a little brother or sister.

And he was popular, for a cop, not only with his fellow officers and the town's upstanding citizens, but also for the most part with the people he encountered on the wrong side of the law. Some of them had been his peers during high school, and had moved on to blue-collar jobs and bar fights, but even among the new crop of teenage hooligans and the permanent Julian underclass that lived, at least partially, by theft, he was afforded a level of tolerance shown to few officers of the law. He had an unaggressive, almost apologetic way of making an arrest or issuing a ticket, he would let an occasional speeder off with a warning, and he was always the "good cop" in the rare cases when a suspect had to be grilled. His unthreatening appearance helped. He was barely five and a half feet tall, with a full head of dark hair and youthful features. Erik Gunn liked to use him as a source for news stories, because he was always polite and never evasive, answering questions in straightforward, easily quotable, complete sentences.

His fellow deputies liked him, too, for his dedication was apparent, and he was always ready with a joke or an appropriately timed wisecrack. He enjoyed his work, which until tonight had given him one or two anxious moments, but not a single nightmare.

Lake Henshaw glowed blackly in the moonlight as he turned the cruiser around and headed back toward Julian. A manmade reservoir for the aforementioned city of Vista, the lake lay at the foot of Palomar Mountain, at the end of a dammed and flooded cow pasture. When tourists stopping at the little store across the road inquired about the cows they saw bathing at the water's edge, the octogenarian proprietor would tell them, "That's how they keep the milk cold."

Blaisdell smiled as he thought of this. He was looking forward to calling it a night. He'd seen all of one car, coming the other way, over the ten miles from the intersection at Santa Ysabel. The dashboard clock read 10:42.

"Just about right," he said aloud to himself, stifling a yawn. The Moon, nearing the apex of its arc through the southern sky, illuminated the road in front of him as he climbed the lip of a hill. The contours of the mountains to his left stood out in stark relief; a barn in the middle of a field cast a long shadow. Behind him, the dome of the main observatory on Palomar Mountain lay bathed in moonlight. It was not a good night for astronomy; he barely needed his headlights.

He turned left at the deserted Santa Ysabel intersection, and gunned the cruiser up the grade toward Inaja Memorial Park, where eleven Julian firefighters had lost their lives battling a blaze in 1956. Inaja was the headwaters of the mighty San Diego River, though even in normal years it could more properly be called the San Diego Trickle, and now, after three years of severe drought and midway through a fourth, it was little more than the San Diego Strip of Still-Green Vegetation. The park's main asset was a half-mile long hiking trail that overlooked the entire Santa Ysabel Valley. Frank had walked it many times as a kid, and more recently with his wife and daughter.

Just past the park's entrance, Blaisdell rounded a curve and saw that the car he had passed on the way down was still there. Coming down, he had been looking into the car's headlights, and in any case had dismissed its presence as routine, but now, from behind, he could see that there was definitely something wrong with the door on the driver's side, and with part of the hood. He pulled to a stop behind it, and turned on his flashers.

The car was a white Volvo; Frank knew he had seen it with some frequency on the streets of Julian. But the door and part of the hood were covered with darker material, as though someone had thrown a bucket of paint at the vehicle. The door lay partially opened, and appeared crooked on its hinges, as if the vehicle had been in an accident, or as if someone very strong or very heavy had leaned very hard on the opened door. He took his long policeman's flashlight from the seat beside him, and shone it at the vehicle's rear window. The car appeared empty.

He knew he recognized the car. And he had an inexplicable feeling of dread, the sense that something was very wrong. Sucking in his breath, he radioed the dispatcher.

"I think you better send somebody down here," he said, and gave his location, the license number of the car, and a description of the circumstances. Within a minute she called back with the registration information, and said that another deputy, Kevin Byars, was on his way.

He should have waited. Later he would remember being torn between the strong desire to wait for Byars, who was built like a bear and didn't seem to be afraid of anything, and the equally strong urge to find out just what the fuck was going on here. Something definitely wasn't right; it was only an abandoned vehicle, but the overpowering sense of wrongness made him feel as jumpy as a cat.

And as curious. Cautiously he got out, his left hand holding the flashlight, his right hand loose at his side but ready, at the first sign of anything weird, to grab his gun, which he had never yet had to use in the line of duty. It was deathly quiet. Almost a thousand feet higher than Lake Henshaw, yet nearly that far below Main Street in Julian, the land here was wooded, and the coastal oaks, unstirred by even a hint of wind, cast pebbly shadows down onto the road. His red and blue roof lights strobed the Volvo and its unnatural paint pattern. He looked at the dark splotches covering door and hood. Neither the Moon nor the cruiser's flashers gave him any accurate indication of color; though bright, the nighttime scene around the two vehicles was playing essentially in black and white. He didn't know what the dark stuff on the car was until he touched it, and it came away wet and sticky on his fingertip.

Blood, he realized, in mounting horror. The car was covered with blood.

He had not been in on the search for Brandy Allen, but he had heard the chilling talk at the substation from those who had seen the body. And of course he knew the family. He was thinking of Brandy Allen now, and the tiny hairs on the back of his neck were standing at attention.

Now he saw that there was more of it on the ground, in the dirt next to the vehicle—big puddles of it, along with scuff marks, and a set of keys. His trembling flashlight followed the marks in the dirt toward the nearby underbrush; obediently, his feet followed the light.

As if from a great distance, he heard the approach of his partner's vehicle. He did not hear the crunch of his own mesmerized footsteps in the roadside gravel, nor did he look up as the sheriff's van, its lights adding to the show, pulled over to the opposite side of the road and Kevin Byars got out. He was looking down instead—at the end of his flashlight beam, and what it had found at the edge of the woods.

In death, Patsy Kittredge could never be called pretty. The body lay on its back, twisted in horrible, unnatural angles. Blood, bone, and torn flesh were everywhere. One half of her face had been entirely ripped away; bare skull stared back at Frank when his flashlight found her. The throat was likewise half gone, gaping redly, and one arm hung loosely from its shoulder by a sinewy clump of gristle. Her shirt had been savagely ripped down the front, and much of the flesh underneath had gone with it. Mute and paralyzed with horror, Frank Blaisdell could not tear his eyes away.

He could feel Byars beside him before he heard him. Byars was a big, no-nonsense type of guy, over six feet tall and powerfully built. His salt-and-pepper crewcut topped a rugged countenance; his nose had been broken at least once, and a jagged scar ran from one edge of his jaw down the side of his neck. He had a deep baritone voice that could give effective orders and get your attention in a second. But that was not the voice Frank heard beside him. The voice Frank heard was pinched and frightened, and barely more audible than a whisper.

"Jesus, Frank," his partner said. "I guess we better get on the horn to San Diego."

# Chapter Eight

PATSY KITTREDGE'S UNTIMELY demise, following so closely the death of Brandy Allen, sent Julian into renewed spasms of mourning and outrage. Though she had few close friends in the area—she lived alone, gently rebuffed most men who asked her out, and threatened many of the town's women with her mere presence—she was no recluse, and would be genuinely missed. Her students, some of whom had called her "cunt" and "dyke" behind her back and penned her name on desks and bathroom walls amid sexually explicit content, showed up en masse for a hastily scheduled memorial service in the graveyard overlooking the town. The school put ads in all the papers and on The Learning Channel on TV, hoping to find a new teacher willing to relocate to Julian on such sort notice and under such grisly circumstances. A grief-stricken pair of parents from New Hampshire showed up a few days later to claim what was left of the body.

Other people showed up too, some with badges, others with press cards. One brutal murder could be dismissed as an unfortunate blot on the face of a quiet community, but two such similar crimes within the span of a month attracted the attention of the outside world. The story ran on page one in Sunday's *San Diego Union*, and led off the County section of the *Los Angeles Times*. Wally Leach got on TV again, this time with tears running copiously down his reddened cheeks; a visibly shaken Frank Blaisdell and a stone-faced, tight-lipped Kevin Byars went before the cameras as well.

Suddenly, cops were everywhere. To the normal sheriff's department contingent and the state highway patrol were added San Diego homicide detectives and FBI investigators, who looked sharp and menacing as they walked in pairs down Main Street in their stenciled windbreakers. The Julian Motel enjoyed steady midweek bookings in what is normally the slow time of the year; the parking lot sported several big, spotlessly white American cars with tentacle-like rooftop antennas that swayed slowly, slowly in the wind.

Since the motel's parking lot was right behind the offices of the *Julian Nugget*, Erik Gunn had a bird's-eye view of the law officers' comings and goings. On Monday, the day after he had skulked around the graveyard taking pictures at the memorial service, and somehow managed to keep from losing it entirely as he tried to hold the camera steady, he approached them, ready to talk.

Gunn was beside himself with grief. Not only had he lost someone he loved; he had no one with whom to share his anguish. His wife had for some time suspected him of having an affair with Patsy Kittredge, and now that she was dead he wished more than anything that her suspicions had been true. Certainly *he* had been willing. Joyce, an attractive woman herself, had set about getting back at him in the most effective way possible, and could not in any case be expected to share his sorrow. His four-year-old daughter was too young to understand.

Patsy Kittredge had walked into the *Julian Nugget* office two years before, during Gunn's third month as editor. She wanted, she said, to start a student newspaper at the high school, and asked if the *Julian Nugget* could help. He took one look at her and said he'd be delighted.

Later, he supposed it was the twin strains of the new job and meeting this attractive schoolteacher that had doomed his marriage. For he was past kidding himself; it was lost beyond retrieving, and he hung in mainly for the sake of their daughter. While he stayed out late two or three nights a week putting together the newspaper, Joyce hired baby-sitters and went out with men, and often allowed one or another of them to take her home. Sometimes he would awaken a baby-sitter at three in the morning on deadline night; Joyce would come in at dawn, without a word to him, and fall asleep in the baby's room. Half the town knew what was going on, and Gunn buried his humiliation by throwing himself into his work.

There was also the coincidence of the date. On the day Patsy Kittredge entered Erik Gunn's life, he had turned thirty years old; he was thirty-two now and had lost most of what was left of the hair on top of his head in the time he had known her. Baldness had hit him early and with no mercy; he was twenty-seven when he first noticed that more hair than usual was staying in his comb in the mornings, and less than three years later, after a nasty sunburn, he discovered that he needed to wear a hat to the beach. Marriage, parenthood, and the continuing loss of his hair made Gunn feel old, and the fact that his wife, five years his senior, had yet to pluck her first gray hair and still turned heads on Main Street, didn't help.

But what really made Gunn feel old was living in Julian, and editing the newspaper. He could see several possible courses for his future, and the path lying straight ahead of him, the one with the gentlest curves and the fewest obstacles, scared the shit out of him because he could see all the way to the end of it. For it was unquestionably possible that editing the *Julian Nugget* was *it,* that he could with a little effort maneuver his life so that he would be putting it out as his own paper by the time he turned forty, that he would be an elder statesman in the community at fifty, an archivist at sixty, and thereafter a gentleman publisher with few real duties, a country grandfather and the subject of occasional soft features in magazines on rural living. He could have that life if he wanted it, and for a while, as he tended his tomato plants and watched his young daughter grow, a part of him thought that he did.

Patsy Kittredge changed that. She didn't do it intentionally, or even knowingly, but she touched the part of him that yearned for adventure. They were very nearly the same age, and both were far from home—he from Missouri, she from New Hampshire. But she had not come to California to settle, at least not yet; her ambitions included teaching overseas, and in her elliptically referred to past she had apparently hitchhiked around much of the United States and Canada in the footsteps of her favorite fictional character, Sissy Hankshaw in Tom Robbins's novel *Even Cowgirls Get the Blues.*

And there was the undeniable fact that she was one of the best-looking women he'd ever met—something that wasn't lost on his wife.

They became friends. He took her to lunch a few times, and when they ran into each other on the street they stopped to talk. He cherished those moments, and did what he could to make them happen as often as possible. He helped her with the school newspaper, which was filled with semiliterate student writings on clothes, foreign affairs, vacations, presidential politics, abortion, birth control, and rock and roll. She got two kids from her classes to cover sports and the school board for the *Nugget*, which meant that he didn't have to, and he sent her an expensive bouquet of flowers in gratitude. Later he supposed that the flowers had been too much, that that was the first time he had crossed the invisible line she had drawn between them.

He would cross it many other times, never knowing its precise location. The result was that she began avoiding him. He encouraged her to drop by the office after school, just to say hello, but she seldom did. He and Joyce gave a party, and he invited her, and was so morose when she didn't show up that Joyce telephoned her the following evening in a drunken rage and demanded to know what the fuck was going on. That, of course, made things worse. He saw less and less of her, and at the same time grew increasingly more distant from his wife, until it seemed to him that his office, on the second floor overlooking both Main Street and the Julian Motel's parking lot, had become his citadel, his fortress from which he could sally forth into the affairs of the town, or in which he could barricade himself behind his desk, his computer, and his telephone, and use the trappings of his job to ward off loneliness.

It wasn't *all* his wife's fault, he rationalized. But most of it was. It was true that his eye had wandered, and that he had maybe neglected her, as she claimed. But a different woman, he thought, would have handled it differently. He hadn't done anything with Patsy, after all, other than cautiously flirt with her and attempt to find out indirectly if she was interested. In the end, his caution had alienated them both.

Joyce liked attention, and didn't care if she got it from a successful young lawyer with a second home in the hills or from a near-destitute crystal head like one-legged Sven. Where Gunn was shy and socially awkward, his wife was vivacious and outgoing, always managing to find the right words or gestures to make other people feel important, no matter who they were. An educated woman who nonetheless valued emotion over reason, she became exasperated with him when he kept his thoughts and feelings to himself. When they met, she had been a successful advertising salesperson for one of San Diego's independent television stations. The souring of the economy, the birth of their daughter, and the move—at Joyce's behest and over Gunn's objections—to Julian had spelled the end of that particular career, and she had come to resent her husband for it.

In Julian, Joyce returned to her roots, so to speak. She had grown up in the sixties, lived for a time in a commune, dropped acid, and had an assortment of sexual partners. Approaching forty, she rebelled against her younger husband by trading the yuppie outfits of the city for long paisley skirts, patchouli oil, and the kind of long, dangly earrings that Gunn was fond of giving her, with bright beads that shone against her dark hair and set off her blue eyes. She was a good-looking woman, easily as pretty as Patsy Kittredge, though by the time Gunn told her this it was much too late, as she was already hearing it from Sven and the young lawyer, among others.

Gunn was powerless to do anything but watch it happen. He worked, he went hiking with his daughter, he called Patsy and talked, more often than not, to her answering machine. He found little joy in anything.

Since the end of the school year, in June, he had barely seen Patsy at all, except to wave to in brief, fleeting moments, as he had on the day she died. Now he faced the grim task of writing about her murder.

The undercover agents who belonged to the big white cars were no help at all. The three men in the parking lot were all wearing pressed dark suits and serious expressions; to a man, they reminded him of the Edward James Olmos character on "Miami Vice." A tall man who had never learned to use his height to his advantage, Gunn approached them timidly, his shoulders sagging apologetically forward.

"You're investigating the murder, aren't you?"

They stared at him silently.

"I'm Erik Gunn, editor of the *Julian Nugget*," he said. "I wonder if I can ask you a few questions."

"You can ask," said the man nearest him, not smiling under his thin, black mustache.

"Doesn't mean we'll answer," said another, who *did* smile, but barely.

"Do you have any suspects?"

"We're talking to a few people, but I don't know that I'd call them suspects at this point," said the first man, as Gunn scribbled in his notebook. "In fact, we're still not absolutely sure that the killer is even human."

"Who are you guys with? FBI?"

"We're with CBS News," said the second man. "What'd you think we were, cops or something?"

Gunn stopped writing. "Come on, gimme a break," he said.

"We're late," growled the third man, who, unlike his rangy partners, was low-slung and broad-shouldered—he looked like a former fullback. He also looked dangerous. Gunn's appraisal was that if the first two guys were the brains of the operation, this guy was the muscle. Of course, appearances can deceive.

The fullback opened the car door, and motioned with his head for the other two men to get in.

"Can I get your names?" Gunn called after them. "Maybe we can talk when you have more time."

"Look, we're not supposed to be talking to the press," the first guy said. "We're in the middle of an ongoing investigation. Call Lieutenant McMahon at Sheriff's Homicide. He'll tell you what you need to know."

Gunn groaned as they got into the car. He'd already spoken to Lieutenant McMahon, who had told him the same things he had told the *Union*, the *Times*, and the television stations—the "official" version of events. He had two days before deadline, four days before the paper hit the streets. He needed a new angle, a hook. He needed *something,* just to keep him going, to keep him from drowning in his own personal ocean of sorrow and not writing the story at all.

# Chapter Nine

TWO MONTHS, TWO murders, and here were the similarities:

Both victims were attractive, unmarried women, one twenty, the other thirty-two. Their photos ran side by side in the *Union*, and later in the *Julian Nugget*, and confirmed something I've observed about women as I have aged. Brandy Allen had that wholesome country look; she had been homecoming queen and Miss Julian as a teenager, and yet, had she lived, in ten years she would have been even more beautiful. Women are at their best in their thirties, when they have learned how to carry themselves and experience has enhanced genetics. In this they are different from men, for whom it's all downhill physically after the age of seventeen.

Both murders took place at night, and both bodies were found in the woods, though Mount Laguna and Inaja Memorial Park are more than twenty miles apart. They are, in fact, on opposite sides of Julian, the small mountain community that both victims called home.

The method used to kill them was the same—and unspeakably brutal. Cause of death in both cases was massive loss of blood from numerous injuries caused by the tearing of flesh by a sharp object or objects. No weapon had been recovered at either scene. In fact—and this baffled investigators—the deaths looked remarkably like animal attacks. The concensus, however, was that the woods of Southern California hold no animal capable of the savagery visited upon the two dead women, not even a rabid mountain lion. A determined Doberman pinscher could do it, maybe, or a Siberian tiger, but the closest zoo was in San Diego, no circus had recently passed through the area, and in any case there would have been sightings, reports of unusual animal activity, *something*.

The police *were* looking at dogs. Every owner of a pit bull terrier in the Julian area, and there were quite a few of them, was questioned. And five investigators spent a full day at the house of Larry "the Wolf Man" Jordan, who owned one hundred acres just south of town, on a portion of which he kept a caged colony of seventeen Alaskan wolves.

Jordan was a biologist by trade, who did much of his work for the Navy in San Diego. But his passion was wolves. Unlike Cyrus "Moondog" Nygerski, the "Wolf Man" moniker was not part of his name, but had been hung on him affectionately by neighbors who had taken to the garrulous Jordan and his unusual pets. His land bordered a Boy Scout camp, and he gave tours of the compound for free, calling each gray or cream-colored wolf by name and keeping up a steady banter of wolf-related trivia.

Jordan was in the middle of a battle with the Julian Community Planning Group that had been the focus of several articles in the *Julian Nugget*. He had begun a series of seminars on wolves and their behavioral patterns, and occasionally played host to groups of students from San Diego State and UCSD. He wanted more than anything to quit the Navy and develop a full-fledged resort and scientific retreat, complete with vacation cabins, guided trails, and an ongoing educational program open to the public. The idea was to use the resort part of the project to fund the scientific research. He had applied for federal grants to participate in endangered-wildlife programs, and could not fathom why anyone would be opposed to such a noble enterprise. But there was opposition. The fifteen-member planning group was split down the middle between no-growth advocates who had moved up from the city, had their foothold, and now wanted to raise the drawbridge, and those who wanted to see the establishment of businesses other than pie and antique shops. A good-natured man who had little patience with the details of county regulations and even less with fools, Jordan had supplied Erik Gunn with many a colorful quote and had made his share of enemies. He tended to brush them off, just as he brushed off his setbacks at the hands of the county bureaucracy, which cost him money and repeatedly scaled down the size of his project. For he loved his wolves, believed in what he was doing, and maintained his faith that the town, once it got over the provincial skepticism with which it greeted new ideas, would believe in the project, too.

He met the suit-and-tie-clad investigators in blue jeans, boots, and a plaid flannel shirt with the tail out. He was a big man whose broad shoulders sloped slightly forward in the suggestion of a shrug; his close-cropped dark hair ignored the efforts of a comb, and his beard was window dressing on a strong jaw. He looked like a professor who had more important things to think about than grooming, and that characterization was not far off the mark.

Jordan carried a cup of coffee to the doorstep; on the mug was a picture of a wolf. "Good morning, gentlemen," he said, cheerfully enough. "What can I do for you?"

The first man out of the two cars, the man Erik Gunn had questioned the day before, introduced himself as Guy Taylor, head of Special Investigative Services for San Diego County. He presented an embossed business card, and said, "We're investigating the recent deaths of two young women in the area. We'd like to speak with you about your animals."

Jordan had known they were coming. Frank Blaisdell had called him the previous evening and asked him to be ready and, above all, polite. Thus Jordan was the picture of congeniality as he led them into his office, where six chairs were arrayed as though by accident among the clutter, and offered coffee.

The office, though not small, was not exactly spacious, either, and its organization could best be described as haphazard. A huge desk dominated the wall by the window, which faced east, toward barren mountains and desert. Wolf motifs were everywhere. A totem pole, about four feet high and topped by a snarling wolf head, stood by the door. Empty Nordik Wolf beer bottles lined the windowsill. Halloween masks hung on the walls, which also displayed colorful photos from various nature magazines and a huge promo poster from the movie *An American Werewolf in London*. A bookshelf near the desk held perhaps thirty volumes, some of them scientific tomes but others occult literature and popular fiction. Taylor's glance picked out *White Fang* by Jack London and *Cycle of the Werewolf* by Stephen King.

"Well," Jordan said, shoving aside some papers and sitting on the edge of the desk. "What would you like to know?"

Taylor was the only one of the investigators who had not taken a seat. Cup of coffee in hand, he stood by the window, alternately looking out at the scenery and around the room. "You have what, sixteen wolves here?" he asked.

"Seventeen," Jordan corrected him. "Fifteen adults and two juveniles."

"And how long have you had them?"

"I got my first pair six years ago," Jordan said. He saw that the visitors were examining the office in minute detail. "As you can tell, they've sort of become my hobby."

"Have any of your animals ever . . . escaped?"

Jordan laughed pleasantly. "I was wondering how long it would take you to get around to that. The answer is no, never. The enclosure is secure. Besides, they're well cared for here, and well fed." He lowered his voice. "It's a terrible thing, Mr. Taylor, what happened to those two girls. But my wolves aren't responsible."

"It must be awfully hot for them here," cut in one of the other investigators, from across the room. "In Southern California. Aren't they used to the tundra?"

Jordan's smile returned. "Wolves are remarkably adaptive," he said. "The wolf's coat, for example, has two layers. The undercoat, which keeps it warm, is shed in the spring and grows back in the fall. And this isn't such a bad area for them, really, because of the altitude. There's a winter here. The mountains and the far north both have long thermometers. In Alaska, the summer days are as much as twenty hours long. It can get up into the eighties. Plus, wolves used to live all over North America, even in warm climates, before people exterminated them. There still are a few wolves in Mexico."

"That answer your question, Slim?" said another of the group. Taylor's mustache twitched; Jordan looked over at him in amusement.

"I could talk about wolves all day," he said.

"So your animals are healthy," Taylor said. It was a question, without being inflected as such.

"Completely."

"Would a wolf attack a human?"

"You know, thinking is kind of divided on that," Jordan said. "A rabid wolf is certainly capable of anything. But rabies in wolves and wolf attacks on people are both extremely rare. It's been said that there's never been a documented attack by a wolf on a human in North America, but they *are* predators. They attack deer, and moose. I don't see why, if the circumstances were right—say, an unarmed man walking through the woods past a hungry wolf—the wolf would not attack. But it almost never happens."

"And wolves kill by ripping their victims, by going for the neck and throat, do they not?"

"Mr. Taylor," Jordan said, "while this may be interesting to you, I really think you're wasting your time. I've already told you that none of my wolves escaped those two nights. And there aren't any free-roaming wolves out there. You'd be much more likely to solve this case by looking for a psychopathic human being, one with a good set of knives, maybe, because humans cause more pain and suffering to other humans every year than the wolf has in all of human history."

If the investigator had a reaction to this impassioned speech, he concealed it. "Your interest in the subject of wolves seems rather, shall we say, eclectic, Mr. Jordan," he said. "You seem to be interested in them not only from a scientific standpoint, but also from the angle of myth and legend. I've seen that movie." He nodded at the poster. "Rather violent, isn't it?"

"Look, someone gave that to me," Jordan said. "And the totem pole, too. I collect wolf paraphernalia. It's not a crime."

Taylor's expression did not change. "May we see your wolves?" he asked.

"By all means. Follow me, gentlemen."

He led them down a gravel path that wound through the sagebrush and around several hillocks until the house was out of view. A rock-strewn dirt road grooved by several large gullies led into the area from another direction. Jordan strode confidently down the narrow path in his boots, well ahead of the investigators, whose dress shoes forced them to pick their way carefully.

The enclosure faced eastward into a breezeway between two mountains, and caught the thermal winds rising off the desert. It was huge, encompassing several small rises and rocky outcroppings that concealed most of the animals from view. The ground, like that outside the fence, was rocky and dotted with small trees and bushy, high-desert vegetation. At a high point within the enclosure near the fence, there was an observation tower, built like a lighthouse with windows all around. The fence itself was at least twelve feet high, and topped with barbed wire.

Those wolves they could see were splayed underneath bushes, seeking the shade they offered. Half asleep, the nearest animal turned an uninterested eye toward the visitors and yawned. On a mound of rocks behind it, a brown and white wolf rose up on its forelegs, stretched, scratched itself behind one ear, and regarded them with gleaming yellow eyes. Two other wolves looked up as the animal yipped.

"Hi, everyone," Jordan called, walking close to the outside of the fence. He addressed each animal by name; they cocked their heads in greeting. This seemed to the investigators to be a daily routine.

Flat patches of wolf scat, smaller and darker than cow patties, littered the inside of the enclosure. There were also a few bones, gnawed white, in evidence. "That fish I've been feeding them gives them the runs," Jordan said cheerfully. "I get it for free down in San Diego. I try to give 'em as much red meat as I can, but it's expensive, feeding seventeen wolves."

"They're smaller than I thought they'd be," Taylor remarked.

"That's because wolves have been enlarged and demonized in human mythology," Jordan replied. "The average full-grown wolf weighs only about a hundred pounds, and many weigh less.

But we've made them villains, and they've grown in our imagination."

"Mr. Jordan, do you ever sell or give your wolves to other people in this area?"

Jordan shook his head. "Not yet, anyway. Wolves aren't for everyone; they don't make great pets. But I might as well save you some time and research. There's a lady over in Henderson Park who's got a couple of wolves. Keeps 'em in kennels, which I think is cruel and unusual. She's got a whole bunch of animals over there. Since you're talking to me, you'll probably want to talk to her as well. Her name's Jane Brock."

"Thank you," said Taylor, making a note.

"But I really think you're barking up the wrong tree," Jordan added. "If you'll pardon the pun."

The investigators weren't through with Jordan, however. They insisted on inspecting the enclosure, and examining his library. They questioned him on his whereabouts on the nights of the murders, which pissed him off, but he managed to answer without showing his anger. Two of them questioned his wife in a separate interview, presumably so that they could not compare notes. They asked for, and received, a copy of his mailing list.

They did not, however, return to Guy Taylor's earlier question about Jordan's interest in the wolf's role in legend and folklore. It seems incredible, to look back on it, but they apparently either disregarded or completely overlooked the other major similarity between the two deaths, which would not receive public airing until Cyrus "Moondog" Nygerski pointed it out, more than a month later, in a newspaper article. None of the investigators seems to have even entertained the possibility that it could have been anything more than a coincidence that both killings took place on the night of the full Moon.

# Chapter Ten

YES, THEY GOT to me, before the week was out. Not all five of them—the gathering at the Jordan Center seemed to have been motivated by a subconscious need for safety in numbers—and not all at the same time. I was visited at my barely furnished home in Sleepy Hollow on four or five different occasions, and once at work. Frank Blaisdell was there at some of those interviews, and I was subjected to the good-cop/bad-cop crossfire I've told you about earlier.

What made it scary was that they wouldn't tell me what they knew. It was established pretty early on that I was a convicted felon, that I'd been recently released from the honor camp and couldn't have killed Brandy Allen unless I had escaped and snuck back in again, that I was still on probation and was statistically likely to backslide. "You really think it's two different guys?" I asked Frank Blaisdell, after he'd conceded my alibi for the first murder.

"We're just checking into every possibility, Joe," he replied, trying to sound as sympathetic as possible. "Now tell us again why you decided to skip work that day and hitchhike to Ramona."

And that was it—I hadn't told them about the grass. I wasn't going to, either, and neither would anybody else barely two weeks out of state custody. I told them that I went to Ramona to go shopping, and they looked in my kitchen and found beer, a loaf of bread, a jar of peanut butter, and a bag of chocolate-chip cookies. "Must've been important," the other cop—the bad cop—growled. "You just can't get this kind of stuff in Julian."

They had the guy from Warner Springs who had dropped me off in Santa Ysabel on the way home. They had the guy who gave me a ride down. They had my boss, and the time of my call. They had someone who said she saw me in front of Dresher's Bakery, reading the paper. For all I knew, they might've found Eddie, the guy who sold me the grass; they might've known I was lying right there; they might be back any hour, any day, with a search warrant and a dark green paddy wagon. I realized later I was being paranoid—they were after a killer, not a dope-smoking ex-thief—but that's what a life of crime will do to you. I still hate cops, all cops, right down to button-cute meter maids in their tight white shorts.

They apparently didn't have the wastrel kids who brought me home in the midst of their drinking-and-driving, rocking-and-rolling, Friday-night jamboree. Nobody seemed to have seen them at all, which meant only that they would live to party another day.

I wasn't the only resident of Sleepy Hollow to be questioned, and the frequent visits by uniformed officers and plainclothesmen made all the tenants edgy. The local cops were well acquainted with the Hollow, whose population was always changing but whose median income, except when a particularly lucrative drug deal went down, never rose. It was a small step up from the Ghetto, a ramshackle collection of beat-up old motor homes two blocks behind Main Street; it was also an improvement over homelessness, jail, and the gang-dominated neighborhoods of East San Diego, where Sleepy Hollow alumni often went when they couldn't pay the rent. But there was upward mobility too; houses occasionally came up for rent in greater Julian, and people at the Hollow with jobs could sometimes afford to move into them. In more than just location, Sleepy Hollow was the gateway to Julian.

On the weekend after Patsy Kittredge met her grisly fate, I saw two of the investigators talking with Haley as he watered his trees. They were telling him, no doubt, that at least one of his tenants was under surveillance, suspected of being involved in a murder. I'm sure they were telling him to keep an eye on me, in particular, since I was new and therefore suspicious. But everyone in Sleepy Hollow had skeletons; it was not the sort of place upstanding citizens stayed for long.

The cops spent a fair amount of time at Blind Ben's house, talking to the people who went through the revolving door there, and they also paid a visit to Tom Keeler. I saw two of them with Sven one day, up at Tanya's; it seemed as though the officers were doing most of the talking while Sven kept carving away on his latest walking stick, staring straight ahead and occasionally nodding.

They kept coming around long after they'd talked to everybody, just cruising through, and it made everybody a little bit nervous. For people who just wanted to deal a little dope or house a few burglarized items, a murder investigation represented an unwelcome intrusion. And I could tell that a lot of them thought it was my fault. I could tell by the cold shoulders, the looks beyond me when I passed my neighbors on the street, the sudden stoppage of invitations to join the horseshoe games, and the fact that Tom Keeler was up all night again, breaking up rocks and looking for gold.

# Chapter Eleven

CYRUS "MOONDOG" NYGERSKI was to have a profound effect on my life, one that continues to this day, though we have gone our separate ways. Had it not been for Moondog, I might have gone back to thievery, because it was tough working for near minimum wage in the steaming kitchen of a restaurant, eating whatever they could spare, when in my former life I had grown accustomed to walking into such places and ordering the most expensive thing on the menu.

Moondog had been and done a lot of things, in a lot of different places. He'd sailed windjammer schooners on the Maine coast, and smuggled dope by small airplane from Mexico into the Southern California deserts. He had played a year of minor-league baseball in Beloit, Wisconsin, in the late 1960s, batting .179 and leading the league's second basemen in errors; he had quit baseball for a career in rock music. By the time I met him, he called himself a writer. It was unclear to me how, or even if, he made his living at the craft, or whether or not he cared, for his was an unconventional lifestyle with nonstandard income requirements. His writing was unconventional, too, which possibly limited his potential audience. He seemed not to care about that, either, and once I got to know him I understood why; he was not a man on whom fame would have sat comfortably.

"I write from the liberating but lonely realization that nobody believes what I say," he told me. "Nobody takes it seriously. I'm an expressionist, not a chronicler. I am the Jackson Pollock of journalism. I throw words at a page, and see what sticks."

He also encouraged me in my early efforts at setting words to paper, and I needed a lot of encouragement. For when I decided to inquire about a job at the *Julian Nugget*, I had done very little writing at all since high school, and wasn't sure I wouldn't get laughed out of the office after turning in my first article. Moondog told me to keep at it, even if I labored under the opinion (which I often did) that what I wrote was shit. "Most people are too timid even to try," he said. "Your biggest enemy is indifference. If you can reach just one person, it's worth doing."

He knew all about indifference. For it was Cyrus "Moondog" Nygerski who first figured out what was going on, and who tried to warn the community. True to his words, nobody believed him.

I finally met Moondog a bit less than two weeks after the death of Patsy Kittredge; unlike Erik Gunn, I don't have a memory for exact dates, and that's one reason, though not the only one, why as a journalist I will never transcend mediocrity. The cops had quit coming to my door, but they still cruised through the Hollow from time to time and gave me the evil eye in town. They made it clear that they still considered me a suspect, though I was free to go back and forth to my job and make my appointed rounds. I was a marked man at work, too; the envelope of air around me was heavy with the pointed silence of my co-workers, most of whom had lived in Julian for years. And my boss was being a real jerk, yelling at me for little things, docking my pay when I was fifteen minutes late, and making me walk home at night even though he drove right past the Hollow on his way home and easily could have offered me a ride.

Maybe he was that way all the time; I once saw him ream out Erik Gunn for parking his car for five minutes in his parking lot to take a picture across the street—but I was getting mighty sick of taking his shit and not saying anything about it. I had figured on hanging in Julian for maybe a year, saving some money, and then possibly heading somewhere else, away from California (where my record was just a computer screen away from any cop who decided to check me out), when the next summer rolled around. But two weeks in, though I didn't miss the honor camp for a minute, I was already thinking about another job. And that was why I went to see Erik Gunn at the *Julian Nugget*.

I'd liked the issues of the *Nugget* I'd seen, especially the latest one, on the murder. Gunn had indeed found his angle. The front page that stared out from newspaper racks at the tourists and the locals was dominated by a huge, black question mark, around which wrapped the copy of a single story. The bold headline at the top of the page read, QUESTIONS ABOUND IN WAKE OF LATEST DEATH.

Gunn had been thorough, getting as much as he could out of the cops, while talking to students, teachers, and the three or four close friends Patsy Kittredge had made in her three years in town. He spoke with Steve Dakota about the tragic loss to the school. He got Danny Taylor at the Chevron station to tell him that her car was badly in need of a tune-up and that she had, in fact, scheduled one for the following week. He even unearthed the boyfriend in San Diego most locals didn't know she had, and with whom she stayed on most weekends. She had been there that evening, the boyfriend confirmed, but had opted not to spend the night.

The murder of Brandy Allen was recounted, and Frank Blaisdell offered a few speculations on what sort of killer the cops were looking for. They had no suspects at present, he added, which made me feel better, until a subsequent paragraph said police were keeping a close watch on all suspicious people in the area. I was, I presumed, among that group.

I couldn't believe the *Julian Nugget* office. It boasted commanding views of the town in two directions, but the windows were the only part of the place not completely overrun with junk, which included stacks of magazines and newspapers, books, clocks, boxes of computer equipment and office supplies, vases and statuettes, hanging plants, fake trees, posters, and a thousand knickknacks that someone apparently thought gave the place character but that worked together to overwhelm the senses of anyone who entered. There were three desks in the room, though no one was sitting at any of them. They were covered with papers, jars of pencils and pens, coffee cups, pictures of husbands and wives and children and grandchildren, and various other items inside and out of bags or packages. Immediately inside the door were two newspaper racks, offering copies of the last eight issues, in retrograde order from the top shelf of the rack nearest the door. Beside these stood a huge metal coatrack, empty save for a wide-brimmed yellow hat of the type worn by Al Capone caricatures in a thousand bad gangster movies. The desk at the front of the room, facing the door like a nose tackle, obviously belonged to the office manager, who wasn't there. Stacks of neatly arranged message pads, subscription forms, and receipt books guarded the front; behind them stood a phone, a calculator, the requisite family photos, an ashtray, and a sign taped to the front that read WHICH PART OF NO DID YOU MISUNDERSTAND? Behind this desk was another desk, also facing out but far less organized, with a couple of tall Budweiser beer cans peering out through the paper jungle. Around this desk were arrayed several chairs; there were, in fact, at least a dozen chairs in the office, though the place was so cluttered I couldn't imagine that many people squeezing into it. A third desk stood to the right of the door, and this one was truly dangerous. It was piled so high with odds and ends, some of them breakable, that one stepped carefully in its vicinity. Anyone sitting at that desk when an earthquake hit would stand a fair chance of being killed by falling debris.

All along the wall behind this Desk from Hell were bookshelves, absolutely crammed with hardcover and paperback volumes and stacks of paper that hadn't found a home anywhere else in the office. Farther along this wall were tables atop which sat a computer, a laser printer, and still more paper, and behind everything, along the back wall, was the paste-up area, which looked more like an Oliver North document-shredding operation than a newspaper production room.

If one stepped carefully, one could perhaps negotiate a path from the door to the chest-high table at the back without knocking over anything, but it was a task that required much care, for at every glimmer of open space and on every available surface there stood an oil lamp, or a bit of handcrafted pottery, or a carved bighorn sheep or a framed engraving of a roadrunner. The *Julian Nugget* office was right above one of the town's many gift shops, but it probably could have opened its doors on tourist weekends and done a decent business without printing a word.

The man hunched over the computer keyboard, tap-tap-tapping away, didn't hear me come in. He was young, bald, and sort of gangly-looking; his upper body disappeared turtlelike into a lightweight suit jacket that was a couple of sizes too big for him. He squinted at the screen during pauses; when he was actually typing, he looked at his hands. A sixteen-ounce can of Budweiser stood in an open drawer beside him. It was about four in the afternoon.

"Excuse me," I said, and he turned. "I'm looking for Erik Gunn."

"That's me," he said. His face bore, I thought, a sort of worried expression. "What can I do for you?"

"My name's Joe Acton. I'm new in town. Wondering if you're looking for a reporter or anything."

His face didn't change. "You got any experience?"

"A little," I lied.

Gunn sighed, and retreated farther into his jacket. Weird that he was wearing a jacket in July, I thought, when it was at least ninety degrees outside. But the air conditioning hummed mightily, working in harmony with the papers it stirred in their various nooks and crannies, and it was actually pretty cool in there.

"You know," he said, "I'd *love* to have a reporter. I'm sick of doing it all myself. It's just a question of getting the publisher to loosen the purse strings a little."

"I see," I said. And where was the publisher, I wondered.

"And I'm right in the middle of this," he said, waving a hand at the computer screen. "Which I've got to get done before the water board meeting tonight. I'll tell you what. Can you come back a little later? We can talk, and see if maybe we can work something out. No promises, but I'll have some time to talk, at least."

"I'm on my way to work right now," I said.

"Where do you work?" he asked me.

"Bucky's Barbecue," I said. "In the kitchen."

"I hear that guy's a real sweetheart to work for," Gunn said, sarcastically.

"He's not so bad," I lied. "I've had worse bosses." *That* part was true.

"What time do you get off?"

79

" 'Bout eleven."

"I'll be here," he said. "I'll leave the back door downstairs unlocked. The rest of the building will be empty. Just come on up."

And so, at just before midnight on a Tuesday, I found myself in the *Julian Nugget* office, drinking beer and shooting the shit with Erik Gunn, the paper's lonely and tormented editor. The office was supplied with a refrigerator as well as a microwave, a coffeemaker, and a toaster oven, though you had to move a stack of *Ranch and Coast* magazines to find the microwave, and the toaster oven sat precariously balanced atop the pile on the publisher's desk. In the first ten minutes of our conversation, Gunn told me he was burned out, he was sick of assigning stories to himself, laying out the paper, and proofing the flats for his own mistakes. He'd taken a week off in June, he said, and driven the coast north to San Francisco, camping in the car and sprinkling resumés at every daily newspaper he passed along the way. He was sick of Julian and the fishbowl of small-town life. He was sick of his publisher, a wealthy woman in her sixties named Claudia Gaines, who liked to throw parties and sponsor events and organizations and wheel and deal with advertisers, but hadn't a clue about how to run a newspaper. Claudia paid his salary and the salaries of a succession of office managers, tossed pittances to the columnists and the guy who developed the photos, and spent the rest of the budget on furniture and decorations for the office, which was fairly bursting with furniture and decorations. Gunn said that if he had his way, he'd hold a huge yard sale in the parking lot, and get rid of everything but the computer, the desks and those chairs that went with them, the coffeemaker, and the refrigerator. He'd use the money to hire one reporter who could show up at meetings and write complete sentences.

He talked about the issues the newspaper covered: the contamination of the town's dwindling water supply, the county's plans to build a huge landfill out near Warner Springs, and of course the murders. He was pretty torn up about the murders—not that he seemed too happy about much of anything—and I told him about my experience with the local cops, leaving out the fact that I had been recently paroled from the honor camp as a convicted ripoff artist. At this he grew interested, and we were talking about this very subject when the downstairs door banged open and heavy, unhurried footsteps began clomping up the stairs.

A moment later a mustachioed face underneath a sailor's cap and a head full of dark hair appeared in the doorway. Our guest was of medium height, and was wearing a black leather jacket, faded blue jeans, and a pair of the black shitkicker boots that some people tromp around in all the time, whatever the season. For the first time since I'd been there, afternoon and night, Gunn's face visibly brightened. "Hey! Moondog!"

"Slaving away as usual," growled the visitor. In one hand he held several loose sheets of paper. "I've been wondering where I left this hat," he added, removing the sailor's cap and replacing it with the yellow hat from the coatrack. "What're you up to?"

"Interviewing potential new talent," Gunn said cheerfully. It was amazing—his whole persona had changed in the few seconds the newcomer had been in the room. "You want a beer?"

"Yeah."

"Moondog, I'd like you to meet Joe Acton. He wants to write for us. Joe, this is the *Julian Nugget*'s premier guest columnist, Cyrus 'Moondog' Nygerski."

"When you deign to print my stuff, that is," said Moondog, fishing a can of beer from the refrigerator and cranking it open. He nodded in my direction. I bobbed my head in return, and our eyes met briefly.

"Come on, we print most of your stuff that doesn't have *fuck* or *shit* in it," Gunn retorted.

"*The Muckraker* doesn't care about that," Moondog replied, taking a swig.

"*The Muckraker*," said Gunn, a trifle stiffly, "isn't a real newspaper."

"Maybe not in your narrow definition of the term, but it sure as hell is more entertaining than this rag of yours."

Gunn chose to ignore this barb. "So, Moondog, where you been? Haven't seen you in more than a month."

"Been busy," the visitor said, and that was all.

"I read your piece on the ants," I said, to fill the awkward silence that followed. "It was very good."

"Shit, that's tame stuff for Moondog," Gunn said happily. "He once suggested dealing with the drought by putting the chairman of the water board down one of the wells, wearing a pair of cement boots. When he stopped talking, that would mean that the water had risen above his mouth and the town could stop rationing."

"Did you print that?" I asked.

"Are you kidding? A lot of people don't even know who this guy is. They think I write his stuff, or someone else around town. They think Cyrus 'Moondog' Nygerski is a *nom de plume.*"

"It *is* a weird name," I said.

Nygerski scowled and said nothing.

"Joe's been telling me that the cops have been after him, asking questions about the murders, especially the latest one," Gunn said. "He thinks he's a suspect."

Moondog lifted an eyebrow. "That's interesting," he said. "I *know* I'm one."

"You?" Gunn looked shocked. "Why you?"

"They found my fingerprints in the Kittredge woman's car."

82

"You knew her?" The surprise stood out in Gunn's voice.

"Yeah," said Moondog, sipping at his beer. "Yeah, I knew her."

He did not elaborate. His face was inscrutable. As I got to know him better, I would come to understand the pain he suffered at Patsy's meteoric flash across his life, but none of it was visible in his features. Erik Gunn's suffering stood out from every pore. They had both loved her, but while Gunn spiraled deeper and deeper into self-pity, Moondog chose instead to go on with his life, bearing his sorrow in silence.

And that was his style, I was to learn. He never lied, but he almost never volunteered unsolicited information, especially about himself. If he had something to say, he wrote a column, and sent it to the *Julian Nugget* or the *Manzanita Muckraker* or one of the other handful of small newspapers and magazines that occasionally used his writing. He did not tell Gunn that the cops had also found his prints in Patsy Kittredge's home, in her bedroom and bathroom, and that three officers had managed to make their way out to his place, where Gunn had never been—where, in fact, less than half a dozen Julianites had been in all the time Moondog had lived there—and grilled him for the better part of three hours. Moondog had finally told them to arrest him or leave, and they had gone off, with threats to return if they uncovered more evidence.

We became friends in part because I'm the same way. I know how to keep my mouth shut and my eyes open and look behind me from time to time. And it's also the reason I'm a lousy journalist. I guard my privacy, and am loath to pry into that of others. I am now almost forty; most of my professional background is in thievery, and I still don't know what I'm going to do with my life, however much may be left of it. I know newspaper reporting isn't it. But I'm kind of glad I gave it a try, because otherwise I might never have met Moondog Nygerski, with whom mutual respect began turning into friendship that very night, when he gave me a ride back to the Hollow and accepted my invitation to come inside for a beer.

"I like it," he said, looking around the nearly empty cabin. "It's . . . bohemian."

# Chapter Twelve

EVERYDAY LIFE IN Julian was becoming more bohemian as well. Summer is usually the slow time of year there, with the weekend tourist crunch picking up around Labor Day, reaching full pitch in October, and continuing its crescendo right through the Christmas season. But for the merchants and restaurateurs, this summer had been worse than usual. The hot, dry weather and negative publicity had kept people away in record numbers.

Wally Leach wasn't just blowing smoke; the town's water really was poisoned. And the culpability of the Chevron station was at least an open question. Certainly the corporate giant was acting as if it had sins for which to atone; without admitting guilt, the company had sent in hydrologists and engineers, sprung for a half-million-dollar filtration system at the central pumping station, and organized two massive giveaways of bottled water to anyone living within the boundaries of the Julian Water District.

Drought gripped Southern California like a vise. For four years the accumulation of rain and snow in the mountains had been far below normal. The town's wells were lower than at any time in anybody's memory, and the new holes the water district's board of directors feverishly commissioned added only a figurative trickle.

Then, in April, at the end of yet another distressingly dry winter, a routine test turned up unacceptably high levels of benzene, as well as several other components of gasoline, in four of the district's eight wells. The water coming out of the taps in town was laden, according to state and federal regulatory standards, with cancer-causing chemicals. Fingers were quick to point at Chevron, which, as one of the few overtly corporate entities in town, was reviled by many of the local neotraditionalists. Chevron, which had had similar problems elsewhere, was quick to respond with what the water district didn't have: money. But there were old underground fuel tanks all over the town site, laid and abandoned many years before such things were ever regulated, and no one had more than a general idea of where they all were. Water board chairman Steve Stephenson threw up his hands and called the drought "an act of God" for which there was no remedy but to wait and pray; Harry Ferguson, his more practical manager of operations, said the low water level meant that whatever chemicals got into the wells were simply that much more concentrated. Chevron announced that it had determined its own tanks to be tight; soon test holes were boring into the Earth at various spots around town in an effort to pinpoint the source of the contamination. "As far as anybody knows, the ground itself could be contaminated," Harry Ferguson said.

It was big news in the San Diego papers. Restaurants that served free rolls began charging fifty cents for a cup of water; their owners bitched that the paper plates and cups kept customers away. A moratorium on new water service, which effectively halted construction, was stiffened to allow negative growth

86

through attrition; when a business or residence gave up its water meter, a new customer could no longer slip in to take its place. Real estate sales, which had been slow, stopped completely. Several Realtors accused the members of the water board of using the drought as a means to limit growth, and Erik Gunn heard more than one suggestion that he soft-pedal the town's water woes in print because he was hurting the business of some of the paper's best advertisers. When deaths that were quicker and more spectacular than benzene poisoning relegated the water problems to secondary news status, Gunn wondered if some of those advertisers weren't secretly relieved. Murder, after all, is often a random thing, akin to being struck by lightning. But people cannot live without water.

August brought still more of the hot, dry weather that had marked April, May, June, and July. The apples on the trees in the surrounding orchards grew to golf ball size and stopped. Leaves turned brown and shriveled; ice cream, Popsicles, and soda pop turned to gooey puddles on the sidewalks of Main Street because no one wanted to be seen hosing them off.

Chevron sank a test well at the street's south end, sending clouds of dust into the air and finding, alas, unacceptably high levels of benzene there as well. Two hundred yards away, on the other side of Main Street and up an embankment, Justin Zak, a San Diego businessman who wanted to build a restaurant and mini-mall on his property there, sank his own well and came up with a few hundred gallons per minute of clear, chemical-free water. At a subsequent meeting of the water board, Leo Vanderbilt, a local geologist, explained to the astonished board members that the Julian town site sits on top of a rock formation called a schist—that parallel fissures run through the rock, and that some of the fissures contain substantial amounts of water. It was a crapshoot whether one would hit a fissure or a dry spot, and Zak had simply gotten lucky. Now the water board, which had spent money it didn't have on a series of dry holes and had three times refused to sell Justin Zak a water meter, was begging to buy his water.

The members of the water board, already under fire from the town's business owners for supposedly manipulating the drought, now were vilified as incompetent. If an out-of-town finance guy could sink a single well and strike liquid gold, the talk went, obviously the water board was either getting bad information from its so-called experts, or else was hoarding what had become the town's most precious resource, for reasons of its own.

Justin Zak's new well should have spelled, if not salvation, at least relief from the deepening crisis of the drought. But the water district had a serious problem: it was very nearly broke. Not even the stringent moratorium it had imposed on the town could account for the state of its finances; there were discrepancies in the books that could not be explained away by the reduction in income. The district had paid out a good deal of money for its new wells and hydrology studies of nearby areas, but it had also dramatically raised its rates and slapped penalty fees on water gluttons. Additionally, the district should have had at least a certain amount of emergency working capital. Harry Ferguson and several members of the board began to suspect that someone was illegally siphoning funds. Suspicion fell, quite naturally, on the two people with the most access to the money: board president Steve Stephenson, who signed the checks, and secretary-treasurer Vicki Bodine, who kept the books.

Steve Stephenson was a man in over his head. A retired truck-driver, he had run for the water board (and in a district as small as Julian, one usually had only to run in order to get elected) primarily out of selfish concern for his own water rates at the home he and his wife planned to spend the rest of their days in, on a ridge overlooking the town. He had no expertise in water matters, and relied on Harry Ferguson, who actually ran the district's operation, for sound advice.

Stephenson and his wife lived well. They had a monstrously large motor home in which they made frequent trips to Baja, where they owned a beachfront bungalow. They'd put in a bunch of expensive landscaping around their home, half of which was now in the process of dying of thirst, because it wouldn't do, after all, to have the chairman of the water board nurture his vines while restaurants had to close their doors two days a week to keep the wells from going dry.

Yes—that last was the recommendation from the water board, one that Bucky's Barbecue followed, giving me every Monday and Tuesday off. Some eatery owners gave up entirely and announced that they would be on vacation in August, before the tourist season started. This was not uncommon even in good years, but Moondog said more places were closed, and for longer, this time around—it had been a miserable summer for business. No one believed that the voluntary five-day work week would stay in effect through September and October, when the town tried to suck up as many tourist dollars as it could, but for now, on Mondays and Tuesdays everybody ate at home.

Stephenson would maintain later that Vicki Bodine had forged his signature on at least a dozen checks, and investigators would have no reason to disbelieve him. The water district would get a portion of the missing money—determined to be close to $100,000—through its insurance company, but it would never have the satisfaction of assigning blame and exacting punishment, because by the time the records were fully examined, everything had changed.

Vicki Bodine was thirty-five and originally from New York—Brooklyn, if I'm any judge of accents. She was popular in town. It was easy to get to know her; she was one of those people who had the knack of turning a ten-second hello into a twenty-minute conversation. Most people liked her—it was hard not to like someone so outgoing—and she had been accepted into the community because she'd passed the five-year residency requirement and worked for the water district. She was a big woman, not fat, but with a physical presence unsuited to subtlety. She was tall, about five-eight or five-nine, and sported a mane of magnificent blondish-red hair that exploded from the top of her head in looping curls that tumbled over her wide shoulders and large breasts and down to the top of her ample behind. She had a husband who worked at a computer electronics firm in San Diego and commuted to and from the city every day. She had two kids, a boy in third grade and a girl in first. She had a house outside of town, and a good many friends. She also had a lover, a rugged tree topper a few years her junior, with his own business and crew, who it was said had fathered at least three children in town with last names different from his.

Vicki Bodine liked to get out; she liked to socialize. She could be found several afternoons a week after work at Quinn's, one of the two bars in town, playing pool with the boys, betting drinks on the outcome. Sometimes she'd go out at night, too, frequently without her husband, either to Quinn's or the Fisherman's Friend, a somewhat rowdier joint ten miles out of town on Lake Cuyamaca.

She worked four days a week, six hours a day, and drove a brand-new, fire-engine-red Toyota Supra. It occurred to me, the first time I saw her driving it through town with the sunroof open and the stereo blasting, that the car must have been a bit of a stretch on a part-time salary.

At the time it was idle speculation; I was slaving away at Bucky's Barbecue, the water district office was across the street, and one hears a lot in a small town if one keeps one's ears open.

But it was soon to be more than that. For the whole water mess was destined to become grist for the local newspaper—and for a new reporter with a wide streak of anarchy and no loyalties to anyone.

# Chapter Thirteen

"WE CAN PAY YOU," Erik Gunn said, "thirty-five dollars per story. You can cover the water board and the planning group, plus whatever stories I assign you. I'll do the sheriff's stuff and whatever other news there is, including the murder investigations. You can come in here and type your stories on the computer, but I need them by Tuesday evening. Okay?"

I guessed that meant I'd passed my writing test—a single typed page on the upcoming Labor Day weekend carnival at the Catholic church. Gunn had given me the assignment, with no pay, to see if I could put complete sentences together, and it was running in the next paper with only a few spelling corrections.

"How many stories a week?" I asked.

"One or two, to start with. That's really all we can afford."

Well, I wouldn't be able to quit my job at Bucky's Barbecue in order to embark on my new career, but seventy bucks a week would sure help, and with the restaurant closed on Mondays and Tuesdays I figured to be able to get to at least some of the meetings. For those that took place on other nights, I hoped I could get my asshole boss to give me some time off. I said okay.

Gunn held out his hand. "Welcome aboard," he said, in the same weary tone. The guy seemed to be in a perpetually lousy mood; the only time I'd ever seen him smile was the night Moondog came into the office. That night the banter had flowed effortlessly; Gunn had actually laughed at the piece of writing Moondog had given him, which appeared in the next paper under the headline LET THE PEOPLE RUN THE WATER BOARD. The thrust of the piece was that Julian's water supply could not be allocated any less efficiently than at present even if it were managed on the communist model for agriculture. Moondog argued that the water should be owned collectively, quotas established, and such a mess made of things that some foreign power—Oregon, maybe—would be compelled to step in out of humanitarian concern and bail the town out.

Gunn drank a lot. The office refrigerator was always filled with beer, and he kept a bottle of Jack Daniel's stashed in the bottom drawer of the file cabinet behind his desk. He haunted the office late at night, several nights a week, even when there was nothing to do that couldn't be put off until the morning. Moondog said Gunn's wife drove him to the bottle, that he hung out in his ivory tower to avoid going home and finding a baby-sitter on the couch while his wife was out on a date. Moondog added that if he were in Gunn's place he'd simply take up with the baby-sitter, but Gunn seemed to prefer self-pity and the deadening effects of alcohol.

Moondog pointed Joyce Gunn out to me one day from the cab of his pickup truck; she was walking down Main Street with one-legged Sven, and made quite a contrast to him with her self-assured walk, shoulders squared and head held high, as he shuffled along beside her. I was struck by how pretty she was, and wondered—like everybody else, I guess—what she was doing with someone so physically unappealing. It was obvious that Sven didn't give a shit about his clothes or couldn't afford to, for he seemed always to be wearing the same torn, faded blue jeans and decrepit leather jacket. The only apparent pride in his appearance manifested itself in his many carefully decorated canes.

I saw Joyce at other times, and with other people: once coming out of the liquor store with a tall, good-looking cowboy type; once with a group of young mothers at the post office; once when she dropped off her and Gunn's daughter at the *Julian Nugget* office; she had a nod for me and maybe two sentences for her husband. I could tell that her presence there was painful for them both. She was invading his sanctuary, and he was communicating to her without words that her standing in the town depended on his job. Joyce had fire in her eyes and was nobody's shadow, and Gunn, introverted as he was, seemed incapable of giving her the attention she felt she deserved. He told me in one of our late-night bullshit sessions that he had once made love to her on the top of his desk, but I had a hard time picturing this and wondered if it wasn't mere male bragging.

I wasn't given a desk; there wasn't room in the office for an additional chair, let alone another working surface. Gunn simply cleared a spot on the publisher's desk (moving the toaster oven temporarily to the production area), excavated a phone from somewhere underneath the pile, and said I could work there when I needed to make calls. Claudia wouldn't mind, he said, because she was never there, at least not during anything that could reasonably be called working hours.

Indeed, almost two weeks passed between the time I was hired and the day I finally met Claudia Gaines, the mostly absentee publisher of the *Julian Nugget*. But I met the office manager the next day. Her name was Karen, and if Gunn was stuck on morose, her meter was permanently set to *cross*. She was a crabby, chain-smoking woman with jet-black hair pulled severely back from her face and compressed into a bun behind her neck, with a knitting needle thrust through it. For six hours a day on Mondays, Wednesdays, and Fridays, she glowered around the office with a look that threatened to take your head off if you asked for anything. Since the main object of her wrath was the publisher, who signed her check and was never there, Gunn and I were the unwitting recipients of her excess anger.

"That woman!" she'd seethe, upon seeing something on her desk amiss. "I don't understand why she can't leave my subscription lists alone! She tries to help, and all she does is mess everything up! She should just stick to her parties and her Republican Club meetings and her art collections and let us do our jobs!"

And at this Gunn would nod silently, having heard it all before.

"We've got to do a story on the new superintendent," he told me on that first day. "It's been kind of put on the back burner, what with all the excitement about the murders. But school starts next month, and people need to know about the new guy at the helm. I want you to go interview him, find out about his background and stuff, his goals for the school, and so on."

"It's gotta be hard for him," I said. "New on the job, and right away one of his teachers is killed."

"Yeah." A misty look came into Gunn's eyes, and he turned toward the window. "Hard on us all," he murmured.

"You want me to ask him about it?"

Gunn stared out the window a long time without answering. Finally he said, "If he brings it up, fine. But we've covered her death pretty thoroughly. I'm more interested in a straight feature story on him. Find out who he is, what he's done, what makes him tick. Get some direct quotes about what he wants for the future of the school system. I'd like it to be a pretty positive story. God knows we've had enough negative news lately."

I met Steve Dakota in his office, where he was eager to talk to

9 5

me and to make a favorable impression on the newspaper's—
my—readers. He poured coffee, and I noticed how awkwardly
his outsized hands gripped the tiny Styrofoam cup. He seemed
always on the verge of spilling it. He spoke at length about the
importance of good public relations, and said his first goal would
be to turn around the high school's image problem in the town.
He would do this, he said, by attending meetings of community
organizations, by encouraging the participation of local businesses in school fund-raisers, and by working with teachers and
parents to see that each student received individualized attention. He didn't mention Patsy Kittredge at all.

He was from the San Fernando Valley, he said, and grew up
idolizing Sandy Koufax and Don Drysdale of the Dodgers and
Jerry West and Elgin Baylor of the Lakers. He had been a history
teacher and eventually an assistant principal in a school district
on the coast north of San Diego, where he and his wife and their
three children still lived, though he said they were looking for a
place in Julian. The new job, he told me several times, was tre-
mendously exciting.

Gunn ran my story on page one, after cleaning up some of the
grammar, alongside a picture of Dakota on a bicycle, riding
through town. "Don't take a picture of me sitting behind my
desk," the new superintendent told me. "I'm not going to be
behind my desk much, once school starts. I'm going to be out
and about, among the kids. I'm going to be an activist, not a
paper pusher." The bicycle photo was Gunn's idea, and a good
one.

Aside from Moondog, Claudia Gaines was the only person
associated with the paper who possessed any visible sense of joy.
Both of them were absent from the office most of the time,
which may have had something to do with it. And though
Claudia Gaines smothered the office with her personality and
Moondog left not a trace of himself there, they each so effec-

tively avoided the newspaper's place of business that they had never even met each other. Moondog told me later that the publisher was not even convinced of his existence, that she signed the thirty-five-dollar checks for his columns—made out to Cyrus M. Nygerski—and handed them to Gunn with a wink, as if to indicate that she was in on his little joke. Gunn dutifully passed the checks along when he saw Moondog, every few weeks or so; Moondog cashed them all at once at a bank in Temecula, which sometimes caused several *Julian Nugget* checks to bounce at local businesses.

Claudia Gaines breezed into the office late one afternoon while I was hunting and pecking around the computer keyboard, working on a story on the water district and trying like mad to get it done before I had to report to work at Bucky's. Gunn was there, nursing a beer at his desk and reading the latest copy of the *Manzanita Muckraker*, a monthly missive published farther out in the backcountry of San Diego County. The *Muckraker*, to which Moondog also contributed, circulated all over the mountains and the desert and seemed to be something of a thorn in Gunn's side. "Look at this," he'd railed, earlier that afternoon. "These guys have no conception of how to write a news story. They editorialize all over the place, and some of the stuff they print is just plain wrong. Here's an article by some redneck complaining that horses are being squeezed out of Cuyamaca Park. They've got miles of horse trails. I don't want to step in horseshit every time I go hiking . . ." Nonetheless, the *Muckraker*, because of its proletarian approach, was a popular paper in the area, with several good ads from Julian, and Gunn worried about the competition.

Moondog's column in the *Muckraker* detailed his long-held suspicion that Ronald Reagan and Margaret Thatcher had been sleeping together, that they had in fact done so in the White House, right under Nancy's nose. As proof, he cited an AP photo showing the president and the British prime minister frolicking together with the Reagan dogs on the White House lawn one cherry-blossomed morning in 1987 or '88. "Look at their faces," Moondog said when he showed me the picture. "You can just tell they spent the night together." The column went on to state that at the Gorbachev summits, Reagan had done nothing but make eyes at Raisa, and that was why Nancy hated her.

When he saw his boss, Gunn took his feet off the desk, closed the newspaper, and set it on top of his open desk drawer, concealing the can of beer from her view. She was carrying several white paper bags; from the top of one protruded an arm-length bouquet of colorful dried flowers. She set them down atop the rest of the junk on her desk, where they balanced precariously.

"I just *had* to get these flowers," she said. "They're having a show downstairs at the town hall, and the place is simply *filled* with them. Aren't they lovely?"

Without waiting for an answer, she took a wicker basket from one of the other bags, put the flowers in it, and began searching the crowded walls for a suitable place to hang it, humming softly to herself. She took no notice of me until she approached the wall above the computer.

"Oh, hi," she said. "I'm Claudia Gaines. I own the paper."

"Yes, I know," I said, rising from my chair and taking her outstretched hand. It was limp, perhaps from the weight of the three large rings and the ponderous wooden bracelets around the wrist. She was a large woman in a body about six inches too short; she was barely, I guessed, over five feet tall. Her graying hair was piled atop her head in a failed attempt at making herself appear taller. She was dressed in a style I would characterize as expensive peasant; her flaming red dress, heavily embroidered across the bosom, reached her ankles. I could tell she had been attractive when she was younger and thinner; she was not entirely unattractive now. Her mannerisms, though, were girlish, learned in the days when the admiring eyes of men bearing gifts had all turned toward her.

"Claudia, this is Joe Acton, the new writer we hired," said Gunn, rising also and coming out from behind his desk. "He wrote the article last week about the new superintendent."

"Oh, yes, I remember that article. It was fine." She smiled at me, and her eyes, I noticed, were pale blue, so pale you could almost see through them. No doubt about it, twenty-five years ago she must have been a knockout.

As time went on, I discovered that everything about the paper was "fine" to Claudia Gaines. I'd already observed that she had very little to do with its day-to-day or even week-to-week operation; it was entirely Gunn's show, and he ignored or modified her occasional suggestions at will. He ran a center spread of children's artwork from a summer day-camp program because it took him about five minutes to lay it out, but any of her ideas that would have caused him additional work he either quickly dismissed or quietly let slide. I perceived that there was some underlying tension between the two of them that was never faced directly, and perhaps that was why she insisted on stuffing the office with trinkets. Gunn would have preferred a more utilitarian workspace, but she had relinquished control of the product and wasn't going to give him the office as well.

Gunn could have written anything he wanted to, and it would have been "fine" with Claudia Gaines. She drew the line at obscene words and questionable language; he had once used the phrase "son of a bitch" in a story, only to see the entire offending paragraph removed, leaving a big hole in the paper. She raised an eyebrow occasionally at some of Moondog's more outlandish pronouncements, but she was essentially uncritical. You would think Gunn would have been happy with that kind of creative freedom, but he was a self-critical bastard who thought every issue should be better than the last. The man carried a lot of self-imposed stress. He'd been trained in mainstream journalism, Moondog said, and it had ruined him as a writer. Whatever imagination he may once have possessed had been *who*ed, *what*ed, *where*d, *when*ed, and *how*ed out of him.

Meanwhile, I was working on a hot story of my own. Gunn wanted me to investigate the water district, to find out where all its money had gone. It was hard to find out much. Steve Stephenson hated talking to the press, and Vicki Bodine, the district's secretary, talked lots and lots but didn't really say anything. I liked her, though—she was friendly to me when I called or dropped by the office, and tossed out a lot of enjoyable town gossip and off-color jokes. Justin Zak was also pretty willing to talk. I think he enjoyed rubbing the water board's collective face in the success of his new well. At the very first water board meeting I attended, Zak got into a huge argument with Stephenson, who accused him of holding the town hostage to his own profits, and then turned to me and told me he didn't want any of his outburst printed in the paper.

"We'll print it all," Gunn told me, when I related the incident the next day. "Who the hell does Stephenson think he is, anyway? You can't shoot your mouth off at a public meeting and then tell the paper not to print it. We *are* the public. If he wants to make an idiot of himself, we're there to help him!"

Gunn clearly liked having someone to boss around, though he wasn't a jerk about authority like my boss at Bucky's. I was doing two articles a week, sometimes three, and Gunn was beginning to smile occasionally, because my being so productive gave him more time to shoot the shit with people who came into the office. You would've thought he'd use the time to be with his wife, but Gunn apparently considered their relationship a lost cause, for they were rarely together. He still hung out at the office late at night, apparently for the primary purpose of avoiding her. I saw them together once in front of the liquor store, with one-legged Sven and Wally Leach and their young daughter. They were arguing about something, and at the end of the argument Gunn scooped up the little girl and stomped off.

Moondog would drop by occasionally, usually around midnight, and we would sit around and drink beer and talk about the news, especially the murders. For all their tough talk, dapper dress, and expensive transportation, the investigators seemed to be getting nowhere, and the town remained very much on edge. Moondog said he had the beginnings of a theory, but would not elaborate further. When he was ready, he told us, he would write a column. Gunn said, with just a hint of sarcasm, that he could hardly wait.

# Chapter Fourteen

ON LABOR DAY, the town ran out of water. That night, there was a full Moon.

Labor Day weekend is the traditional beginning of the Julian tourist season. The town's popularity as a day-trip destination probably owes a great deal to the number of transplanted Northeasterners in San Diego and Los Angeles. When the calendar turns to September, their thoughts turn to fall—to the colored leaves, the crisp, cool air, and the smell of woodsmoke, experiences that are available in Southern California only at high altitudes. Julian milks this to the hilt, offering horse-drawn carriage rides, hand-pressed cider, tours of the apple orchards and the gold mine, and enough apple pie to feed an invading army, which the stream of cars coming up the two highways in a pincer movement from the southwest and northwest often resembles.

The town, like most tourist towns, has a love-hate relationship with its visitors. Shop owners expect to make three-quarters of their money in one-third of the year. Realtors cheerfully keep their offices open long hours on Saturday and Sunday, with panoramic pictures of holdings in the hills taped to the windows. But on weekends in the latter part of the year, many of the locals not directly involved in the tourist trade simply stay home. For there is no way to get to Julian from anyplace far away save by automobile, and the town's narrow roads simply cannot handle all the cars. By midmorning there is no place to park within half a mile of Main Street, and anyone trying to get through town on the way to somewhere else can face a half-hour wait in traffic, while dogs and kids and bicyclists and people who got there earlier dodge back and forth among the crawling vehicles. Running to the store for a six-pack or a loaf of bread can become an ordeal, and occasionally there are harsh words between a cowboy liquor-store regular and a Bermuda-shorts-clad, camera-toting, Mercedes-driving yuppie sightseer two places in line in front of him.

Despite the bad publicity about the murders and the water situation, the curious and the bored still came to Julian on this Labor Day weekend, and promised to continue to come all through the fall. St. Anne's Catholic Church held its annual street fair in its parking lot, two blocks west of Main Street; the annual country music jamboree remained scheduled for mid-October, at the peak of the tourist crunch. Stafford Emerson of the Julian Bicycle Emporium led two-wheeled tours of the area each day of the three-day weekend, and the numbers of bicycles sharing road space with automobiles added an element of danger to the sport of mountain biking, Julian-style. Wally Leach assumed his post outside the town hall, in hog heaven with hundreds of new people to talk to each day. Business boomed at all of the restaurants, most of which, despite the continuing water crunch, would now be open seven days a week until the tourists stopped coming, sometime after the end of October.

The water was flowing late Sunday night; though it had been a busy weekend, the restaurants managed to get their dishes washed, and Mariah's was serving margaritas on the deck until the wee hours of the night. Early Monday morning, someone found enough water to hose the dried ice cream and pie off a stretch of sidewalk in front of the hardware store. But when water board chairman Steve Stephenson arose later that morning in his house near the top of the ridge and wandered into his bathroom to splash his face, the faucet coughed and spat at him, and after a few seconds managed to heave up a foul-smelling mixture of water and brown sludge. "Uh-oh," he said to his unshaven reflection in the mirror. For him at least, he knew, Labor Day would be no holiday.

Some thirty minutes later, Harry Ferguson called to inform him that the pumps in the district's three functioning wells were "sucking mud," and added the observation that they had better figure out what the fuck to do pretty quickly, as the town would be filling up with tourists in just a couple of hours. Stephenson didn't need to be reminded of the severity of the situation. He'd already received two calls from residents who, like him, lived at the district's high end and had likewise run out of water. They were not pleased. He imagined that the restaurant owners would be less than thrilled if forced to close their doors on Labor Day, one of the big days of the year—especially since the board had twice raised rates since May.

Having few other options, he called Danny Taylor at the Chevron station. Taylor in turn called corporate headquarters in Los Angeles, and in less than an hour they worked out a plan. Taylor informed Stephenson that Chevron had agreed to pay Kenny Walls, a tanker-truck operator based in Santa Ysabel, to cart as much water as the town needed from Palomar Mountain. Walls was already en route; he would be paid twice his normal rate. Stephenson groaned; while Chevron would initially foot the bill, he knew that they would find a way to get compensated down the road. Big companies, he reflected, always do—that's why they're big.

There was more bad news. The water would need to be siphoned out of the tanker truck and into the water district's tanks. This would take time, and would require the help of the Julian Volunteer Fire Department. Taylor said that depending on traffic, Walls was expected to deliver his first load sometime shortly before noon, and the water would not be ready for consumption along Main Street until around one o'clock. He, Stephenson, would have to call the restaurants and ask them not to open until one, so that the entire town would not run dry. Stephenson thought that Taylor, as president of the chamber of commerce, should make the calls, but Taylor was adamant in his refusal. "This is about water," he said. "It's your baby. Besides, I've already got people lined up at the pumps."

Though it was still early in the day, Stephenson already felt tired. The restaurant owners were, predictably, furious. Stephenson listened to a series of harangues about his incompetence, many of them laced with colorful language. After about the fourth or fifth call, he began mentally composing the first paragraph of his resignation.

The ensuing day can only be described as an adventure. The town never did completely run out of water; only about a dozen residences, like Stephenson's, at the higher elevations, experienced an interruption in service. But it was a close thing. Until the Sun went down and the tourists started to leave, the town consumed water as fast as Kenny Walls could truck it in. Stephenson and Ferguson sweated out each delivery. Just when it seemed the tanks would run dry and they would have to shut everything down, the truck would appear, and the firefighters would set feverishly to work transferring its precious cargo. No one dared think what would happen if a major fire broke out.

The fire department had a cache of unpotable water in reserve, but to get at it would have required the efforts of everyone who was helping to keep the town in drinking water, and the streets were hopelessly clogged.

Kenny Walls made ten trips to Palomar Mountain and back in a span of sixteen hours, quit at midnight, and got up at six on Tuesday morning to start again. By Tuesday afternoon the worst of the crisis was over. Several of the restaurants closed their doors that day, recovering, as the midweek semi-calm descended and the water level gradually stabilized. By then everybody was talking about something else anyway.

Traffic on that Labor Day had to be seen to be believed. Walls fought lines of cars, RVs, and cycle-toting pickup trucks heading for the desert as he pushed to get the water through. He himself was responsible for some of the congestion, for a fully loaded tanker truck negotiating climbing, curving roads can only achieve and maintain so much velocity. Once he went the long way around, down into the high desert and up Banner Grade, approaching Julian from the east, but that route proved too steep to maintain anything over fifteen miles an hour, and he more than lost the time he gained by avoiding the traffic from the city. Highways for miles around were a mess all day; parking in Julian was an impossible dream. It got hot, and tempers flared. Blasts from horns, middle fingers thrust rudely in the air, and epithets shouted from vehicle to vehicle rang out across the countryside. A few cars overheated during the uphill crawl and pulled to the side of the road; some of their drivers waited hours before an available tow truck could get through. Diners snarled at waitresses when they finally found seating; frustrated restaurateurs reamed out an obnoxious customer or two. Store owners who depended on tourist dollars nonetheless grew surly. There was an incident on Main Street when a local drunk deliberately rammed his pickup truck into the back of a double-parked

Pinto, perhaps hoping it would explode. The cops came, tied up traffic further, and hauled the guy away as Wally Leach, the only person in town who seemed happy about the chaos, heckled him from across the street.

Leach, in fact, enjoyed the day so much that he became falling-down drunk before nightfall, and was mercifully driven home just before dark by two local rednecks in the back of their pickup truck before a couple of beefy-looking visitors, weary of his derogatory verbiage, could carry out their threat to beat the shit out of him, bad legs and all.

The atmosphere of anger that lay over the town all day did not affect Vicki Bodine, the blond, buxom part-time secretary/treasurer who may or may not have been tapping into the water district's bank accounts. While the members of the board and their technical staff ran around town making sure the flow of water continued, Vicki Bodine was nowhere to be seen—at least until that evening, when she showed up at the Fisherman's Friend on Lake Cuyamaca with her woodcutter.

It was ironic, but not surprising, that the area's most popular watering hole looked out on a lake that provided not a drop of water to Julian when the town was dying of thirst. Ten miles from town, the bar attracted customers from several mountain communities, and since everyone had to drive to get there, it had been, over the years, indirectly responsible for its share of late-night highway carnage. There were occasional fights there, especially when bikers arrived on the weekends, and the odd stabbing or two, but the bar was frequented mostly by rednecks who were used to this sort of thing, and so far there hadn't been a murder, which was about the only thing that would get a joint closed down in this neck of the woods.

Lake Cuyamaca, a man-made reservoir whose water slaked the thirsts of customers in the Cajon Water District in San Diego, and whose depths were stocked regularly with trout and catfish, sat in the middle of a high valley between the Cuyamaca and Laguna Mountains. The valley was a dozen times bigger than the lake, and fell away beyond it in a series of rolling hills kept treeless by grazing cattle. In flood years—and many people in the area could not remember the last one—the lake rose to fill the valley, creating a handful of grassy islands on which cows were sometimes stranded. Held in place by a dam on one end and a large earthen levee leading to a wooded hill on the other, the lake was at its lowest level in years. A flock of about forty ducks and geese made the lake their home; there were owls and golden eagles in the area as well. On the near shore, across the highway from the bar, a store and park operation offered fishing gear and boat rentals from a metal dock now almost completely out of the water. It wasn't much of a lake at all, really, but in the light of the full Moon, even the smallest body of water can look quite romantic.

Vicki Bodine thought so, too. By the time the round Moon rose above the trees on the far side of the lake, she and Vern Whittier had been there for several hours and had enjoyed several margaritas. Vern Whittier shared her love of booze. He was about six-four, always wore red suspenders and flannel shirts, and was missing the ends of three fingers on his left hand, lost to a chainsaw during an unfortunate attempt to remove a limb from a tree after he'd had too much to drink. Perhaps he could perform erotic feats with those stubby digits that other men could only dream of; for whatever reason, women—especially married women—found him irresistible. He'd been with Erik Gunn's wife, among many others; he had even, in the throes of a monumental drunk, slept with Claudia Gaines, and had studiously avoided the *Julian Nugget* office ever since.

The band onstage was thumping out a loud country-rock tune, the type of music generally preferred by the bar's redneck clientele. Vicki Bodine had won several games of pool earlier in the evening, good for three or four drinks, and was trying to coax Vern into playing. They were seated at the bar; conversation, music, and laughter roared all around them.

"C'mon, you shmuck, one game," she urged. She was teasing him; he sucked at pool. His impaired hand couldn't properly hold the cue, and she always won. He usually didn't mind, because he always ended up fucking her afterward, but he was in a mellow mood, kicking back at the bar, listening to the music. He didn't feel like shooting pool.

"C'mon. We'll play for funsies." It came out sounding like "funsheesh."

Vern gently pushed her shoulder, and Vicki swayed precipitously on her barstool. He laughed. "You're too drunk to play, babe. Quit while you're ahead."

"Drunk or not, I can still beat you." But she let it drop. He was feeling no pain, either, and the game would likely be lousy. Instead she swiveled on her stool, leaned back against the bar, and gazed out the window, where the moonlight made a glittering path across the surface of the tiny lake.

"Look at that Moon!" she cried. "Aah-ooooh!"

The whole valley lay bathed in moonlight, the lake a pool of silver at its near end. The gentle hills beyond were accented by their shadows; the bare rocks and stately pines likewise stood out in a light that almost seemed to emanate from within.

"Hey, Vern," she said, nudging her mate. "Let's take a walk, okay?"

"A walk? Where?"

"Down by the lake. C'mon, ish a beautiful night." She was already up, tugging at his arm.

He looked down at her from his perch on the barstool. "You need some air, babe?" he asked.

She stood on tiptoes, looped an arm around his neck, and put her face close to his ear. "I need *you*," she whispered.

A wolflike grin spread over his face; he felt the beginnings of a hard-on behind his scrotum. "Let's go," he said, rising from his stool. He winked at the bartender as he steered her toward the door.

The noise of the bar and the band faded behind them as they crossed the highway and maneuvered stumblingly down a dirt path toward the water's edge. The store and dock, illuminated by a pair of streetlights, lay far to their left; they could see the aluminum boats, tied up for the night, bobbing in the moonlight. The operation shut down at sunset, but sometimes someone from Fisherman's got the inspiration to borrow one of the boats and go for a midnight joyride. A couple of years before, two people had drowned during such an escapade, and since then the store and dock had been guarded by a padlocked chainlink fence running all the way to the water's edge around both sides.

The shore of Lake Cuyamaca was fringed with reeds and cattails taller even than Vern Whittier. Vicki grabbed his hand and led him along the path that threaded its way through them toward an open area near the lake's narrow south end, a deep spot favored during the day by fishermen who preferred to cast from shore rather than rent a boat. After the noise of the bar, it was almost unnaturally quiet; the only noise was Vicki's heavy breathing as she hurried along.

They came at last to a small point of land, defined by lunchbox-size rocks and gravel leading down into the water. Vicki stood at the tip of this tiny peninsula, hands on her hips, gazing out at the lake.

"Nice night for a swim, don'tcha think?"

"A swim?!" *That* wasn't what Vern had in mind at all. "Vicki, you can't swim in here, it's a reservoir!"

There was a rustling in the weeds behind them. Vicki seemed not to notice. Vern turned his head.

"Oh, who cares about city peoples' drinking water? *I'm* going swimming." She pulled off her top, undid her bra, and treated Vern to an excellent view of her fine tits as they fell free. His prick stiffened. She'd started to undo her jeans, when he heard the rustling noise again.

"Vicki!" he hissed. "Stop! I think someone's following us!"

"Oh, don't be so paranoid," she said. "Come on, get naked." And taking her own advice, she wriggled out of her blue jeans and panties, and suddenly there were two full moons over Lake Cuyamaca.

"Jesus, you are the craziest goddamn female . . ." But he was lowering his suspenders and unbuttoning his shirt as he said this, for the sight of her naked body never failed to arouse him, and he had a full-blown erection which the cool water of the lake would do little to dampen.

Something crashed in the reeds quite close to them. This time she heard it too. She was at the water's edge, poised to immerse herself. She turned back toward him in alarm. "What was that?"

"I'll look," he said. He took two steps toward the path down which they had come—and then something hit the side of his head so hard he was knocked to the ground and momentarily blinded. He'd been in fights and in accidents, but the tuning fork in his head told him he had never been hit so hard in his life. For several seconds all he saw were stars. Through the ringing in his ears, he heard Vicki scream. He got groggily to his knees, in time to see his girlfriend thrashing wildly in the ankle-deep water, a huge shape on top of her.

His first thought was that she was being raped, and he had to protect her. Adrenaline kicked in then—he rushed at the attacker, leapt up on his hairy shoulders, pounded at the back of his head. The man rose as if Vern himself weighed nothing; Vern landed on his back and rushed him again. Another haymaker came out of nowhere and smashed against his cheekbone. His head snapped back.

Vern felt himself falling, falling in slow motion, unable to do anything but watch himself fall. He saw the Moon, looking as big as a cantaloupe; he saw the reeds, as tall as redwoods; and then the back of his head smashed into something hard and he saw no more.

When he came to, it was still night, and the Moon was still in the sky, though in a different place. There were other lights as well, the lights of several powerful flashlights, probing the reeds and the water. He heard the tramping of dry vegetation, and he saw legs—legs in blue pants and black boots. Down by the water, two men were bundling something. Voices spoke in low, baritone murmurs; other voices crackled over radios. His head felt as though someone had driven a javelin through it.

He remembered that he'd gone drinking with Vicki at the Fisherman's Friend. He hadn't wanted to play pool. He'd had a lot to drink—his brain was oatmeal. What were those guys doing in the water?

It was only when they lifted their bundle, when he saw the tumbled mane of hair cascading down from one end, that he recognized it as the dead body of his lover.

# Chapter Fifteen

"SHE DIED, ERIK," I argued. "Let's let her rest in peace, huh?"

Erik Gunn leaned back in the great black armchair that was one of the few visible perks of his position, and sipped on his Budweiser. "If she was embezzling money from the water district, that's a legitimate story," he said. "Our readers have a right to know. Certainly the water customers in the district will be interested."

"But she's *dead!*" I maintained. "What would be the point?"

It was Wednesday night in the *Julian Nugget* office, two days after Vicki Bodine's death and two days before the paper would hit the streets. Once again the daily papers had come to Julian to play the town's latest misfortune on page one. Once again, Gunn was trying to figure out his angle, to give his local readers some new twist on the fact that their quiet little town had become a haven for a psychopathic killer. It was all anyone was talking about. Gunn had spent most of the past two days on the phone, or listening to the parade of people who had come through the office, wondering aloud what in hell the world was coming to when something like this could happen in Julian.

But the victim this time was no young, outwardly perfect college student or aloof professional newcomer. Vicki Bodine had lived a lifestyle that was at least interesting, even to the less judgmental people along Julian's gossip grapevine, and she was not to be spared in the press. What she was doing at the Fisherman's Friend on a Saturday night with the town's most notorious womanizer was to be addressed in Gunn's exhaustive story; he wanted me to uncover the other major scandal in her suddenly abbreviated life.

"The point," Gunn said, "is good journalism. We don't conceal information simply to protect people, even dead people. We're in the business of information. You think her husband likes reading that she was found naked, with her head practically ripped off, next to a guy who had his clothes half off himself? You think he likes seeing quotes from people who saw them leave the bar together? All that information was in the San Diego papers. Maybe they're uncomfortable about his feelings, about her relatives' feelings, and how it might affect the children—but they don't let their discomfort prevent them from doing their jobs. And neither should you."

"They haven't mentioned anything about the water district money," I pointed out.

Gunn leaned forward and set the beer can down sharply on his desk. "Exactly!" he said. "But you know they'll find out about it, and soon. I just hope they don't find out before Friday. We've got to break the story this issue. It'll be a scoop."

I swear, the man was almost giddy at the prospect. I guess he hadn't gone to sleep at night thinking about Vicki Bodine, as had been the case with the previous victim, but nonetheless I couldn't help feeling that there was something ghoulish about getting pleasure from printing dirt on a dead person, newsworthy or not. I think it was about at that point that I began to dislike my new career—and Gunn, too—when I grasped his attitude that a person's right to privacy did not extend beyond the grave, or beyond the need to "scoop" the competition.

"Well, Stephenson says she stole the money," I said. "And he's got a bunch of receipts and canceled checks and stuff he says is proof that she did. I guess there was going to be an arrest pretty soon. It's just—"

"Just what?" said Gunn, crumpling his beer can and tossing it, in a short arc, into a nearby cardboard box, where it bounced around among several others.

"Well, it's awfully convenient for him that she died, isn't it? She can't defend herself. What if he was in on it, too? It *is* his name on the checks."

"Which he says she forged," Gunn reminded me. "Come on, Joe, one of those checks was for a down payment on her car."

"He's got a new car, too," I said. "And that big ol' motor home. And up until now he's been awfully secretive whenever I've asked him about water district stuff. Almost like he's got something to hide."

"Are you saying that maybe Stephenson killed her, to cover up his own involvement?" Gunn stared at me, astonished.

"No, I'm not saying that."

The cops had, in fact, questioned Stephenson about his whereabouts that night. He had been home watching TV with his wife. They also paid a friendly little visit to my humble abode at Sleepy Hollow, and later to Bucky's Barbecue. Fortunately for me, at the time Vicki Bodine's throat was being slashed by a set of sharp objects, I was scrubbing burnt-on chili beans off the bottom of a cast-iron pot.

But I still didn't want to write the story, and I couldn't get across to Gunn why not. I'd dealt with both Vicki Bodine and Steve Stephenson; my conversations with her had been fun, while those with him had been a drag. Stephenson was a taciturn, suspicious man who frequently gave one-sentence inter-views. That sentence was "I'm not gonna say anything for publi-cation," or some variation thereof. Now that Vicki was dead, he was willing, even eager to talk, and I found that at worst dis-honest and at best distasteful.

And part of my reluctance had to do with my own past. Hav-ing spent a fair part of my life on the wrong side of the law, I empathize with thieves and embezzlers. I know why they do it, because I've done it myself. There's a code of honor among outlaws, even reformed outlaws, and writing the type of story my editor was asking me to write felt like a violation of that code. I guess I was letting my personal preconceptions color my judgment, as Gunn would have put it.

We didn't carry the discussion further, however, because at that juncture the downstairs door creaked open, and familiar footsteps on the stairs were followed a moment later by the ap-pearance in the office doorway of Cyrus "Moondog" Nygerski.

He had a new hat, a crushed red velvet job adorned with several feathers; it would have been somewhere around number 480 in *The 500 Hats of Bartholomew Cubbins*, by Dr. Seuss. He had a thing for hats; he changed them every so often, he told me, to keep from being readily recognized. Otherwise he was dressed almost exactly as he had been on the night I met him. Now, as then, he held several sheets of paper in his hands, cov-ered by carefully chosen words painstakingly typed on his Smith-Corona manual typewriter. I'd watched him type; his prolific output was all the more remarkable because he used no more than four or five fingers and worked methodically. In other words, he was slow.

"Moondog!" For some reason Nygerski, alone of all the peo-ple who came into the *Julian Nugget* office, had the ability to cheer Gunn up.

"Got any beer?" Nygerski growled.

"Of course. Help yourself."

"This," he said, waving the papers in front of him, after liberating a beer from the icebox and taking a healthy swallow, "is perhaps the most important column I've ever written."

"All your columns are important, Moondog," said Gunn. "Even the ones I can't use. You know I consider you a major literary figure." He held out his hand for the article.

"Not so fast," Moondog said, pulling it away. "I presume the two of you are here at this time of night, not only because you have nothing better to do, but also because you are planning your coverage of the latest, uh, incident."

He looked at Gunn, and then at me. He had the damnedest eyes—dark, dark brown and at least half pupil, as if he'd embarked on an acid trip from which he'd never entirely returned. He looked at you as if he could see things not visible in the ordinary spectrum. Neither Gunn nor I said a word.

"Let me tell you what it is that we are dealing with," he said.

"You mean, aside from a nutzoid serial killer?" asked Gunn.

Moondog took a long draw off his beer before answering. "We are dealing," he said, "with a werewolf."

If he was joking, there wasn't a hint of it in his features. Gunn and I stared at him.

Finally, after several seconds of silence, Gunn began to chuckle. "You know, Moondog," he said, "you are really too much."

"I'm not trying to be funny," Moondog said.

"Like hell," Gunn retorted. "A werewolf! Jesus Christ! Only you could find humor in three people being brutally killed. A werewolf! Sheesh!"

"Moondog, whatever drugs you're doing, can you get me some?" I put in. "They must be pretty good."

"I don't care whether you two assholes believe me or not," Moondog said.

117

"We don't," Gunn replied quickly.

"You will," Moondog told him.

Silence hung in the office for several seconds, until Gunn said, "Ah, Moondog . . . is this what this column of yours is about?"

"Yup."

"You know, Moondog, I've always appreciated your sense of humor, but given the circumstances, I'd think even you would agree it's in kinda poor taste, you know what I mean?"

"I told you, I'm not trying to be funny," Moondog said. "I'm deadly serious. The cops, the investigators, the other papers—they're not going to solve this case until they realize there's another element involved. A man who becomes something other than a man when the Moon is full. A werewolf."

Gunn got up from behind his desk, and fished a beer out of the icebox. "You want one, Joe?" he asked.

"Sure." Gunn tossed a can my way; I reached out and made a pretty decent one-handed grab. Moondog, the former second baseman, nodded approvingly.

"A werewolf." Gunn sat back down at his desk and stared at Nygerski, awaiting an explanation.

"Yup."

"Oh, come on, Moondog! You expect me to print something like that? We've got some sicko on our hands who hates women. These are appalling and disgusting crimes. The whole town—anybody with any sensitivity in the whole region—is outraged. And you want to talk about a *werewolf?*"

"Look at the way the victims were killed," Nygerski said. "They weren't just killed, they were brutalized. They were savaged. They weren't raped, which someone who hates women would surely do. They were almost like animal attacks—by a huge, deranged animal. I don't know if you know this, but the same night Vicki Bodine died, two cows near Lake Cuyamaca were killed in much the same way. The cops think *that's* pretty strange. They're talking about Satan worshipers, and shit like that. But here's the clincher: all three murders—every one—happened on the night of a full Moon."

"Coincidence," Gunn said. "Or maybe it's some misguided misogynist who *thinks* he's a werewolf and acts it out."

Moondog shook his head. "I think it's the real thing," he said. "Unfortunately, I have some firsthand knowledge on the subject."

Gunn stared at him. "What do you mean?"

"I had a girlfriend once who turned out to be a werewolf."

"Jesus," I said. "What did you do?"

"Well, when I found out, I dumped her, of course," Moondog said. "I was lucky to get out of that relationship alive."

Gunn was staring at him in disbelief. "Is *that* how you got the name 'Moondog'?" he asked.

"Shut up," Nygerski said casually. "There *are* werewolves—not many, but more than most people think. A small percentage of murders every year can be attributed to them. And I think one has reared its ugly head in Julian."

"Did she ever bite you?" I asked.

"No, fortunately not," he said. "But that's a good point. A person who is bitten by a werewolf and lives becomes a werewolf. Which means that Vern Whittier should be watched very, very closely."

"I'm going down to see him tomorrow afternoon," Gunn said. "He promised me an exclusive interview."

Whittier was in Pala Meadows Hospital with a fractured cheekbone, a dislodged retina, and multiple lacerations about the head and neck. He was also recovering from a severe concussion, incurred when his head hit a rock. None of the major papers had yet been allowed at his bedside, and Gunn, ever alert for his angle, had extracted a promise from the woozy woodcutter to deny them access until after the *Nugget* came out.

119

"Would you mind if I tagged along?" Moondog asked. He held up his hand at Gunn's startled expression. "Don't worry, I won't step on your journalistic toes. I'd just like to hear what he has to say."

Gunn leaned back in his chair, looking suddenly exhausted. "All right," he said.

"I'd like to come, too," I said.

"Finish your story on the water district first," Gunn told me.

"Whatever you say, boss."

"Wait a minute," Gunn said suddenly, leaning forward and looking at Moondog. "Vern Whittier's a pretty big guy, I know, but he couldn't stop a werewolf, could he? Aren't they supposed to have superhuman strength?"

"They're strong," Moondog admitted. "They've been known to overpower several strong men at one time."

"If that's the case, then why is Vern Whittier still alive? Unless our killer is just a woman-hater, like I said. Werewolves don't discriminate between the sexes, do they?"

"Not that I'm aware of," Moondog said.

"Then why is Vern Whittier still alive?"

"I don't know," Moondog said slowly, twisting one end of his dark mustache in his fingers. "But I intend to find out."

The next morning, sheriff's deputy Frank Blaisdell, completing some paperwork at the office before his shift, received an unusual phone call.

"Deputy Blaisdell, this is Cyrus 'Moondog' Nygerski of the *Julian Nugget*," the caller said. "You and some of your pals visited me out at my place in Mesa Grande a while back. Remember?"

"Sure," Frank Blaisdell replied pleasantly. "What can I do for you, Cyrus?"

"Actually, sir, I prefer Moondog, if you don't mind."

"Not at all, Moondog. What's up?"

"Well, like everybody else, I'm concerned about these murders."

"It's a pretty frightening thing," Blaisdell said, his voice appropriately grave. It wasn't an act; he would never forget the sight of Patsy Kittredge's mutilated corpse as long as he lived.

"What I want to know is this—last Saturday night, when the Bodine woman was killed, she was with a guy, right?"

"Yeah. He was pretty roughed up, too."

"Right. Now, was he by any chance wearing any kind of jewelry, anything silver especially, on his hands, or around his neck?"

"Yeah—as a matter of fact, he was," the deputy said. "He had a little silver cross, with Jesus on it, on a chain."

"And the cross was around his neck when you found him?"

"Yeah. On a silver ch— Wait a minute! How the hell did you know that?"

"I didn't," Moondog said. "Thanks."

"Now wait just the hell a minute!"

But the caller had already hung up. The line was dead. Frank Blaisdell held the receiver at arm's length, and frowned deeply.

# Chapter Sixteen

## THE BEAST OF JULIAN

Cyrus "Moondog" Nygerski

Who is killing the women of Julian?

In the past three months, at exactly 29-day intervals, three local women have met their deaths in savage fashion. So far, there have been no arrests.

This is not news to anyone who reads a major Southern California daily newspaper or watches the news on TV. What is alarming, however, is that investigators continue to ignore the obvious.

What do the three killings have in common? They have been carried out with extreme brutality, at night in the woods, and the victims have all been female. Is that significant? Perhaps. But far more telling is their timing. Police say that the killings resemble nothing so much as animal attacks—by a huge and incredibly savage beast. *And every attack has occurred on the night of a full Moon.*

There is only one possible conclusion: A werewolf has come to Julian.

Werewolves are real. They exist, and the horror that has come to the backcountry this summer is proof of their existence.

This is why the murders remain unsolved. It is very difficult to catch a werewolf. Between full Moons, werewolves live ordinary human lives, showing no outward manifestations of their affliction. Occasionally a werewolf will exhibit telltale signs—a blackened fingernail, an index finger longer than the middle digit, an excess of body hair, elongated teeth. The trouble with these signs is that they are ambiguous—they can be exhibited by non-werewolves as well. And in werewolves they may not appear until many transformations have taken place. Since the killings began just three full Moons ago, we are either dealing with someone new to the area, or a local person who has only recently become a werewolf.

A person can become a werewolf in one of several ways. There are legends from Europe—especially Russia and northern Scandinavia—of so-called "ly-canthropous rivers." Drinking from their waters near the time of the full Moon can bring about the transformation. So can, apparently, certain spells and incantations, though how much of this is folklore rather than fact is open to speculation.

The surest way to become a werewolf is to be bitten by a werewolf and survive the attack. And in extremely rare cases, a person can be so evil, can have so little love in his heart, and so little righteousness in his soul, that the spirit of a werewolf can enter the body spontaneously. This generally happens only at the moment a werewolf's human host dies, when the malevolent spirit must then seek a new body or go into limbo, a sort of halfway house for restless souls between life and death.

Werewolves generally don't know what they are, because of the amnesia associated with the phenomenon. It is extremely probable that Julian's killer does not know that he or she is a werewolf. Typically, the person will wake up the next morning, sometimes in a strange place, with a groggy feeling not unlike a hangover. He will not remember the events of the previous night—events that too often include the deaths of innocent victims.

For a werewolf under the influence of the full Moon has but a single instinct: to kill. And the werewolf in turn cannot be killed by ordinary means. An Uzi will not stop a werewolf when the Moon is full. In the beast state, a werewolf can be dispatched only by a silver bullet through the heart, or a silver dagger in the same location.

Vern Whittier survived the attack that killed Vicki Bodine because of a small silver crucifix he wore around his neck. Werewolves are repelled by silver, and, because they are creatures of the spirit world, by religious symbols as well. They also have an aversion to garlic and certain other plants, including wolfbane, which was often cultivated in European villages where werewolves were said to be prevalent.

Knowing that there is a werewolf among us, what can we do? The next time the Moon is full, stay in-

side. If you must go out, wear something silver, pref-
erably a cross or other religious icon. The sheriff's
department should double its patrols when the Moon
becomes round, and issue silver bullets to all its deputies. So far, they have scoffed at this suggestion. In
doing so, they are risking the lives of everyone in the
Julian area, including their own.

THAT ARTICLE APPEARED in the October issue of the *Manzanita
Muckraker*, which hit the streets near the end of September,
shortly before the next full Moon. Within three hours of its ar-
rival, Connie Burbage, the woman who sold advertising and
delivered the paper to Julian, Santa Ysabel, Palomar Mountain,
Borrego Springs, and points beyond, received a phone call from
Tim Pemberton, owner of the Corner Market. "Get this paper
the hell out of my store," he said.

The *Muckraker* was a freebie, laid out for all takers on store
counters throughout the mountains and desert over a geographi-
cal area larger than Rhode Island or Delaware. Its publisher was
a man with many opinions and not a single qualm about express-
ing them or letting his writers express theirs. He also possessed
a keen eye for publicity. When Connie Burbage called him,
he called a reporter at the *San Diego Union*, and pretty soon the
news that the paper had been "Banned in Julian," including the
reason why, was delivered to metropolitan doorsteps from
Tijuana to Oceanside. Erik Gunn, who had refused to print
Moondog's column, would have killed for that kind of expo-
sure.

Moondog himself was out of town when the paper came out;
the publisher of the *Muckraker* had sent him to Alaska to do a
piece on Exxon's efforts to clean up the mess it had made the
previous spring. Before he left, however, the cops and the shirt-
and-tie investigators, curious about his phone call to Frank Blais-

dell, had paid another visit to his home in Mesa Grande. According to Moondog's account, it hadn't been a social call.

"You asked Frank here if Vern Whittier was wearing a silver crucifix," Guy Taylor snapped, jabbing his cigarette in Moondog's direction as he paced the long living room. "That information wasn't made public. It's something only the killer would know."

Moondog was seated on his couch; Blaisdell and Kevin Byars stood at either end like sentinels. A second plainclothesman, the sleeves of his white shirt rolled up, like Taylor's, to the elbows, guarded the door, as if they were afraid that Moondog might at any minute bolt upright and make a run for it. "What did they think I was gonna do, leap onto the back of a cow and go galloping off into the sunset?" he said, much later, when we discussed it.

To the cops, he said, "I didn't ask specifically about a crucifix. I asked if he was wearing anything silver, particularly around his neck."

"Which he was," Taylor said. "And you, alone among all the people we've talked to, knew it."

"Look, if I did kill that woman, why would I call you and help you guys out? I mean, if you were a murderer, would you volunteer clues to the police?"

Taylor leaned down close to Moondog's face, so close that Moondog could smell his tobacco-laced breath. "The world's full of psychos," he said menacingly. "I don't have a clue what makes you tick. You live way the fuck out here by yourself at the end of a ten-mile dirt road. You don't seem to like other people. The last time we were out here you told us to get lost. You've got this weirdo nickname—'Moondog.' And now you're calling us on the phone with this wacko theory that it's a werewolf committing these murders. You expect us not to be a little suspicious? Who *are* you?"

"You're blowing smoke in my face," Moondog said quietly.

"You're blowing smoke up our ass!" Taylor shouted. He whirled, and began pacing the room again.

"How'd you get the name 'Moondog'?" Frank Blaisdell asked, trying to sound as offhand as he could.

"None of your business," Moondog told him.

"Oh, you're cute," Taylor said, turning toward the couch again. "You're a real beauty. You just better hope you don't get too cute for your own good."

But in the end, they had to leave, although Taylor wanted to take Moondog down to San Diego for a lie-detector test. While it was true that he had no alibi for the night of Vicki Bodine's murder ("I was at home," he'd told them, without elaboration), no one had seen him at the Fisherman's Friend, or out near Lake Cuyamaca, or in town. No one had seen him at all, in fact, and in the life of Cyrus "Moondog" Nygerski, that was not at all unusual. There wasn't a shred of evidence that he had had anything to do with any of the three murders, and if it wasn't for the nickname and the fact that he liked to express himself in print, the cops would most likely have left him alone.

I didn't go with Moondog and Gunn to see Vern Whittier, for the excellent reason that I hadn't finished my story. When I did get it done, the next day, it was a shoddy, ambiguous piece of work that nonetheless left my conscience relatively clear about repeating accusations whose truth I didn't know or really want to know. The chick was not around to tell her side of the story, after all—and payments on her Supra were now something of a moot point. Gunn hadn't even started his story, but he was the editor and could do what he damn well pleased. So while his wife was out about town with one-legged Sven, he sat at the foot of a hospital bed, interviewing a man who'd once balled her, and apparently considered it simply part of the job.

Moondog told me about the interview. Whittier was apparently still pretty drugged up and not very articulate. And Gunn was no help at all. "Every time I tried to ask a werewolf question," Moondog said, "Gunn cut me off. I asked him if he was sure it was a man, and Gunn said, 'Of course it was a man, he already said it was.' 'Well, did you get a good look at him? Did you see his face?' I asked. 'No, it happened so fast,' he said. 'I've never been punched that hard in my life.' I asked him if the guy was all hairy, if he had, like, hair on his shoulders. He said he didn't remember."

"Was he bitten?" I asked.

"Don't know," Moondog said. "He had some nasty scratches on his face and neck, but they could've been made by bushes as easily as by claws."

"Or by Vicki Bodine," I said.

"In any case, we'll know by the next full Moon. He'll be out of the hospital in a week."

Now, I've got to admit that I took Moondog's werewolf theory with a pound or two of salt. Like everyone else, I've seen the old movies—I've seen a couple or three episodes of "Dark Shadows" as well—but to listen to somebody talking seriously about a werewolf in the here and now was something else. People got ticked—people like the owner of the Corner Market, and Vicki Bodine's husband, and Guy Taylor and his crew—because they thought Moondog was putting them on, that he was using the tragedy of the three deaths to have his own private joke at public expense. But it wasn't that way at all—that would've been sick, which is what everyone accused him of. I didn't necessarily believe his interpretation of events—not then, anyway—but I believed from the first that *he* believed it, and didn't deserve the storm of criticism that came his way, or the hassle he got from the cops.

# Chapter Seventeen

"MAN, HOW DO you put up with that?"

Chink, chink, chink. Tom Keeler's midnight gold-mining operation was in full swing on the night Cyrus "Moondog" Nygerski first visited me, and Moondog, who lived so far out in the brush that the only ambient noises at night were made by animals and the wind, picked up on it immediately. It was unconscionable, given the town's water woes, that the guy was allowed to run a sluice to separate gold—if indeed he ever found any—from the slurry of broken rocks. But Bill Haley paid the water bill, and although the operation surely added to it, half the toilets at the Hollow leaked, and he himself squandered gallons upon gallons watering his precious young trees. As far as the noise went, Derek had spoken to him a couple of times, and Tom had left off for a couple of nights on each occasion, but he either had a short memory or flat-out didn't care, because he always took up his nocturnal pounding again. Besides, he had the look of an ax murderer, and Derek probably didn't want to hassle him so much that he might push him over the edge. He was inexhaustible, too; he could keep up the hammer blows for hours, like the crazed Jack Nicholson character in *The Shining*, sitting at his typewriter day and night, typing the same sentence over and over again.

Tom Keeler didn't work. I guess the family was on welfare, but he dealt a little crystal, too. I knew, because the people who visited him, day and night, had the same faraway look in their eyes, though not the same glint of madness. Sven occasionally limped on down there to get his nose filled, though more often than not he shopped at Blind Ben's, which had a twenty-four-hour operation too.

Chink, chink, chink. "Add a bass line," said Moondog, as Keeler kept chipping away, "and some tasteful lead guitar, and maybe it'd be halfway listenable. Right now it's driving me nuts."

"It bothered me at first," I told Moondog. "But now it's just part of the background noise. You get used to it. You know, like city traffic."

"Yeah, but it jams you up," he said. "You don't realize it, but your brain has to work to tune things out. That creates a permanent level of fatigue, through which it's difficult to think clearly. It's kind of like alcohol," he said, looking at the beer in his hand.

I offered to roll up a joint, but he shook his head. "I gave up pot," he told me. "Nice high, but a bad drug for a writer. It's disorganizing. Makes it hard to get anything done. If I took up grass again, I'd hardly ever write a word."

When I visited his place, I was to learn how serious Moondog was about his writing. The stuff he wrote for the *Nugget* and the *Muckraker* was just the tip of the iceberg. I discovered that he had completed at least five novels—none of which had been published—and was working on a sixth. He also wrote sports articles, mostly about baseball. The man had three or four loose-leaf notebooks filled with poems, compilations of published and unpublished columns, and hastily penned music and lyrics to better than two hundred songs.

"I had a couple of bands once, back in Boston, in the sixties," he told me. Moondog owned five or six guitars, an upright piano, an assortment of wooden flutes, xylophones, and chimes, and several small stringed instruments I could not name; perhaps he had invented them himself. The main room of his house was filled to overflowing with books, papers, and musical junk. Since his only immediate neighbors were cows, squirrels, and coyotes, I imagined him sitting out in the evening on his porch, hypnotizing his four-legged listeners with song.

I guess it was a week or so before the death of Vicki Bodine when Moondog first took me out to his place, for which "remote" is too cozy a word. Though he actually owned only five acres, those five acres were sandwiched between two open grazing ranges so vast and uninhabited that when you were there you felt master of all that you could see. To get to the beginning of the long dirt road that led to his place, you drove north out of Santa Ysabel and then turned left down the seven-mile, up-and-down, constantly curving road to Mesa Grande. If Julian is a town and Santa Ysabel is a crossroads, Mesa Grande is a spot on the map where someone felt it necessary to place a name. There was once a store there, but the four cars a day that passed by couldn't support it, so it closed, and the California sun was fast fading the letters from the front of the abandoned building. At the center of population density in Mesa Grande, the houses are within sight of one another; the name, however, refers not to the settlement but to the land itself, a large mesa or table that rises between the Santa Ysabel Valley to the south and Lake Henshaw to the north. Some of the land is wooded, but much of it is open grassland, kept that way by the free-roaming cattle that have claimed the mesa as their own. Sometimes the cows would turn up in Nygerski's front yard, staring indolently into the windows;

at other times days would pass when he wouldn't see any cattle at all.

Moondog's place lay at the end of a winding, washboarded dirt road unsafe to travel at speeds over fifteen miles per hour. It was fully ten miles from his house to pavement. Along the road's course, other dirt roads branched off, some leading to ranch homes, some to abandoned cabins, some to clearings where someone had once had a contract to cut wood. There were no signs, and all the roads were the same width and in the same state of disrepair. How the cops had managed to find him was a mystery to Moondog and, once I saw the place, to me as well.

His house was wide, wooden, and low-slung—it could once have been a barn—and set to the side of a grove of coastal oaks that supplied his winter firewood. To the south he had a view of open, rolling hills, and because there were no nearby trees in that direction, the place got a lot of sun. He'd built a porch onto this side of the house, where he'd installed three cable-spool tables and several rusting metal chairs that had once been covered with white enamel. It was the primo place to sit and talk, or just tune in to the harmony of nature.

The interior of the house was wide open; bedroom and kitchen lay semi-enclosed on opposite ends of a huge main room dominated, as I've said, by books and musical instruments. There were two massive desks, one piled high with manuscripts and magazines, the other fairly neat, with a manual typewriter and a stack of blank white paper on its uncluttered surface. There was also a woodstove, a couch, a couple of comfortable chairs, a stereo, and a small television. "I get two channels," Moondog said, "depending on the weather."

The walls were sparsely decorated, but what pictures there were offered clues to the man. There was a giant photo of the Earth taken from space; a scowling portrait of the Ayatollah Khomeini; a two-page sideways spread from the *Los Angeles*

*Times* on Manute Bol, a seven-foot-seven-inch Dinka tribesman from the Sudan who had been recruited to play basketball, first at some small college in Connecticut and then in the NBA; and a representational drawing of Bob Dylan in which Dylan, in profile, appeared as a tree. In the roots below his neck were the names of his influences: Pete Seeger, Leadbelly, Woody Guthrie, Little Richard; in the branches of his hair were the names of acts for which he in turn had been an inspiration: the Byrds, Donovan, Jimi Hendrix, the Turtles. There was also a huge poster showing four young, long-haired guys leaning against a stoop on a city street, an electric guitar perched between them. Big block letters at the bottom of the poster said: APPEARING FRIDAY MARCH 15 AT MARIO'S PUB—THE BLOODHOUNDS. The name of the group was in red.

"That's a real collector's item," Moondog said, when he caught me looking at it. "That was my first band. We were all about nineteen. We played straight-ahead, three-chord rock and roll. We sucked, really." He laughed, and pointed to a young man, sans mustache, on the poster. "That's me. I played bass."

"Did you ever make any records?"

"Nah. We broke up after about a year. Then I was in another band for a while. We had this crazy lead singer—Phil Urbina was his name. He got a pair of those José Feliciano glasses, you know, the wraparound kind that blind people used to wear? And he painted red streaks from his eyes down both cheeks, and we called ourselves Oedipus Rex. We were punk before the Sex Pistols were out of third grade."

Moondog had inherited his place, he said, from a friend with whom he used to smuggle marijuana from Mexico into Arizona and the Southern California desert. About ten years ago the guy had crashed his plane into the Chocolate Mountains, east of the Salton Sea; Moondog, who by this time had abandoned the smuggling business for a job as a stuntman in Hollywood, was named in the will. He'd given up city life and retreated here permanently a few years after that, he said, though he still liked to travel. The place had its advantages. No one knew when he was here or when he was in Boston or Mexico or even overseas; and it was, he said, a great place to write.

I picked up one of the loose-leaf notebooks from the cluttered desk. Taped to the front was an index card that read, THE COL-LECTED POEMS OF CYRUS "MOONDOG" NYGERSKI, 1970–1980. The notebook contained at least two hundred pages. I flipped through it, stopping randomly at a poem entitled "Thoughts for a Rainy Night in Maine."

> *Rain keeps the Earth from dying of thirst*
> *Surprises keep Life from being rehearsed*
> *Art makes Death seem less than the end*
> *The Universe glows with a smile from a friend*

> *I love you*
> *whoever you are*
> *and when and wherever I'll meet you*
> *Keep smiling*
> *you radiant star*
> *Don't let the distance defeat you.*

Touching stuff, I thought, for such an obvious loner. There was no sense of a woman's presence, now or in the recent past, in the house. During the two days I spent there, the conversation once or twice turned to love and sex; he told me of his one-night tryst with the recently departed Patsy Kittredge, but on the subject of the women in his life he was for the most part close-mouthed, steering the talk in other directions when the subject came up. But I had a chance to glance at his novels. The first was called simply *Joan,* and described a year-long romance in a small village on the south shore of Lake Superior; as winter closed in, the couple became more and more absorbed with each other and oblivious of the outside world. It was almost pornography; at least half the book described in great detail the two main characters having sex. Moondog could make an orgasm last five pages. At the end, the lovers forgot to eat or fuel the stove as the snow piled higher and higher around the windows; they were found frozen to death in bed, in the act of copulation.

Another novel chronicled the life and loves of a woman who kept changing names and identities, moving on when a man or men threatened to tie her down. It took place all over the world. I took this character to be a female version of himself; her names, for instance, became more and more unwieldy as the book went on. She was Mary at the beginning, but after eleven or so relocations she called herself Chrysanthemum-Marie. Still another book was a darkly humorous story about a ritual priestess in Los Angeles who has children smuggled up from Mexico for sacrifice to Satan.

I didn't read all of Moondog's novels in those first two days, of course. I read them in pieces, and there are a couple I haven't gotten all the way through yet. And they weren't all serious or heavy-handed. He was big on baseball, having played, and one of his books was a science-fiction story detailing the workings of the game on the Moon, Mars, and the moons of Jupiter and Saturn, where visiting teams had to adjust for different gravities and surface conditions. And Moondog was quite excited about his current project, of which he had completed about two hundred pages. Called *Tartabull's Throw*, the entire story took place during a few minutes of August 27, 1967. It revolved around a single play in a single major-league game played between the Red Sox and the White Sox in Chicago. Moondog was weaving together the lives of a dozen Red Sox fans listening to the game on the radio, using the play to peer backward and forward into their destinies from this one shared moment. There was a ten-year-old boy on the Maine Coast, a wealthy gynecologist in Cambridge, a lonely widow in Providence, a ski bum in Vermont, a fetching coed at New England College in New Hampshire, a convicted murderer in a Massachusetts prison, and so on, all listening to the game on pins and needles, all involved in Moondog's portrait of New England in 1967, the year the Red Sox won the greatest pennant race in history.

I asked him where he got the title.

"It was the defining play of the season." he said. "There were five teams in the race at that point, and the Red Sox and Chicago were tied for first. The Red Sox had a four-three lead in the ninth, but they were just hanging on; Chicago had scored a couple of runs in the seventh to make it close, and had a rally going. Man on third—Ken Berry, outfielder, good speed—one out. It was a crucial game. Duane Josephson's up. Pretty good hitter. All they need is a sacrifice fly to tie it up. Josephson hits a fly ball to José Tartabull in right. Now Tartabull doesn't have a great arm—he's playing only because Tony Conigliaro got hit in the head by a fastball earlier in August and is out for the season. So Tartabull catches the ball and Berry tags up and takes off for home. And half the population of New England tenses—knuckles go white from Providence to Presque Isle. The throw is high, but Elston Howard, who's catching, goes up to get it, and comes down and makes the tag. Game over."

He was going through the motions as he said all this, and finished by making a fine tag on a knee-high stack of newspapers.

Moondog went to several baseball games a year on both the major- and minor-league levels. Sometimes he'd show up at Julian High School baseball games, wearing dark glasses, and stand off to the side and leave before the game ended. March he spent in Arizona, watching spring training, and he wrote an annual season preview, which several papers, including the *Julian Nugget*, picked up. "I love baseball," he said. "I couldn't give a shit about any of the other sports—I don't even pay attention. But baseball . . . you know, if they didn't have this unreasonable prejudice against left-handed second basemen and if I could've hit the curve ball, who knows what might have happened?"

His seasonal preview, like everything else he wrote, was fun to read. He hammered the Dodgers for letting Steve Sax sign with the Yankees, whom he loathed, and expressed the hope that Sax would name a son after ex-teammate Orel Hershiser. A kid named Orel Sax, he said in print, could not miss media stardom. Erik Gunn got several letters to the editor on that one.

Moondog picked the Giants to win the National League and the Red Sox in the American; the Sox, he predicted, would win the World Series in seven games. "You're picking the Red Sox to go all the way?" I asked skeptically. "What've they got for pitching, beyond Clemens?"

"Nobody," Moondog said. "I pick the Red Sox every year. I told you, I've got a credibility problem—nobody believes what I write."

"But, Moondog," I said softly, "the Red Sox never *do* win it all."

"Not yet," he said. "They haven't won the Series since 1918, in fact. But the year they do, I want to be the first person to say 'I told you so.' "

The Red Sox did not win in 1989, but I'm sure that Moondog's faith is undiminished. Anyone who has the patience to live out at the end of a road that leads to nowhere, writing six novels without landing a publisher, also has the patience to wait for the near-impossible to happen, or for the answer to a mystery to be revealed.

# Chapter Eighteen

As is the case with most small towns, Julian's most efficient vehicle for information was not the local newspaper but the conversational grapevine. Much of that conversation took place over breakfast or coffee, before the tourists and through-travelers invaded, and before the business of the day grew pressing enough to interfere.

The denizens of downtown Julian could be politically divided with fair accuracy according to which of the two early-morning eateries they frequented. Mariah's Café was in a new building across Main Street from the *Julian Nugget* office; its large windows faced out toward Main Street and its spacious sundeck offered a view of much of the town. The fare included some forty varieties of omelettes, some with exotic ingredients like cactus and okra; the lunchtime menu was equally imaginative. Inside, Linda Ronstadt or Bob Dylan or maybe a demo tape by a trio of local folksingers, who sometimes performed there at night, dampened the echo underneath the wooden cathedral ceiling.

The walls were covered with artwork that sometimes chased away potential customers who were born-again Christians, because there were occasional nudes and depictions of nondoctrinaire themes. A framed Richard Nixon campaign poster, circa 1948, hung at an angle on one wall; the restaurant's ponytailed, fortyish, graying, balding, chain-smoking owner and head chef—a refugee from Berkeley—explained that Nixon just wouldn't fit in a frame that wasn't crooked.

Nevell's Restaurant was a block up a side street and had been there forever, just like many of its patrons, the bulk of whom had voted for Nixon in 1968 and 1972, and 1960 too, if they were old enough. Its owners, a couple in their fifties who were getting ready to open a second restaurant in Borrego Springs, so they could live in the desert, served bacon and eggs, buffalo burgers and fries, and in the morning offered up many varieties of doughnuts and sweet rolls, easily their most popular items. There were few pictures of any kind in the low, booth-lined dining room, though a few small frames amid the wallpaper held sepia prints of Julian scenes from the early 1900s. It was remarkable how little the town had changed.

Mariah's served coffee in environmentally correct washable mugs; Nevell's offered Styrofoam cups in three sizes, from regular to jumbo, and would fill up a thermos for a dollar. Nevell's also had a porch, but there were only two or three tables on it, and one was usually claimed during the first hour of the morning by the first shift from the sheriff's department.

The two clienteles were not really divided by age or income level, but more by philosophy. The rich realtors and the starving artists went to Mariah's; the old-timers, the cops, and the young blue-collar workers chose Nevell's. Larry "the Wolf Man" Jordan, Claudia Gaines, and Danny Taylor were Mariah's customers; Vern Whittier, Stu and Derek, Steve Stephenson, and Harry

Ferguson could all be found occasionally at Nevell's. The older restaurant felt the loss of Vicki Bodine keenly; Patsy Kittredge was mourned and missed at Mariah's.

Erik Gunn liked to enjoy his morning coffee and newspaper on the deck at Mariah's, where he could keep his eye on his office across the road and on the unfolding scene on Main Street. Occasionally he'd take his little girl there for breakfast before dropping her off at day care, but usually he'd drop her off first, and relax for an hour or so before going to work.

He must have been paying a lot for baby-sitters; he was always working, it seemed, and his wife was getting more and more flaky about coming home at night. One morning in mid-September he decided to skip Mariah's and stop off at Nevell's for some doughnuts to take back to the office. There at one of the tables on the porch was his wife, chatting cheerfully with one-legged Sven and two of his buddies. He hadn't seen her since the previous day, and I guess there was a bit of a scene. Gunn called her a whore, among several other epithets, and he didn't speak them softly. I heard about it later, from a couple of different sources. I guess it gave everybody something to talk about, for a day, besides the murders.

It was tearing him up inside, I knew, and yet he showed few outward signs that anything was wrong. He checked with news sources, went to meetings, wrote good stories and strong editorials, and tended to the myriad details necessary to putting out a credible newspaper, week in and week out, on schedule. He listened politely to everyone who came into the office; he helped the real-estate ladies make changes in their listings, even when it was past deadline; he gently reminded Claudia Gaines to write checks to Lyle the photo guy, me, Moondog, and anyone else who helped in any small way to lighten his workload. Yet sometimes he'd just sit at his desk, sipping a beer or a glass of something stronger, and stare out the window. He could do this

140

for the longest time, even at night—especially at night, when there was nothing there to see. Erik Gunn was not a happy man that summer and fall. Perched on a precipice at least partially of his own making, he waited for responses to the job feelers he'd put out on his trip up north, a few weeks before I came to town, while a lurid story of mystery and death unfolded, month by month, on the streets and in the woods beyond his office window.

And, month by month, things changed in Julian, though the pace of change was slower there than in the congested cities down the hill. Frank Blaisdell's wife grew rounder and more radiant as her pregnancy progressed; friends stopped her on the street to discuss possible names for the baby and other happy things. The elementary school hired a long-term substitute for her forthcoming leave of absence. The high school hired a new English teacher, a fresh-faced young woman of twenty-two who looked young enough to be a narc, to replace Patsy Kittredge. Steve Dakota shmoozed with business owners in town, and invited the entire staffs of both schools down to his place by the beach for a massive school-year kickoff party. The new superintendent, driven as always by the athletic image my story and Gunn's photo had reinforced, bought a new mountain bike from Stafford Emerson and started a men's basketball group that met Monday nights in the high school gym. Some of the kids from the high school played, and their parents thought it a wonderful and wholesome activity the school's new leader had begun.

There was a big fire on Palomar Mountain, twenty miles away, and for two days the town was choked with smoke. Moondog, who lived a lot closer to the blaze, was out of town.

In my small slice of Julian, things changed also. Two of the three party girls in the lower cabin went off to college, the third moved back in with her parents, and Bill Haley rented out the place to one of the new cooks at Bucky's Barbecue, a guy about six feet tall, completely bald, with a bushy red beard and tattoos up and down both arms. I tried to make friends with the guy, but how can you strike up a conversation with someone whose vocabulary consists almost entirely of grunts? After a few attempts, I left him alone.

I did make friends with Darlene, my next-door neighbor, the woman who was always arguing with Derek about the condition of her cabin. I would have paid a fair amount of money to see a wrestling match between her and Bill Haley, but the two of them just occasionally shouted at each other when he wasn't avoiding her, and that was all. It wasn't that she was fat—well, she *was* fat, to be completely honest—but she was *big* all over. She stood close to six feet tall and had broad shoulders and big bones, and a deep voice for a woman. She had a boyfriend, whom she dwarfed, and she drove a light blue Volkswagen sporting a bumper sticker that read, DON'T LAUGH, IT'S PAID FOR.

Sometimes she'd invite me over for coffee in midmorning; we both had evening jobs, and we'd sit on her tiny front porch and watch the action of the complex unfold before going off to face our respective days. The Mexicans were forever trudging back and forth to the laundry room while their kids roamed the complex on skateboards and tricycles. The Keeler kid played in his muddy yard while his father prospected for gold. Several times a week Sven would show up at Tanya's, often looking haggard and unshaven; she'd offer him a shower and a steady stream of beer afterward, while he sat on the front steps and played his guitar or polished a new cane. At about ten, Montana Bill would rumble on by in his rattletrap car, heading for the liquor store. There was usually something going on at Blind Ben's, be it music—and Sven would sometimes hobble over there and jam—drugs, or a simple get-together for his many friends.

Darlene wanted out. "I've been here a year and a half," she told me, "and the only reason I stopped here at all was because my car broke down on the way from Phoenix. I was on my way to Northern California—I've got family there. Now I've got this little place, my car's fixed, and my job just barely covers rent and expenses." She shook her head sadly at her surroundings. "It'll probably be another year and a half before I can get out of here."

She worked at the dinner theater at the Cedar Mountain Inn, building stage sets and tending bar. One weekday morning she informed me that she had been able to score me a free ticket for one of the Friday-night performances. I called in sick, which predictably pissed off my boss, and caught a ride with her—she had to be there hours before the show and stay hours after. By the time the evening was over, I had discovered that the occult was alive and well in Julian.

The Cedar Mountain Inn lay at the end of a winding, four-mile road that left the highway near the spot where Moondog had found Patsy Kittredge and her stalled car in the rain those many weeks ago. That road itself split into a bewildering array of narrow winding roads just before it reached the Inn. There were many homes in the area; Cedar Mountain is sort of a separate enclave of Julian, with its own water district and a homeowners' association, dominated by weekenders from San Diego. The houses, many of them quite expansive and expensive, lie scattered in this labyrinthine road system. The inn is more or less at the entrance to this maze; once you're there, it's easy to get back to the highway, but God help you if you make a wrong turn. Some people have lived in Julian for ten or more years and still don't know where all the roads go.

The whole place had an eerie feeling about it. There was very little sunlight, even though we drove out there in the late afternoon, because the cedar forest for which both settlement and inn were named ranged fairly uniformly over the area. The place was ripe for a devastating forest fire, I thought, but apparently one had not occurred there for some time, for the biggest cedars were truly massive, and old pines and oaks seemed to be thriving as well. A few of the pines had turned brown, victims of a beetle whose appetite for tree bark had become more voracious with the drought, but they were not the dominant trees here as they were on Palomar and Mount Laguna, and thus the forest retained its dark, foreboding quality, even in summer.

The inn itself, it seemed, lay in the very densest part of the woods. Compared to most California lodging establishments, it was positively ancient, half stone and half wood, with vines crawling all over the walls and stone terraces. The dinner theater was in a converted gymnasium, down two sets of stone steps from the main body of the inn. Ribs and steaks sizzled on a long row of grills set up outside the building; patrons filed by and loaded their plates with salad, potatoes, and the main course, which they ate at tables inside, arranged in rows for optimum view of the stage.

Sven was there, sitting on a low stone wall behind the grills, his pale eyes boring into everybody. I guess the cook was one of his buddies and Sven had come down to bum a meal, for I didn't see him at intermission or after the show. He seemed to be everywhere, always on the fringe of whatever was going on; for a guy with one good leg, no car, and no visible means of support, he got around pretty well.

And then the show started, and it was too much. The offering that night was *The Mystery of Irma Vep*, by Charles Ludlam. Two guys played four parts each—women, men, and beasts—and they did a good job with all the quick set and character changes of what proved to be a spoof of the entire gothic horror genre.

This play had everything: a mansion on the moors of Scotland, an evil ghost, a hunchback, a mummy who came to life in a cursed Egyptian tomb. It even had a werewolf. The actor transformed right on stage. I couldn't believe the synchronicity of it. We had talked of werewolves in the *Julian Nugget* office only days before. Moondog's column had not yet hit the streets; when it did, one of its unintended effects was to boost attendance at the show, which, since it was in the third month of a four-month run, had been lagging.

Afterward, I went up to the bar in the main building of the inn and drank beer while I waited for Darlene to get off work and give me a ride home. The lobby of the place was the second whammy. Dark wooden bookshelves surrounded a deep stone fireplace; in front of the fireplace were a leather-covered couch and several matching chairs you could have lost a child in. A glittering crystalline chandelier hung from the beamed wooden ceiling, directly over a handcrafted wooden table positioned at the focal point of the couch and chairs. A chess set, its carved, three-inch pieces looking fierce and Oriental, stood on the table, set up for a game although no one was playing when I walked in. Books filled only half the shelves. The rest of the space was taken up by a huge collection of crystal balls, figurines of witches and wizards, amulets and wands, and other symbols of magic. There were tooth necklaces, crystals of various shapes and sizes, even a pentagram or two. The overall effect wasn't frightening—I didn't feel as though I'd entered the Bates Motel—but I sensed that there were powerful forces at work here in the middle of these old, old woods.

The collection belonged to Nat Barrows, the owner of the Cedar Mountain Inn, a small man with white hair, a white beard, and an elfish expression in his eyes. He looked something like a wizard himself. Barrows was helping Darlene tend bar as the crowd from the theater streamed in; she introduced us.

"Did you enjoy the show?" he asked me, setting down the bottle I'd ordered.

"Very much. Especially the werewolf. I have a friend who believes in werewolves."

"And you don't, I take it." His eyes looked directly into mine; I couldn't tell whether he was kidding or not.

"I'm not sure," I said. I thought I'd better shut up, because the murders were on everybody's mind, and the last thing I needed to do was get involved in a weird and easily overheard conversation at this decidedly strange bar. I had come to Julian, after all, intending to keep a low profile, and shooting off my mouth about werewolves in the wake of three unsolved murders certainly wasn't the way to do it.

Fortunately, Darlene came to my rescue. She turned to Barrows. "Tell him about the ghost," she prompted him.

"What ghost?" I asked her. "Are you going to tell me this place is haunted?"

Darlene looked at her boss. "It's true," he said. "Back in the late forties or early fifties, this place was owned by a couple from Los Angeles, in the movie business. Harry and Joan Blackburn were their names. They had their Hollywood friends and business partners down here quite often—of course, there was no theater here then, but it was a popular spot for movie people to come and relax, get away from it all. Well, right before Christmas in 1952, or maybe 1953—I don't remember—Harry was out one night fixing one of the lampposts. There had been a storm, and the light had blown out. There was ice all over everything. He slipped, and broke his neck. He died."

I sipped at my beer, and looked over at Darlene, who nodded.

"Since then," Barrows went on, "he's lived here, at the inn. His wife finally sold the place to a San Diego businessman, who sold it to me, ten years ago. But his ghost hung around. Guests have seen him, in their rooms and outside. *I've* seen him, on several occasions."

"But not recently," Darlene put in.

"No. Joan finally died, earlier this year, up in Los Angeles. I haven't seen him since then. So I think maybe their spirits joined."

"Wow," I said. It was all I could think of to say.

The bar didn't close until just before two in the morning, by which time I was exhausted. "That place is outrageous," I told Darlene in the car on the way home. "That crazy play, and all those crystal balls and ornaments, and that guy's tale of the ghost who lives there! Have *you* ever seen it?"

"No, but I don't doubt that it exists," she said. "Nat's no crackpot. If he says he's seen it, he's seen it."

"He looks like he should be a part of that collection himself," I said. "Don't you think he looks like a wizard?"

She laughed. "You didn't get a chance to meet his wife. She looks like Morticia on 'The Addams Family.' But Nat's a sweetheart. They both are. They started that theater from nothing. It's a real gift to a redneck town like this. They're good people."

When we pulled in to Sleepy Hollow, we were almost blinded by flashing red-and-blue lights. Three cop cars surrounded Tom Keeler's cabin and gold-mining operation, and just as we pulled up, two uniformed sheriff's deputies led Keeler, handcuffed, out the door of the cabin. He was wearing ripped blue jeans and a T-shirt; his boots were unlaced, as if he had hurriedly put them on. He kept his head down, away from the lights.

Most of our neighbors were in their doorways or outside, watching the action. At least two other cops were in the house; one was talking to Keeler's wife, who was trying to comfort her screaming son. Off to one side stood Derek, the manager, and Frank Blaisdell, talking casually as the two officers opened the back door of one of the cars and shoved Keeler in. Darlene and I got out of her car and approached them.

"What's going on?" I asked.

"Dope bust," Derek said. "The guy's been dealing metham-phetamine out of here."

He turned his head, and squirted a stream of tobacco juice onto the pavement. "You rent from me, you better keep your nose clean."

# Chapter Nineteen

THE *FARMER'S ALMANAC*, which catalogs the movements of the planets and the phases of the Moon, reached the newsstand at the back of the Julian Pharmacy on September 30, a few days after the *Manzanita Muckraker* came out. Its calendar for the next year began with October of this one, and I saw as I flipped through the pages of my purchase that the Moon would be full on October 2. Though the midafternoon temperature on the sidewalk was still in the eighties, I shivered when I saw the small hollow circle on the page, and wondered what, if any, preparations were being made to guard against some new horror. Mind you, I was not yet convinced of the veracity of Moondog's theory, but copies of the *Muckraker* were floating around, and people were talking. I hadn't seen Moondog in over two weeks; he had given me no hint of when he might return.

A siege mentality gripped the town, even as the tourist season swung into high gear. Guy Taylor and his cop crew solidified their residence at one end of the first floor of the Julian Motel, which inconvenienced a few weekenders but greatly increased the volume of doughnut sales at Nevell's. The expected confrontations between locals and visitors over things like parking and the length of the line at the liquor store seemed more tense this year than in the past. Proprietors of eateries and knickknack shops who ordinarily were friendly eyed each unfamiliar face with suspicion. The cops made a point of cruising past Sleepy Hollow and the Ghetto at all hours of the day and night, and the people who lived there, whose poverty was always inducing them to break some law or other, reacted with predictable paranoia. There was an incident at the Ghetto in which a baseball-sized rock was thrown through a window of a cruiser; two men were taken to the Vista jail and charged with criminal mischief, but there was little visible progress on the murders.

And each day the Moon grew larger, rising later in the afternoon sky and hanging over Main Street, mocking the town with the impossibility of halting the march of its phases. Moondog's article was widely read, and either vilified or ostensibly ignored, but the whole town was on edge, waiting for something to happen.

On the second of October, I spent the afternoon at the *Julian Nugget* office, conducting telephone interviews with the three candidates for Steve Stephenson's soon-to-be vacated spot on the water board. Gunn was there, sipping beers, morose as usual. It was his wife's birthday, and he was wondering aloud what to get her.

"Sometimes I think," he said into his beer can, "that the best present I could give her would be to go back to Missouri and stay there. If it weren't for Diana, maybe I would."

"What about flowers?" I suggested. "I've never known a woman yet who doesn't like flowers." Really, I wanted him to shut up. I was trying to work, and he was making it difficult.

Gunn sighed. "Yeah, I suppose flowers would be all right.

Predictable, but all right. I was trying to think of something special, though. Something to show her I still care."

"Do you?" I asked. It was maybe not the most tactful thing to say, but fuck, I hadn't taken the job to listen to his personal problems.

Gunn's answer was to look out the window and take another sip of beer. "Small towns are brutal," he said. "I don't know why I let her talk me into living up here. I thought California would be good for me as a writer. You know, L.A., Hollywood, that whole trip. But nobody takes you seriously when you write for a newspaper that maybe two hundred people read. Julian's in California, but it may as well be the Ozarks."

"I'd get her a piece of jewelry," I said. "Something silver. You can't be too careful—and the Moon will be full tonight."

"Give me a break," Gunn said. "For one thing, I can't afford jewelry. For another, there are no such things as werewolves, no matter what Moondog says. I know it, you know it, and everybody else knows it. Moondog's having a great time, playing his little joke on everybody, stirring up controversy like he loves to do, but have you noticed that he hasn't shown his face around here lately?"

"He's in Alaska," I said.

Gunn set down his beer can and laughed joylessly. "Alaska, huh? Must be nice. What's he doing, wolf research?"

"He could do that here," I said, just to be obnoxious. I had less than an hour to finish my interviews, and Gunn was getting on my nerves. What I really wanted him to do was leave me alone, go buy a present for his wife or whatever he had to do, and get out of the office for a while. He was *always* there. No wonder his marriage was failing.

"Moondog doesn't do research," Gunn said, with as much humor as he seemed capable of mustering. "He just makes stuff up. That's what I love about the guy. Not that I take what he writes too seriously. I mean, come on, Joe, you don't believe in werewolves, do you?''

No, I didn't. But I felt like giving him a hard time, don't ask me why. Maybe because his depressive manner seemed to ask for it. So all I said was, "We'll see tonight."

I didn't see much of anything until nearly midnight, except the inside of the kitchen at Bucky's Barbecue. Guy Taylor and two of his assistant investigators came in to eat; our eyes met when I brought a stack of cleaned dishes into the main dining area. I wondered if they were staking me out, and if, despite the official dismissal of Moondog's piece as superstitious nonsense, the cops were on special alert under the full Moon. I know my senses were heightened as I walked home under its baleful eye; despite myself, I walked faster than usual and kept glancing into the trees to my right, ready to make a run for it if I glimpsed anything even remotely frightening.

I had almost reached the entrance to Sleepy Hollow when the cop car screeched to a halt on the roadside dirt behind me. My first impulse was to run into the woods. Years of training as a criminal had given me a greater fear of Johnny Law than of any mythical creatures that might be lurking in the shadows. Common sense prevailed over the desire of my feet to flee; given the tension in the mountain air, running probably would have gotten me shot, and I wasn't doing anything wrong. I turned around and stared into the cruiser's headlights, blinded.

"Where you going, Joe?"

I recognized the growl as belonging to Kevin Byars, who had been among the officers to question me on several occasions.

"Home," I said to the lights. "Is that a crime?"

"Don't get smart, Joe," came Frank Blaisdell's voice out of the darkness. I heard two car doors slam, and Blaisdell's silhouette approached me from in front of the headlights. The Moon was behind the car; I couldn't see either officer's face. "You coming straight from the restaurant?"

"Yes!" I said, annoyed. "What's this all about?"

"Nothing, I hope. You haven't been wandering around up on Main Street, then?"

"I'm just walking home," I repeated. "What, did you guys find another dead body or something?"

"It's too bad having a big mouth isn't against the law," Byars said. "Otherwise I'd take your ass in. I don't like you."

"No bodies," Blaisdell said, his tone a good deal less menacing than his partner's. "But somebody put a brick through the window of the jewelry store, and made off with a bunch of stuff. That wouldn't be you, would it, Joe?"

"I told you, I'm just walking home. I got off work about ten minutes ago. If you don't believe me, ask my boss. I bet he's still there."

Static crackled over the radio in the cop car, and another vehicle, going downhill, whizzed by in the night. Blaisdell walked back toward the car where his thickset partner stood, hands on his hips, ready for anything.

"I suggest you go home and stay there," Frank Blaisdell said. "Keep out of trouble. People are a little bit nervous around here lately. And I can't blame them."

The two officers got back into the car, and Blaisdell pulled a fast U-turn and gunned it back up the hill into town. I did what he said—I went home. There was some sort of a party at Blind Ben's cabin, and the light was on at Darlene's but Tom Keeler's gold-mining operation was silent and the house was dark. Following Keeler's arrest, Bill Haley had immediately evicted his wife and child, removed most of the crap from the yard, and rented the place to one-legged Sven. While I welcomed the quiet that came with Keeler's absence, I felt for his wife and son, who were now probably homeless somewhere in greater San

Diego, and I viewed Sven with some trepidation. It wasn't that I was afraid of him so much as unnerved. He had that stare—if Charles Manson had had blue eyes, he would have looked a lot like Sven. And he came and went at weird hours, often, like Blind Ben, disappearing for days at a time. He was probably over at Blind Ben's now, keeping the watch with the other revelers, under the watchful eye of the full Moon.

I couldn't sleep. Wired from the confrontation with the cops, and possibly affected by the gravitational influence of the Moon, I drank several beers and listened to the radio, changing the station every time the Doors came on. At about three o'clock a cop car screamed by with its siren blaring; shortly afterward, I fell asleep in the chair. When I awoke it was light, and I was disoriented at first, because there was no metallic tapping. I got into bed and slept until noon, with the Moon safely on the other side of the planet.

# Chapter Twenty

ERIK GUNN STOPPED in at the Banner Stage Stop soon after it opened for the day. They had fresh coffee on the counter; he poured himself a large cup, and also bought a granola bar. This was his breakfast, consumed in the front seat of his car in the store's parking lot.

His head hurt, and so did the ankle he had evidently twisted, walking around in the desert. Beer cans littered the floor of the backseat; before heading up to Julian, he reminded himself, he needed to round them up and put them in the trunk. One of the cans, he observed, was unopened, but he had no desire for the hair of the dog. He had work to do, both at the office and at home, where he'd try to repair, or at least mitigate, the damage of the previous evening.

He tried to remember what the argument, the latest in a series of arguments, had been about. It had had something to do with her birthday, and his being late, or not making an elaborate dinner or taking her somewhere or being somehow deficient in some area of husbanding. The flowers hadn't helped; she had seen them as a last-minute gesture that was supposed to make up for three hundred and sixty-four days of neglect. Besides, a much more expensive bouquet had been sitting on the table in the good vase when he walked in. She had refused to tell him who they were from.

He remembered seeing four-year-old Diana cowering in the doorway of her room, and hating himself in that moment for losing his temper in front of her; he remembered Joyce accusing him of frightening their daughter, even though Joyce herself had initiated the fight. She started them all, he thought, yet once they had begun he seemed powerless to stop them, flinging her words back in her face and adding a few choice ones of his own. He was, after all, a man of words, unprepared to meet a verbal assault with silence. In the end he had just left, as he usually did, before things turned violent. But something had broken on his way out—her oil lamp maybe, or, worse, the stained-glass picture made for her by a former husband that she hung in the kitchen, cherished above all other possessions. He'd lugged that thing from house to house during their marriage, always under her suspicious eye, knowing that if he slipped it would never be considered an accident.

He had gone to the desert, his preferred refuge in times of stress, taking the curves too fast, opening it up to seventy-five when he hit the bottom of the grade. He'd spent the rest of the day wandering among the cacti and sitting atop windswept rock outcroppings, drinking one beer after another, until the argument and its deeper implications faded into the euthanasia of drowning brain cells. He didn't remember eating any dinner; a bag of Doritos lay crumpled on the backseat, and he guessed that had been it. His mouth tasted horrible.

He drove slowly up Banner Grade, not wanting to hurry the onset of the confrontation he knew was inevitable. On his way through town he saw that there were two cop cars in front of the jewelry store, and that the entrance was blocked off by yellow tape. The journalist in Gunn made a mental note to call and check on it; had his mind not been in such a state of turmoil, he would have stopped. But right now he didn't give a flying fuck about the paper. His head throbbed, and the coffee hadn't agreed with his stomach at all. He wanted to go home.

Joyce was in the driveway when he pulled up, putting bags into the back of her Subaru. Her face hardened when she saw him; she turned and walked back toward the house.

"Hey," he called, and started after her. She disappeared into the doorway to the kitchen, and reappeared a moment later with a cardboard box full of pots and pans.

"Joyce, what's going on?" He knew, but he asked anyway. He had always asked. He was a masochist that way.

She looked at his face, her eyes clear and cold. "I'm leaving," she said. "I can't take this anymore."

"Joyce, look, I'm sorry about yesterday . . ."

She set the box down in the back of the car and turned to face him. "You broke my oil lamp," she said evenly. "I've had that lamp for fifteen years."

"Look, I'm sorry. I'll get you a new one." He sounded lame as hell; besides, it was at least half her fault, so why was he apologizing?

"This isn't about last night, Erik," she said. "I've wanted to leave for a long time. Last night was just another of many nights. I don't like you anymore."

He stared at her in silence.

"Where did you go, anyway?"

"To the desert."

"To the desert," she repeated. Her face was inscrutable. He didn't know whether she believed him or not.

"Yeah."

He was surprised he didn't feel more, as he looked at his still-desirable wife, her steely blue eyes glaring dryly at him from under her dark mane of hair. It had been her impetuous, head-strong nature that had attracted him to her in the first place, and now the wrath that was never far below the surface was aimed directly at him. It made him tired, more than anything else, tired of having to defend himself daily from one attack or another. He always felt the victim in their arguments, which had been going on regularly for a year or more. She made him feel that way, with her infidelities, her accusations, her ever-increasing de-mands on his time. He had known that he was losing her, and here it was. But at this moment what he felt was not loss but instead a queer sense of relief, augmented by fatigue, that the arguments were finally ending. He wanted her out of his face, so that he could think. The time for tears would come later.

"Where's Diana?" he asked.

"She's inside, watching TV. I've told her."

"Where will you go? Are you taking her with you?"

"I'm going to stay with my mother in Escondido for a while, until I find a place," she said. "And yes, I'm taking her with me. You don't have time to spend with her anyway. You're always at that damn office!"

Gunn felt his eyes grow moist. "You are taking my daughter away from me," he said pitifully.

"She can come see you," his wife said, her voice softening for the first time. "Sven's taken a place in Sleepy Hollow, and he wants me to visit him. I'll bring Diana when I do. Look, Erik, let's make this as easy on her as we can, okay? It's no good for her, the two of us at each other all the time."

But this last bit of information was too much. "What the fuck," he cried, "do you see in *him?*"

"He cares about me, Erik!" she flared. "He talks to me, and listens to me! All you care about is that fucking newspaper! If we didn't have a daughter, you'd never come home!"

"That's not true . . ." he began.

"It *is* true! People call here at all hours of the day and night, and you act like they're doing you a favor! If something happens, you're there, and to hell with your family! You stay out all night . . ."

Gunn heaved a sigh at old wars. "It's the nature of my business," he said.

"Nature of my business, nature of my business," she railed. "Well, you know something? I'm sick of your business! I'm sick of being Mrs. *Julian Nugget*! I have a life, too, and talents, and dreams, and they're *just as important as yours!* I'm sick of being your shadow!"

She was shouting now; at a nearby house, a dog barked. "Joyce, can't we talk about this?"

"Oh, Erik, we've talked and talked. We always end up fighting. There's nothing left to say. It isn't working anymore. Can't you see that?"

He felt the first sting of tears. He hated crying in front of her. She thought it was weak, and on occasion rubbed his self-image in it. But for him there was a great deal left to say, about why she hadn't tried harder to *make* it work, why she had flaunted her affairs to humiliate him in front of a town where so much of his work was public, why she was deliberately breaking apart their home and condemning their daughter to a schizophrenic future between two parents who loved her but could not, or would not, get along with each other. He wanted to take the time to analyze what had gone wrong, and make an effort to repair it, and she refused to try.

But at that moment the phone rang, and Gunn broke away from his wife to answer it. It was Claudia Gaines, telling him about the robbery at the jewelry store.

After several minutes, Gunn put down the phone. He looked out into the driveway, where Joyce was still putting her belongings into her car. He heard the television in the other room. He would go and speak quickly to his little girl, tell her that everything was going to be all right and that he would see still see her. Then he would take a shower and go to the office.

But everything was far from all right. His head throbbed, and his heart ached. It seemed that his life was coming apart at the seams. He couldn't even remember when it had started, and now it had gone too far to do anything about. He couldn't even remember last night, and he didn't want to face today. But he would face it. He would. He was strong, and there was no time for despair. He had work to do.

# Chapter Twenty-one

WALLY LEACH WAS the next Julianite to suffer a disaster. It happened on Thursday, two days after the full Moon, and in broad daylight, in front of everybody on the street. Erik Gunn had perhaps the best view of anyone, for he was in front of the town hall, engaged in a mostly one-sided conversation with Leach, moments before it happened.

It had now been more than a month since the death of Vicki Bodine; full Moon had come and gone without another murder. *The Mystery of Irma Vep* concluded its run at the Cedar Mountain Inn, and the Julian Melodrama and Olio, an annual event featuring a corny play set in the town's pioneer days, with campy song-and-dance acts during intermissions—all performed by locals—opened for weekend performances at the town hall throughout October, and drew good crowds. Danny Taylor was in the play, as a hillbilly; Larry Jordan played the villain. A petite, dark-haired woman named Kathy Boles was cast as the fair heroine, and did a decent job with the part, but everyone remembered the role of the heroine in the previous year's melodrama;

she had been played with precocious poise and youthful impudence by Brandy Allen.

The theft of several necklaces, rings, and crucifix pendants from the jewelry store remained officially unsolved, though the cops suspected a group of wayward, aging hippies from Ranchita who wore animal skins and indulged in LSD and hallucinogenic mushrooms. Two members of the group had apparently been staying at the Ghetto that night; all had records and none a legitimate source of income. Sheriff's deputies told the owner, whose insurance had been fully paid up, that they expected to make an arrest soon; the owner was told not to reveal the specific items that had been stolen, as that was something only the thief would know. Gunn asked, and asked me to ask, and both of us were stonewalled.

The local cops were secretly pleased with the theft, for it was an eminently solvable crime that would take some of the heat off of them for the murders—or so they thought. But Guy Taylor and his crew were still around, and they didn't care about some two-bit burglary. They were after a murderer, and they made it clear that they would not leave until the killer was in custody. No one seemed to think that there was any connection between the break-in at the jewelry store and the deaths of Brandy Allen, Patsy Kittredge, and Vicki Bodine.

Wally Leach had been absent from his customary post on the town hall steps for several days. He was usually there by ten in the morning and drunk by midafternoon, in time to shout greetings to the teachers as they showed up at Quinn's or the liquor store following the end of the school day. However, that first week of October he was nowhere to be seen until Wednesday afternoon. When he appeared, he looked as though he had been in a fight; there was a scratch down one cheek and assorted bruises on his hands and arms. His manner was subdued, too, at least for him, until one-legged Sven showed up and bought him a bottle. By five o'clock he was his old, loquacious self.

He accosted Gunn on Thursday, when the editor was on his way to the Corner Market for a sandwich. Leach had a lot to say about the murders and Moondog's article in the *Muckraker*, just as he had a lot to say about every other topic. Gunn listened politely, knowing that to argue was simply to prolong Leach's verbosity.

Gunn couldn't help noticing how bad Leach looked. "Wally, did you hurt yourself?" he asked. "Your face is all cut up, and that fingernail looks like it's about to come off."

Leach looked down at his massive, swollen hands. The fingernail on the left index finger was purplish black; dark fluid was clearly building up behind it, pushing it upward. "I hit it with a hammer," he said, making the motion with his other arm. "I was building some steps for my parents, and wham! Hurt like a son of a bitch."

"Were you drunk?" Gunn asked.

"Me? Drunk?" Leach guffawed, and slapped Gunn hard on the back. "Nah, I wasn't drunk then, but I was that night, when I fell down the steps I'd just built. Hey, you know what you should write in your story? You should find out why the guys who hit the jewelry store only took things made out of silver. Especially crosses. They took every cross in the place, and they left a whole case of gold rings alone! Know what I think? I think your friend Nygerski inspired that theft. I think someone was trying to protect themselves! I think—"

"I've already written the story, Wally," said Gunn. "It'll be out tomorrow. Besides, they're not giving out information on the specific items that were stolen. You're just speculating. Wildly speculating, I'd say."

"Yeah? You read the *Union* today?"

"No. Why?"

"There's a story in there about the robbery. It says the thieves took nothing but silver."

"What?"

"Says the cops have several suspects, too."

"Get outta here! They told me they weren't giving out information about the specific items that were stolen, because it would hurt their case!" If there was one thing Gunn hated, it was getting scooped.

"Got a quarter?" Leach replied. "I'll prove it to you."

"Yeah." Gunn reached into his pocket, and flipped a quarter to the big man. Leach got up, and steadied himself with his crutch. "I'll be right back," he said, and he waddled out into the street, toward the row of newspaper racks on the other side.

Neither of them saw the RV rounding the corner until it was too late. The retiree at the wheel gave a blast to the horn, and a swifter man might have been able to get out of the way. Leach spun around and froze, as the huge vehicle bore down on him at perhaps fifteen miles an hour.

"Wally, watch out!" Gunn cried. A second later, Leach's bulk went sprawling across the pavement; his crutch clattered to the pavement, and his head fell on top of it.

Automotive and foot traffic screeched to a halt. "Get an ambulance!" someone shouted, and two people bolted into the drugstore while another dashed to a nearby pay phone. The driver of the RV opened the door and stared numbly down at Leach's prostrate form.

Gunn didn't move, either. From the sidewalk, he could see the pool of blood begin to spread from Leach's downturned face toward the storm drain near his own feet. And then he saw something else—a blood-covered, roundish object—rolling in the same direction as the flow of blood. The thing stopped rolling, and Gunn realized what it was. He sucked in his breath, and bit his lower lip, to keep from screaming.

It was an eyeball, and it was staring sightlessly at him.

# Chapter Twenty-two

INSISTENT POUNDING ON my door woke me from a sound sleep. I looked at the face of the digital clock beside my bed: two-thirty in the morning. Jesus. "It better be important, whoever you are," I grumbled, as I pulled on my pants.

The pounding kept on. "Yeah, yeah, just a *minute!*" I flipped on the light switch and opened the door.

"Hey, dude," said Cyrus "Moondog" Nygerski.

It was the second week of October; I hadn't seen him for nearly a month. "Hi, Moondog," I said, as cheerfully as I could. I'd gotten home at eleven, smoked a joint and had a beer with Darlene when she got home at midnight, and dropped into my pillow forty-five minutes ago. Most of me was still there. "How was Alaska?" I asked him.

"Oily," he said. "Which, I suppose, is better than being late."

I stared at him blankly.

"It's a joke, stupid," he said. "Although, I admit, not a very good one. I didn't wake you up, did I?"

"What the fuck do *you* think?"

"*They're* still up." He pointed toward Blind Ben's cabin, where the lights were blazing and four or five bodies could be seen milling around behind the curtains. Rock music, barely audible from my place but surely loud enough within the walls, played on the stereo.

"That's 'cause Ben's away, and the mice are playing," I said. Darlene had told me that Blind Ben had departed the previous week, his backpack stuffed with food, on one of his extended hikes. His many friends, as was the custom whenever he took off, were taking care of the place in his absence. Say what you will, Blind Ben probably did more than anyone to ease the problem of homelessness in Julian.

Moondog reached around behind him on the porch, and came up with a large rectangular box. "Here," he said. "I brought you a present. Got it on the way back through British Columbia."

It was a case of Molson ale. And the bottles were cold, too. "Just don't let Gunn see it," Moondog said, handing me the beer and seating himself in the one chair. "You'll be lucky to drink three of them if he does."

"He never comes over here," I said. "Especially since he might run into his wife." I told him about Tom Keeler's drug bust, and the subsequent and swift eviction of his wife and child. I told him that one-legged Sven had snapped up the vacancy, and that Joyce was a frequent visitor. I told him that she had taken her daughter and moved out of Gunn's house; he didn't seem surprised.

He told me about Alaska—how big, bold, and beautiful it was—and he said that if the shit ever hit the fan in Mesa Grande, if they put the landfill in, or if the cops kept coming around every time something happened because they didn't like his name or his writing, he might chuck it all for the Great White North. He spoke of the Aurora Borealis, and of oil-coated rocks

167

on once-pristine beaches. He spoke admiringly of the redneck oil workers and disparagingly of their overweight, citified bosses. He described endless stretches of evergreen forest, snow-capped mountains, and glaciers that pressed down to the edge of the sea. He recalled moose utterly unafraid of humans, and the howls of real wolves in the night. And finally, when he was through, he asked, "And what about *our* wolf? What happened when the Moon was full?"

"Nothing," I said. "At least nobody died."

I pulled out the latest issue of the *Julian Nugget*, which featured Gunn's story on the robbery of the jewelry store, my story on the vacuum at the top of the water board, and a tepid update on the murders that contained little new information. Moondog read through it all before he looked up.

"It looks like you're going to have to abandon your werewolf theory," I ventured.

"What about Vern Whittier?" he asked.

"He's back," I told him. Vern Whittier had, in fact, been drinking heavily that night at Quinn's, threatening to kill "that fucker Nygerski" if only someone would tell him where Moondog could be found. When the Sun went down and the full Moon rose, the only change that came over Whittier was that he became more drunk and more belligerent, and he ended the evening on the losing end of a fight with the boyfriend of an attractive tourist he tried to hit on. He sported a black eye and a fat lip the next morning; his silver crucifix had not been able to save him from that.

"And nothing else?" Moondog asked anxiously. "No dead cows or coyotes or deer?"

"Not that I've heard of," I said.

"Hmm. Was it cloudy?"

"No, I don't think so," I said. "In fact, I know it wasn't, because the Moon was high in the sky when I walked home."

"You walked home? Alone?"

"Yeah, I always do. Look, Moondog, I think you're going to have to get off this werewolf thing. It was good for a few laughs, but—"

"It's not a joke, Joe. I'm glad no one was killed, but now we've got to figure out why."

"Maybe because the killer doesn't want to be caught."

"Werewolves in the beast state don't have that kind of consciousness," Moondog said. "Everything is subjugated to the overpowering instinct to kill."

"Moondog, it's late. My head hurts."

"Listen to me. Just because nobody died on the last full Moon doesn't mean we should let down our guard. Any number of things could have happened. And the next full Moon is likely to be the most dangerous one yet."

"Why?"

"It's a question of how the werewolf phenomenon works," he said. "Of exactly how full the Moon has to be."

"What do you mean?"

"Well, full Moon does not occur on a *night*," he said. "It occurs at a precise moment, like the solstices and the equinoxes. At the moment the Moon is at the point in its orbit exactly opposite the Sun from the Earth, that's full Moon."

"So? What's your point?"

"So a werewolf isn't a werewolf for a moment, he's a werewolf, as far we know, for an entire night. Don't you see? We say there's a full Moon on the date that moment occurs, but a Moon that's ninety-nine percent full is, in most cases, able to bring on the transformation. Now, the calendar says the next full Moon is on October 31, Halloween. But the time of exact full Moon is around ten in the morning. That means that the Moon is fuller at midnight on the thirtieth than it is at midnight on the thirty-first. Essentially, there will be a full Moon for two consecutive nights. No one knows how close the Moon has to be to perfect fullness in order for a werewolf to transform. It probably varies from werewolf to werewolf."

"Moondog, there is no werewolf! No one died on the last full Moon. No one even came close to dying. I'm sorry, but I think your theory has been disproved."

"Or," Moondog said, "the werewolf was away at the time."

"*You* were away," I said, just to tease him.

"Yes, I was," he said seriously. "Who else?"

"Well, Vern Whittier was here," I said. "So was that crazy cook. So was I."

"How about our gold-digging friend over there? The guy they busted for dealing crystal?"

I shuddered, remembering that crazed look in Tom Keeler's eyes. "Jesus, do you think—wait a minute. He was in jail. If he turned into a werewolf in jail, don't you think someone would have noticed?"

"Do you *know* he's in jail?" Moondog asked.

"No," I admitted. "But I saw them take him away in hand-cuffs."

"Joe, you know they can't keep a lot of those guys," Moondog said. "The jails are full—they're more than full. A lot of people get released on their own recognizance, even for serious crimes. How serious is dope? Maybe our guy is down in San Diego somewhere, wandering the streets. Maybe he wolfed out on somebody down there."

We sipped our beers quietly as we contemplated this possibility. "His wife's gone, too," I said. "Maybe *she's* the werewolf. Or maybe it's the kid. I always thought there was something strange about that kid."

Moondog shook his head. "No," he said. "A small person would turn into a small beast. Not something big enough to knock a guy like Vern Whittier senseless." He paused. "Does he really want to kill me?"

"Your article offended a lot of people," I said.

"Well, that's too damn bad," Moondog replied defiantly. "At least they read it, didn't they? That's an accomplishment these days. Most people don't read newspapers. They just skim the headlines. They're like someone with a remote control on the TV, skipping from channel to channel, spending two seconds looking at the picture before changing the channel again. I'd rather offend people than be ignored. Any response is better than indifference."

He took a long pull off his beer, draining the bottle. "Besides," he said, "I still think I'm right."

"If you *are* right," I asked him, "then who's the werewolf?"

"That," my friend said, "is what we have to find out."

# Chapter Twenty-three

WHEN IN DOUBT, hold a meeting. That seemed to be the modus operandi in Julian in times of crisis, whether the emergency involved water, trash disposal, or violent death. In my job as a cub reporter, I'd already been to several such meetings. Water issues were handled, of course, by the water board; matters of land use were the purview of the Community Planning Group. Because the wave of deaths threatened the town's economic base as a Mecca for visitors, the special meeting held a few days after Moondog's return was sponsored by the chamber of commerce.

They'd invited representatives of the sheriff's homicide detail to come and speak that evening; these weren't the local boys, but suit-and-tie higher-ups from San Diego. In a show of solidarity, however, the entire contingent of the Julian substation turned out, too, and occupied the entire first row of chairs facing the town hall stage. It would have been a good time to commit a burglary somewhere in the Julian area. Only the highway patrol was out on the streets, and they had something like one officer for every hundred miles of backcountry road.

The town hall was packed. Gunn was there, near the front, notebook and pen out and ready. Claudia Gaines sat with several of the wealthy realtors who supported her paper. Larry Jordan and his wife were in the audience; so were Nat Barrows and his. My boss was there, with a few of the other restaurant owners. I recognized several of my neighbors, including Derek and Cindy and their two boys, the monosyllabic cook I worked with, Joe, and Stu and Tanya. At the back of the hall, Sven stood with Vern Whittier and several other men I'd seen frequently clustered around the front of the liquor store. Gunn's wife was not there; neither was Cyrus "Moondog" Nygerski, who avoided all public gatherings.

Danny Taylor gaveled the meeting to order. He was an awkward public speaker, and clearly he hadn't envisioned his job as chamber president as including the formulation of the town's response to a kind of violence not normally associated with rural communities. Historically, as I've noted earlier in this narrative, Julian was a violent place. Moondog would argue in the next issue of the *Muckraker* that the werewolf attacks—if that's what they were—were a throwback to the past as well, to a time when human civilization was new on the Earth and the spirit world, including the dark spirits that could become werewolves, was more active and acknowledged.

Taylor thanked everyone for coming, and made a few remarks, aimed at the business community, to the effect that despite the recent tragedies Julian was still a nice place to visit, and should continue to be promoted as such. He said the large turnout at the meeting indicated that this was a caring community, committed to protecting its own, and he expressed complete confidence in the sheriff's department on its handling of the three still-unsolved murders. Then he turned the meeting over to Lieutenant Keith McMahon of Homicide.

McMahon was a short, stocky man, dressed starchily in a gray suit whose shoulders ended at militarily correct right angles. His hair, combed tightly back from his forehead, matched the color of the suit. He looked as if he'd shaved fifteen minutes ago and combed his hair ten minutes after that. He looked almost stereotypically like an office cop, and he spoke in a crisp voice that snapped off syllables like the ends of fresh green beans and did nothing to blur the image.

He spoke briefly and matter-of-factly about the deaths of the three women, not glossing over the brutality of the crimes but not providing any lurid details, either. He summarized the facts of each case, stressed that the investigations were ongoing, and said that anyone with any information that *might* be relevant to any of the three crimes should not hesitate to come forward. He repeated the official line that investigators were proceeding on the assumption that there was a single killer, but said the possibility of copycat crimes could not be ruled out. "That's where we stand," he concluded. "Mainly, I'm here to answer any questions you may have, and to solicit your assistance so that we can do our jobs."

There were many, many questions. One of the first came from a member of Sven's group, one of the young cowboys at the back of the hall. "You guys have been poking around a lot up where I live," he said. "I kinda get the feeling you think the killer is someone local. That true?"

"We don't know," McMahon said. "We do know that in each case the victim was killed where the body was found. The crimes were committed locally, against local people. A transient or someone passing through would not likely return a month later, and again a month after that, to commit similar crimes. It could be that it's someone from the city who comes up here when the urge to kill comes over him. More likely it's someone who lives here."

"Have you checked to see if there have been other people

killed in the same way, in other areas?" someone else asked. "Maybe this sicko travels around."

"Good question," McMahon responded. "And the answer is that we have checked, throughout Southern California, and we haven't come across any reports of any other women killed in this manner since the beginning of the year. The killer seems to be confining himself to this area."

Erik Gunn raised his hand. "Lieutenant, it seems that the nature of the crimes—you know, the messiness, for lack of a better word—well, it seems as if there would be a lot of evidence left lying around, like bloody fingerprints and clothing and so forth. It doesn't seem that the killer cares too much about covering his tracks. Yet three people are dead, and you don't have a single suspect. How come?"

"Yeah, what are you guys doing?" shouted a member of the group at the back. "Besides eating all the doughnuts in Julian?"

This brought a round of derisive laughter—dangerous, because it could turn ugly, but illustrative of the tension in the room. McMahon raised a hand in the face of the audience's discontent.

"We *have* been gathering evidence," he said. "Much of it must remain confidential until we are able to make an arrest. Because, as I'm sure you know, an arrest is only half the battle. We need enough evidence to be able to go into a court of law and put this maniac away."

"Do you have a suspect, then?" Vern Whittier asked.

"No, but we—"

McMahon was not permitted to finish. "This meeting is a joke!" someone cried, and he was immediately joined by a chorus of jeers and other shouts of indignation. I halfway expected someone to throw something. People were uptight.

Danny Taylor rose from his seat in the front row and joined McMahon at the podium. He held his arms high above his head, motioning for quiet, and after a minute or two the shouting subsided.

"We called this meeting because a lot of you said you wanted to ask some questions," he said. "The lieutenant admits that he does not have all the answers. But he agreed to take the time to come here and talk to us. Let's at least give him the courtesy of listening to what he has to say."

"Lieutenant, were the victims sexually assaulted?"

The question came from the middle of the room, and it was a woman who asked it. I turned, and recognized Marla Atherton, proprietor of Europa Bookstore, a second-floor shop on one of the small side streets, which specialized in feminist literature and had a hard time turning a profit. She ran a business-card-size ad in the *Nugget*, and was about four months behind in paying for it.

"As far as we can tell, no," McMahon said, as the hubbub died down. "The most recent victim was found nude, but according to our witness she removed her clothes herself, to take a swim." At this point a lot of eyes turned toward Vern Whittier, who seemed to be trying, despite his size, to melt into the crowd standing at the back of the hall near the door. "With the first two victims," McMahon continued, "we found no evidence of sexual molestation, although the bodies were pretty well torn apart."

The questions went on. The frustration level of the audience remained high, and Taylor remained beside the podium, in a silent show of support for the lieutenant. I listened carefully for any clues that the cops might actually have uncovered something useful or out of the ordinary, but it became increasingly clear, as McMahon continued to speak in the same clipped, unemotional monotone in response to each question, that the primary purpose of the meeting was to prevent the town's angrier citizens from forming a posse and meting out their own brand of vigilante justice on whatever stranger seemed convenient. The police weren't hiding anything, because they had nothing to hide. They had no answers at all.

I found myself wishing that Moondog was there. *He* wouldn't have been embarrassed to ask the question—the one question that no one else seemed willing to ask, for fear of ridicule or for whatever other reason. He had already asked it in print, it was true, and would ask it again, but at this meeting it was being ignored, as probably he had known it would be. I hadn't expected to see him there, for to expose the question at that forum would have required Moondog to expose himself, and there would have been no easier target for the town's wrath. Public debate wasn't Moondog's thing, anyway. He was a reclusive, secretive son of a bitch, who had mastered the art of talking and being talked about without being talked back to.

Still, the question hung there, unasked, and I wasn't sure that anybody other than myself could feel the weight of it. My palms were sweating—a telltale sign of nervousness. I blew on them softly, and then raised my hand. McMahon pointed to me about five minutes later.

"Officer," I said, standing up, "what about this werewolf business? There was a column in one of the local papers—"

"Does someone have a *serious* question?" McMahon asked, looking around.

"I *am* serious," I insisted. It had taken some nerve to pose the question; I wasn't going to back off now. "You've described the attacks as vicious and animallike, and there was a full Moon on the night of each murder. You told us you were considering every possibility."

"Sit down," someone behind me said. "You're making a fool of yourself." I looked quickly over at Gunn; he was studying his notebook and slowly shaking his bald head.

"A werewolf isn't a possibility, it's fantasy," McMahon said, looking straight at me. "We're not responsible for some idiot writer who thinks it's funny that people are being murdered. Besides, there was a full Moon about ten days ago, but no murder. That tells me the killer knows exactly what he's doing, and is laying low for fear of being caught. I have every reason to believe we'll catch him before he kills again."

"Maybe he's left the area," I offered, motivated more by loyalty to my friend than any belief in the supernatural. "Before the Moon was full."

Anger flashed briefly in McMahon's eyes. "One thing I would hope to see during our investigation," he said, "is fairness and good judgment on the part of the press. We can't disclose every piece of evidence we have, for obvious reasons, but we try to maintain a cooperative and cordial relationship with the media. Crackpot stories by people who don't know anything about police work not only hurt our investigation, they might give other sick people ideas. I would hope that responsible newspapers would refrain from printing that kind of garbage."

"Amen," said a voice in the crowd. I sat down.

But Moondog was soon to have his vindication.

The following weekend, as long lines of tourists ate their way up one side of Main Street and down the other, a young couple went hiking by the old Bailey Mine, near the bottom of Banner Grade, where the mountains meet the high desert. Banner Creek, a spring-fed stream that bubbles down the mountainside all year long, even in drought years, runs past the piles of rock and falling-down cabins where men once camped and dug into the Earth with dreams of riches. People still pan for gold in its shallow waters, and every so often someone comes up with a few flakes or a pebble-sized nugget that's actually worth something.

The young man and woman were walking along the creek, noting with dismay the proliferation of shotgun shells and dis-

178

carded beer cans littering the area, when they spotted, half-buried in the fallen leaves on the creek's far side, a man's leather jacket. Taking a closer look, they saw to their horror that the jacket had not been lost or discarded: a hand poked out of one of the sleeves.

The badly mutilated and partially decomposed body was that of a human male, between thirty and forty years old. The throat appeared to have been slashed several times. The man's long hair and beard were caked with blood. The chest cavity had been ripped open; maggots and other small creatures of the woods had moved in and made a home there. The face was ripped to the bone; one ear lay detached on the ground beside the body. The eyes were gone, too, but that would not have been a tremendous loss to this particular victim.

The body was that of Blind Ben, who had not been missed because he frequently disappeared for days or even weeks at a time. The autopsy revealed that he had been dead for a bit less than two weeks; the best estimate was that he had met his grisly fate on the second of October, or the day before.

# Chapter Twenty-four

"*Now* DO YOU believe me?"

We were sitting in the *Julian Nugget* office—Moondog, Gunn, and I. It was late at night. We were all nursing beers; Gunn was maybe on his sixth or seventh. The brand was Old Milwaukee. Like talk, it was cheap.

"I've told you before, Moondog, we've got a nut case on our hands," said Erik Gunn. "Like the Hillside Strangler in L.A., or that Gacy character in Chicago. Sooner or later he'll slip up, and the cops will catch him. But there's no proof—none—that the killer is a werewolf."

"Well, your misogynist theory is certainly blown to hell," Moondog said. "There's no way in hell Blind Ben could have been mistaken for a woman, even in moonlight."

"And why the full Moon?" I put in. "Every single one of these murders has been committed on the night of a full Moon."

"They don't know about Blind Ben," Gunn said. "They can't pinpoint the exact day he died, or even if he died at night."

"They can come pretty close to pinpointing it," Moondog

maintained. "It's within a day or two. Maybe even on the day. And the method of killing is identical to the three women. I'm willing to assume that it was done under the influence of the full Moon. I'd say the circumstantial evidence is pretty strong."

"Circumstantial evidence of *what?* I can't believe I'm sitting here in my office talking with two otherwise rational people about a fucking *werewolf!* Listen to me. *There are no such things as werewolves!"* Gunn ran his hands over his balding head in exasperation. "And if you think I'm going to print anything about a werewolf in this newspaper, you're out of your fucking minds."

"Erik, I like you," Moondog said. "But you have a closed mind about some things."

"I need another beer," Gunn replied. He pushed himself up from his big desk chair, but fell back, wincing. "Ow! Son of a bitch!"

"What's the matter?" I asked.

"Oh, this damned ankle. I twisted it, walking around in the desert a while back, and every time it starts to get better I forget about it and put too much weight on it and hurt it again."

He got up slowly this time, and limped over to the refrigerator.

"Why don't you go see Dr. Sohn?" I asked him.

"Nah, I don't believe in doctors. Besides, this job doesn't give me health insurance. I'm sure it's nothing. I'll just keep taking these painkillers." He sat back down, opened the can of beer, and raised it to his lips.

"Erik, werewolves *do* exist," Moondog said gently. "I know that for a fact. And all the evidence points to a werewolf. You're letting your own prejudices get in the way of honest reporting."

Gunn sighed. "Moondog, I'm not calling you a liar," he said. "But I will believe that werewolves exist when I see one transform before my eyes, or when someone brings the body of one into this office. I want to be shown. I want proof. It's the same problem I have with the Loch Ness Monster, or Bigfoot. People insist that they're real. Well, if they exist, there has to be a breeding population. Nothing lives forever. Why hasn't anyone ever found a Bigfoot skeleton? We have dinosaur skeletons millions of years old, yet if there are Sasquatches in the California woods, as some people maintain, where's the physical evidence? Where are the bones, or the piles of Sasquatch shit? If someone wants to prove that Bigfoot exists, all that person has to do is shoot one and put the body on public display. But that hasn't happened, because people are in love with the supposed mystery rather than the reality. And the reality is that Bigfoot is a myth."

Moondog listened intently as Gunn spoke, and considered his argument for several seconds before replying. "You know, it's healthy to be skeptical," he said. "Especially for a journalist. But your Bigfoot analogy isn't entirely accurate. I agree, Bigfoot and the Loch Ness Monster are probably myths. But a werewolf is different. Werewolves aren't animals. They're temporary physical manifestations of the supernatural. That's why they can be fought by supernatural means, like the symbol of the Christian Jesus on a cross. You can't just shoot one and bring in the body. If I were a werewolf, I could be sitting here talking to you now, just like I am, because the Moon isn't full. You could shoot me—you wouldn't even need a silver bullet, because the beast in me would be dormant between full Moons—and it wouldn't prove a damn thing."

"But werewolves are the stuff of legend," Gunn said. "Like the Greek gods and goddesses. If they were real, wouldn't there be more than one of them? Wouldn't people be killed all the time, every time the Moon is full?"

"People *are* killed all the time," Moondog said. "Do you know how many murders there were last year in Southern California alone? Just in Los Angeles there were several hundred. And lots of murders go unreported, unprosecuted, unpunished.

Bums, winos, homeless people—people that nobody misses when they die. Most people live in cities, so that's where most werewolves are, too. The carnage they create just blends into the overall background of violence. It's pretty rare that a werewolf gets into an upper-class neighborhood, or a rural area like this, where it's more likely to be noticed."

"He's got a point, though, Moondog," I put in. "Why *isn't* there any documentation, like a werewolf on videotape, or anything?"

"Because werewolves are myths," Gunn said.

"Have you ever seen a California condor?" Moondog countered, looking at each of us in turn.

"No," I said. Gunn shook his head.

"But you don't consider them mythical creatures, do you?"

"Come on, Moondog, they're breeding them right down at the Wild Animal Park," said Gunn. "They show them on TV."

"But you've never *seen* one, have you? Videotape can easily be faked. Yet you take it on faith that the condors are real, and the werewolf photos in the supermarket tabloids are bogus. There are only about twenty-eight condors left on Earth. I'd be surprised if there were that many werewolves. Mankind is evolving beyond the primitive instincts that give rise to such beasts. It's quite likely that werewolves will one day be extinct. Most people who become werewolves are tormented souls; quite a few of them commit suicide. Others die natural deaths, and the beast within them goes into limbo or, if the bloodline is wiped out, dies. So werewolves are rare, as rare as the condor. The difference is, werewolves aren't herded together in captivity. They're free to roam among the masses, and to kill people when the Moon is full."

"But—" Gunn began.

"And as for myths," Moondog went on, "well, how many so-called myths have later turned out to be true? Heinrich

Schliemann found Troy. That astronaut was pretty sure he knew the location of Noah's Ark. The jury's still out on the Shroud of Turin. Never underestimate the power of myths. They come from somewhere."

"*Somewhere* more often than not being the human imagination," Gunn argued. "People make things up. Like astrology. Or the Greek myths. Okay, so maybe there was a city of Troy, and maybe there was a long war there, like the one Homer describes. That doesn't make it literally true that Achilles's mother dipped him in the River Styx and held him by the heel, or that Aphrodite guided the arrow that killed him to the one vulnerable part of his body. It's symbolism. And that's what werewolves are—symbols. They're representations of evil, or something. They're not real."

"Your problem is that you're a complete rationalist," Moondog said. "If you can't latch on to something with one of your five senses, then for you it isn't there. Do you believe in God?"

"I'm an agnostic," Gunn said uncomfortably.

"Ah! In other words, you're hedging your bets. Do you believe in life after death?"

"I hope so."

"But you're not *sure*, are you? You don't have any direct evidence, do you?"

"People have had near-death experiences—"

"Circumstantial," Moondog said. "Do you believe in ghosts?"

"No."

"Extrasensory perception? Telepathy?"

"I don't think anyone can do it consistently," Gunn said. "I think ninety-eight percent of this so-called psychic stuff is bunk."

"Only ninety-eight percent? That's interesting. Have you ever had a telepathic experience? When you and someone else were each thinking the exact same thing at the exact same time?"

Gunn squirmed in his chair. "It's happened to me once or twice. But—"

"But you dismissed it as a coincidence. Because it wasn't like algebra, or grammar. It wasn't something you could learn, and apply all the time, whenever you wanted to. It wasn't something you could control. It came from outside yourself."

Gunn sighed loudly; his shoulders sagged forward. He looked down into his beer can but did not drink from it. "Moondog, what's your point?"

"My point is, you shouldn't be so quick to dismiss things you don't understand. Werewolves are beyond logic, beyond the three-dimensional time capsule of existence that has been given to human beings. They interact with this world, often with deadly results, but their origin is elsewhere, on an entirely separate plane. Erik, I know this sounds incredible to you, even crazy. But I've studied this. I know. Somehow, some way, a werewolf has turned up in these mountains. And in less than two weeks he's going to strike again. I hope we're ready for him."

# Chapter Twenty-five

AT SLEEPY HOLLOW, the death of Blind Ben was observed first with an extended wake, followed by what promised to be permanent occupation of his living quarters by an extended family of mourners. Ben had lived with few material possessions, but one of the most precious was a thirty-day rental agreement signed by Bill Haley, and he had friends who knew how to parlay such a document into free shelter for months. Haley waited three days before mentioning to several of the dozen or so bereaved squatters that they would need to find other housing. He was told by one of the group that Ben had had an arrangement with Dave, who was now in Arizona, to share rent, and that the rental agreement should automatically transfer. Haley didn't see it that way, and Derek, not wanting to encourage such open-door policies, slapped up a thirty-day eviction notice, without much hope that Ben's friends would willingly move. After a decent interval following the discovery of Ben's body—a week at the most—the parties began again and life, Sleepy Hollow style, went on.

Sven spent a lot of time there, and at Stu and Tanya's, and a lot of time away from the Hollow as well; I'd sometimes pass him on the road as I walked up to town in the morning. Many times he looked hung over out of his mind, and barely recognized me as I wished him good morning. Sometimes he'd stagger out of his cabin around noon and shuffle off to town, but really, he was hardly ever there. Gunn's wife visited him from time to time, sometimes with her little girl, but more often without. A pile of manzanita sticks, raw material for future canes, began to grow in the yard that had once been nothing but rocks and mud and old boards.

Montana Bill suffered a heart attack, probably from all that drinking; the ambulance came in one night and whisked him away. He was not seen for the better part of a week. When he returned, an old woman, a sister, perhaps, was with him. She drove the car to town now, while he sat out on the porch, or inside the cabin watching TV.

On the weekend of the annual country music festival, Derek and Cindy told all the tenants to park their cars at the back of the complex, and made over a hundred bucks by charging the concertgoers three bucks a pop for all-day parking. The traffic was as bad as it had been on Labor Day, but this time there was no full Moon or bicycle event to complicate things, and the water held out. Justin Zak made out like a bandit that weekend, too, for the new chairman of the water board had made him an offer he couldn't refuse. My big story that week, which Gunn ran on page one, was that Julian would be getting its new shopping center after all.

At the Methodist church, about a mile west of town, carloads of visitors were being flagged down by men in orange vests, holding out apple pies with one hand and rubbing their tummies with the other. Although it looked a little ridiculous, the theory—that people would be so starved for apple pie after driving for more than an hour that they would not be able to wait until they got to downtown Julian to choose between a dozen pie outlets—apparently worked, because the Methodists exhausted their weekend supply before noon on Sunday. By that time the traffic was so bad that they too were charging for parking, in the church parking lot, and people were willingly paying, even though it was warm and a mile-long uphill walk awaited them.

Wally Leach returned to his post on Main Street with a patch over one eye, a sewn-up gash running from one cheekbone to the side of his chin, a worse limp than ever, and a continually more embellished story about the foray across Main Street through traffic that had cost him his depth perception. He continued to drink and to heckle people in his loud and distinctive manner, but people noticed that his grooming habits, never great to begin with, had taken a turn for the worse after the accident. He rarely shaved, and missed large patches when he did. In addition, he seemed to be growing more hair around the collar of his T-shirt and on his hands, which were still swollen and bruised. He looked terrible. People told him he should be home eating healthy food and laying off the booze; their sympathy was good for rides home before nightfall, but did not bring about any real change in his behavior.

Julian High School held its homecoming, with a parade of old pickup trucks on the back of which perched football players, cheerleaders, and displays from the 4-H Club, Future Farmers of America, and other student organizations. The football team put its undefeated record on the line in a game dedicated to the memories of Patsy Kittredge and Brandy Allen. They were soundly defeated by a team from a small private school in San Diego. The game turned ugly in the fourth quarter. The visiting team had a fabulous running back, a lithe black kid with moves like O.J. Simpson, and he shredded the Julian defense for something like three hundred yards. Julian had lots of Indians but virtually no blacks; there were two black families, I think, in the area, and no black kids at all in the high school. As the frustration of a losing effort mounted, the racial slurs came out, both from the Julian bench and the stands behind it. The Julian coach, an intense young math teacher whose quest for a league championship the previous season had been denied by this same team, did little to diffuse the situation, pacing the sidelines and doing his best Mike Ditka impersonation. "Hit him!" he'd yell, as the star running back reeled off another long gain. "Goddammit, stop standing around out there! He's running circles around you guys! I want to see some *hitting!*"

He saw plenty. The game ended with a fistfight and a bench-clearing brawl with three minutes left on the clock. Since the game was hopelessly out of reach anyway, the officials sent both teams to the showers and imposed one-game suspensions on three Julian players. The next day the coach met with Steve Dakota and the president of the school board; when the meeting was over he was no longer the coach. The whole affair received a generous write-up in Monday morning's San Diego paper by a sports reporter who did not attend the game.

Julian, it seemed, couldn't buy favorable press—and this was a town with a long tradition of fluff pieces on its country ambiance, its neighborliness, its desirability as a place to get away from it all. But the news these days was all about contaminated water, crippling drought, malfeasance and chicanery, racial intolerance—and death upon death upon death. It was as though a curse lay over the place, bringing pestilence and suffering like that visited upon Thebes during the reign of Oedipus. And still the tourists kept coming. They talked about the murders, yes, and they talked about the water shortage, but these were not things that affected them personally; at night they could simply go home. Besides, for many of them, an autumn visit to Julian, to a fantasy hamlet of sweet-smelling cider and crisp yellow leaves, was an annual tradition. Very few of them actually saw the place for what it was; rather, it lived in their imaginations as a remnant of a simpler and somehow better time, and even after negotiating miles and miles of clogged roads and looking at three blocks of stores and restaurants unremarkable for anything except the crowds of underdressed city people milling in front of them, most were loath to allow reality to intrude on the preconceived image. They came because they were supposed to, or because they always had, or because other people did, and they saw what they wanted to see. They saw the mountains, but little of the dark shadows all around them.

# Chapter Twenty-six

DAYLIGHT SAVINGS TIME ended two days before Halloween; by six o'clock it was completely dark. Everyone noticed the waxing gibbous Moon hovering above Main Street while people were still out and about, but no one seemed much inclined to talk about it. The nights had grown colder, too, and even the days seemed brisk, as the long thermometer began its downward plunge and the winds of autumn swept over the mountains.

Moondog left for Mexico a few days after Blind Ben's body was found; he said he had to drop off an article for the *Muckraker* on his way out of the country, but I suspected he did not want to undergo another interrogation, another violation of the sanctuary of his home.

A television crew from "Unsolved Mysteries" showed up in town, but since it was October they couldn't find any hotel rooms to rent, and ended up staying in Ramona and driving the twenty-two meandering miles up the hill each day. They talked to Vern Whittier and to Blind Ben's friends, who told them their stories; they talked to the sheriff's people, who told them nothing. They taped a lot of loose talk on Main Street. They asked repeatedly where they might find Cyrus "Moondog" Nygerski, but no one could help them. They found the *Julian Nugget* office, one day when I wasn't there; Gunn told them little more than the cops did. They spent an hour with Wally Leach, who told them a good deal more than they wanted to know, and then they bought an apple pie for each member of the crew and went home.

The *Julian Nugget* came out, and came out again. Erik Gunn had always complained that he never got letters to the editor; now he had more than he could print. He censored the ones that talked directly about werewolves or about Moondog's column in the *Muckraker*, but many of the published letters contained phrases like "speculations about monsters," "supernatural phenomena," and "extraordinary talk on the street."

The hardware store, the drugstore, and the liquor store decorated their windows for Halloween, and the same volunteer crew that had ghosted and goblined up the tiny jail for years and years brought the papier-mâché monsters out of the closets and wove fake spider webs in preparation for the big night. The students and teachers at Julian Elementary School busied themselves decorating classrooms and preparing games and attractions for the annual Halloween carnival.

On the second-to-last day of October, Moondog surprised us all by showing up at the *Julian Nugget* office in midafternoon. "Can I help you?" Karen snapped at him. She didn't work at night, and so had never met him.

"Karen, this is the famous Moondog Nygerski," Gunn said, getting up to shake his hand. "How you doing, Moondog? You want a beer?"

"Beer? In the middle of the day?" Karen sniffed.

"Think I'll pass," Moondog said. "What are you writing over there, Joe?"

I swiveled my chair away from the computer screen. "Just an update on the water situation," I said. "With a few potshots at the water board from Justin Zak. Pretty boring stuff, actually."

"What're you doing tonight?"

"I have to work."

"I'll pick you up after," he said. "Got something to talk with you about. Besides, it's not safe for you to walk home after dark."

"What do you mean, it's not safe?" Karen asked. She had been eyeing him suspiciously ever since he entered the office. Maybe it was the hat—a red plaid hunting cap with flaps that snapped down around the ears.

"You know what tonight is, don't you?" Moondog looked around the cluttered office. "It's full Moon!" he said. "Our werewolf is likely to be out and about. It's best to be careful."

Gunn sat back down at his desk, folded his hands in his lap, and looked out the window. Across the street, a survey team was marking out measurements for Justin Zak's shopping center.

"*Now* I know who you are," Karen said, fixing him with a baleful stare. "You write all those weird, left-wing columns for our paper and that . . . that *Mudslinger*, or whatever it's called."

"*Muckraker*," Moondog corrected her.

"Right. Well, anyway, I hate your columns. What are you, some kind of Communist?"

"Communist?" Moondog feigned shock, but he was smiling. "No way. Anarchist, maybe, but certainly not a Communist. I hate all bureaucrats."

"Well, I think your columns are obnoxious. So does my husband. He refuses to even read them anymore."

"Speaking of columns, Moondog," said Gunn, "we haven't had one from you in a while. How about it?"

Before Moondog could answer, however, another figure appeared in the doorway, rapped gently on the wood, and entered

193

the office. He was tall, handsome, well dressed. I turned, and recognized Steve Dakota.

"Hi, Erik," he said to Gunn. "Hello there, Joe. You look like you're hard at work." He smiled broadly.

"Always," I replied.

"Well, Steve, it's good to see you," said Gunn, who was feeling friendly, possibly because Moondog was in the room. "To what do we owe this unexpected pleasure?"

"I wanted to see if I could pick up a few copies of the issue with the story Joe did on me," said the superintendent. "My wife really likes the picture you took of me, by the way. On the bicycle."

"I'm glad," Gunn said. "Karen, can you find Mr. Dakota a few copies of that paper? It's one of the August issues, I believe."

"August twenty-ninth," Dakota said.

"August twenty-ninth," Gunn repeated. "How many copies do you need?"

"Oh, four should be fine," Dakota replied, reaching for his wallet. "Yeah, my wife likes that picture a lot. Haven't seen you out bicycling with us lately, Erik."

"I've been kind of busy," Gunn said uncomfortably.

Karen found four copies of the paper in the file cabinet, and handed them to Dakota without a word or a smile. He handed her a dollar and said, "Thank you very much." Then he turned back to Gunn.

"We're having a ride tonight," he said. "We're doing the Engineers Road loop. You should come. Ride starts at five-thirty."

"Well, I'd like to," said Gunn, "I really would. But I haven't done this week's editorial, and I kind of hurt my ankle a while back, and—"

"You're going bicycling *tonight?*" Moondog asked.

Dakota looked at him, and his permanent smile faded. "This evening, yeah," he said.

"Do you think that's wise?" Moondog asked.

"We've all got headlights and flashers," the superintendent said. "It's perfectly safe."

"It's also full Moon."

Dakota stared at him for several seconds, his smile replaced by a look of genuine puzzlement. "Who are you?" he asked.

"No one special," Moondog said. "Just a concerned citizen."

"The Moon is full tomorrow night," Dakota said. "At least that's what the calendar in my office says."

Moondog and I looked at each other; we'd had this conversation before.

"It's actually full at ten in the morning," Moondog told him. "Effectively, the Moon will be full tonight *and* tomorrow night. It could be very dangerous. You might even want to consider calling off the Halloween carnival."

Dakota actually looked offended; his head snapped backward as though he'd been slapped. "Halloween is always dangerous," he said. "It's an unfortunate fact of life in today's world that sick people do sick things. That's why we have the carnival at the school, to get all the kids together, with adult supervision, in a safe place. The whole thing's been carefully planned."

"That makes no difference," Moondog said, "to a werewolf."

All traces of Dakota's public-relations smile vanished. "You don't really believe that crap, do you?"

"I think it's smart to take precautions," Moondog said.

"And I think it's stupid to scare people needlessly, especially impressionable children," the superintendent countered. "The sheriff's people will be there. I'll be there, and so will all of the teachers. If parents are frightened because of . . . because of what's been going on, they can keep their kids home. There's no reason to ruin Halloween for everybody."

Moondog shrugged, giving up. "Well, we'll see what happens," he said. He turned to me. "See you after work, right, Joe?"

"I'll be there," I told him. And an instant later, Moondog was gone, his footsteps fading methodically down the stairs in the quiet building.

"Who *was* that?" Dakota said to the office at large.

"That was Cyrus 'Moondog' Nygerski," Gunn told him.

"The guy who wrote that crazy article in the *Manzanita Mudslinger*," Karen added.

"Oh, him." The superintendent shook his head. "What a nut."

"You got that right," Karen said humorlessly.

"Well, thank you for the papers," the superintendent said awkwardly to Gunn. His smile returned, but there was unease behind it. "You oughtta send Joe over to the school one of these weeks to do a story on our two new teachers. They're both dynamite."

"I'll do that," Gunn said. "Thanks for coming in."

"See you around the campus," Dakota said, and left.

Moondog picked me up at eleven; we took the back way out of town and rejoined the highway four miles west. "The cops are all over the place tonight," he observed. "It's interesting that they don't believe me about the werewolf, and yet they're doing double duty on the night the Moon happens to be full."

The Moon at the moment was behind a bank of clouds. It was almost completely overcast, but there were gaps, and as we rolled over the curving, up-and-down road toward Mesa Grande, the luminous orb peered through periodically. After months of relentlessly clear skies, the weather had become unsettled over the past two days; there was a different feel to the wind, and the pressure had dropped. Satellite photos in the San Diego and Los Angeles papers showed a series of storms heading south from the Gulf of Alaska; the San Francisco Bay area had gotten rain that day, and there was hope that some of it might reach the parched southern mountains soon. Sunny Southern California was anticipating the onset of winter. When the Sun shone during the day, it was still summery, but there had been one or two days lately when gray clouds had moved in and sat on top of the mountains, the wind had whipped up from the north, and sweaters had popped up on Main Street amid the shivering visitors from the city. Moondog, who was from Boston, told me he liked the Julian area because it experienced an autumn not unlike that finest of seasons in New England. As for me, I like it warm, and I was a little bit bummed that summer was over.

"How do clouds affect werewolves?" I asked him.

"No one really knows," he said. "You'd be amazed—there's very little literature on what makes werewolves tick. Go to the library—any library, even downtown—most of them have piss-poor werewolf sections. There's a crying need for more scientific research."

"In that Michael Jackson video," I remembered, "he only becomes a werewolf when the Moon comes out from behind the clouds."

"Shit, what does Michael Jackson know?" Moondog shook his head. "Unfortunately, though, that's about the level of general knowledge available. I would think, however, that clouds would have little or no effect. Maybe a real thick cloud cover, or a socked-in rainy night like we sometimes get up here in the winter, would block the effect. But I'd think the cloud cover would have to be pretty damn thick for that to happen. The Moon's still up there, after all, and other lunar cycles, like the tides and oysters opening and closing and women's periods, aren't weather-dependent. Besides, a werewolf can't keep from transforming by staying inside, and what's the difference between a roof on a house and a roof of clouds?"

"What about an eclipse?" I asked. "The first girl died during an eclipse."

"Yes. And it would be interesting to know the exact time of the attack. Was it after the eclipse was over, or would that matter? It's an interesting question." He thought for a moment. "Of course, it comes down to the same thing," he said. "Is it the *light* from the full Moon that causes the transformation, or its gravitational influence? Or some resonance in position between Moon, Earth, and Sun? The Moon isn't actually blocked from view during a lunar eclipse, it's just in the Earth's shadow. Does the shadow negate the effect? Or if you put a werewolf in a mineshaft, with a chunk of Earth between him and the Moon, would that do it? It might, because during the day, when the bulk of the Earth is interposed, there's obviously no werewolf effect."

"Sounds like there are more questions than answers," I said.

"That's because of the denial factor. As long as the skeptics and the disbelievers are running the show, you can bet there won't be a penny of government money available for werewolf research. It's blatant discrimination. There are funds available for self-esteem studies, and photos of bullwhips in people's assholes, and weapons in space, but people don't want to put a cent into studies of the paranormal. Until that attitude changes, you can forget about answers, let alone a cure. It's a shame, too. Think of all the lives that could be saved."

We were now rolling slowly down the washboard dirt road that led to Moondog's home. The clouds had left a large hole over Mesa Grande, and the rolling fields and stands of oak were bathed in moonlight. There was condensation on the windows of Moondog's truck, a sign that the nights were getting much cooler now that we were past the autumnal equinox. We rode silently and slowly over the curving dirt road, until Moondog spoke again. "Well, at least I know it isn't you," he said.

"What?"

"And you know it isn't me. The werewolf." He looked over at me and grinned.

"Oh. Oh, yeah." I laughed uneasily.

"I thought it might be you at first," he said. "New in town, traveling light, no past . . . at least not one you talked about."

"Like someone else I know," I said.

"Right."

"And you were away for a month, when it looked like nobody was killed."

"But somebody was."

"I know. Moondog, it's true, isn't it?"

"What?"

"The murders. It really *is* a werewolf. Isn't it?"

Moondog looked over at me from the driver's side of the cab, a quizzical expression on his face, almost as if he were offended that I hadn't believed him from the first. "Look in the glove box," he said.

I opened the glove compartment, and saw, on top of several maps and other papers, a revolver, and next to it, a small leather bag tied at the top with a thong. I sucked in my breath.

"Open it," he said.

I did so, and reached into the bag to remove several bullets. The moonlight from outside the truck's window glinted off their shiny surfaces.

"Are these what I think they are?" I asked.

Moondog nodded. "Silver bullets. Got 'em in Mexico. A silver bullet through the heart is the only thing that will stop a werewolf."

"Moondog, what are you planning to do?"

"Planning? Nothing. I just think we ought to keep our eyes

and ears open. And be ready to protect ourselves if the need arises."

There were several moments of awkward silence, during which Moondog retreated into his own thoughts—perhaps about the cruel death of Patsy Kittredge, with whom he had been briefly intimate—and I into mine. I'm not that comfortable about guns, despite my criminal past, and Moondog seemed to sense my apprehension.

He leaned forward and flipped on the radio. A burst of static filled the cab. He twirled the dial past several stations, finally settling on "Message of Love" by the Pretenders. "Reception's great out here at night," he said. And he cranked it up.

When the song ended, he turned the radio down and said, "I went to see Larry Jordan this evening. You know, the Wolf Man?"

"Yeah," I said.

"When I introduced myself, he burst out laughing. Said he loved my stuff, but he didn't think I was real. Said he thought Gunn wrote my articles. He couldn't get over seeing me standing at his door, in the flesh."

I said nothing.

"Anyway, he invited me in, and we drank some Nordik Wolf beer," Moondog continued. "He's got a real good collection of werewolf literature. We talked for a while, and then he took me to see his wolves. I got 'em to howl at the Moon." He laughed, remembering.

"Weren't you scared?" I asked him.

"No." He pulled something from underneath his shirt. "I'm wearing a silver good-luck piece. Bought it in Alaska. Had it tested and everything. Pure silver."

I leaned over to look. It was a snarling wolf's head, beautifully crafted, barely more than an inch long.

"Besides, Jordan's come to the same conclusion I have," he

said. "Werewolves aren't wolves at all. They're associated with the mythology of wolves, not the animal itself."

"What do you mean?"

"Wolves have been pretty maligned in myth," he said. "They're made out to be fearsome, evil creatures that kill for the sadistic pleasure of it. In truth, they're not that way at all. They're predators, and they survive on cunning, but they pretty much leave humans alone. *People* have had it in for the wolf, for most of human history. That's why some species of wolf have been hunted almost to extinction."

"But doesn't a werewolf turn into a wolf at the full Moon?" I asked.

"He turns into a beast," Moondog corrected me, "that only superficially resembles a wolf. The beast will attack like a wolf—going for the throat to kill—but werewolves also use their claws to tear a victim's flesh, like the big cats do. And there's evidence to suggest that a werewolf can stand and walk upright, like a man. They have tremendous upper-body strength. Vern Whittier's a big guy, yet he was knocked senseless by a blow to the head."

"So *werewolf* is really a misnomer."

"Exactly. They have about as much to do with wolves as vampires have to do with bats."

I was about to ask him if he believed in vampires too, but at that moment we came around the last curve in the road and into view of the house. Moondog parked the truck near the woodpile and said, "Come on in."

Moondog's place looked different. The picture of Khomeini had been replaced with an incredibly tacky black velvet rendering of the crucifixion, in lurid purples, oranges, and reds, which could only have come from south of the border. On each of the four walls hung a garlic wreath, and Moondog had drawn a large pentagram—a five-sided star inside a circle—in chalk on the brick chimney into which the cold metal of the dormant wood-stove fed. The poster of his old band, the Bloodhounds, was gone, too. In its place was a U.S. Geological Survey map of the greater Julian area. In red magic marker, Moondog had drawn several small pentagrams on the map, and written a date under-neath each one. There was a star on Mount Laguna, one near Inaja Memorial Park, one at Lake Cuyamaca, and one at the Bailey Mine. They represented, of course, the locations of the previous attacks, and as I looked at the map I was struck by the symmetry of the pattern they made. If one connected the dots, the lines formed four sides of a pentagon, with its center very near downtown Julian. The missing dot would be out in the Cedar Mountain area, beyond the end of the paved road east of the Cedar Mountain Inn, where few people lived, and fewer people ventured after dark.

# Chapter Twenty-seven

ABOUT AN HOUR before Moondog would lead Larry Jordan's wolves in their lunar chorus, half a dozen bicyclists gathered in the failing daylight outside the Julian Bicycle Emporium on the south end of Main Street.

It is something of an unwritten business directive that virtually every commercial establishment within ten miles of Main Street must work "Julian" into its name, in order to draw customers from among those outsiders attracted to the town's projected image. When a developer went before the planning group, for instance, with plans for a third downtown lodging facility, he told the group he planned to call it the Julian Inn. "That's nice," quipped the planning group chairman. "So we'll have the Julian House, the Julian Motel, and the Julian Inn. Think people will remember where they are?"

Stafford Emerson had seen the wisdom of this directive when choosing a company name two years earlier, upon moving to Julian from the commuter jungle of Orange County. He had done well since, combining bicycle sales and service with guided tours and special events for weekend visitors longing for open vistas and fresh air. Julian is in a magnificent location for bicycling. Elevations range from near sea level in the desert to the east to over a mile atop Mount Laguna and Cuyamaca Peak. Away from the oft-crowded highways there are miles and miles of quiet back roads and dirt trails on which a person with a strong set of legs and a decent bike can commune with nature and his or her own physical stamina. Emerson was held in high regard by parents of junior high and high school students, who would rather see their kids get into bicycling than drugs, petty crime, or hanging out; he was also admired by many of the town's women because bicycling kept his six-foot frame lean and trim, and because he was young, solvent, and resolutely single.

Emerson wrote a column on bicycling for the *Julian Nugget*, which he regarded as free publicity; at the end of each piece he listed the schedule of that week's community rides. A core group, which sometimes included Erik Gunn and Steve Dakota, had begun to grow around these rides, and most of that group, though not the newspaper editor or the school superintendent, now milled around the small parking lot, testing gears and brakes and headlights in preparation for departure. The Moon had not yet risen, but there was a chill in the air, and scattered patches of clouds scooted across the sky over the jagged mountaintops to the east, pushed by the modest but definitely discernible wind.

Emerson dragged his own bike out of the shop and locked the door. He specialized in mountain bikes, but since tonight's ride was to be entirely on asphalt and hard gravel, he'd selected an ultralight, thin-wheeled model with twenty-one gears. He wore the latest in bicycling equipment: the sleek black padded pants, special bicycling shoes, fingerless gloves, a Day-Glo shirt that would reflect car headlights better than a highway sign, and a helmet with a powerful, tight-beam light attached to the top.

The others were similarly attired; he'd sold them most of their equipment, including their bikes.

"Small group tonight," he observed.

"Well, you know, maybe people are superstitious," drawled Kyle, a lanky Southerner who lived out by Lake Cuyamaca and had already biked the ten miles into town. "There *is* going to be a full Moon." (Moondog's column in the *Muckraker*, which nobody professed to believe, had nonetheless been widely read and talked about.)

"Don't worry about that," Stafford Emerson said. "I guarantee we won't have any problems."

"Why is that?" asked Kathy Boles, the tiny heroine from the Julian Melodrama. She weighed maybe one hundred pounds, all of it muscle, and stood next to Kyle. She had a thing for pink—her bike frame was pink, as were her body-tight pants, shirt, and helmet. About the only things that weren't pink were her tires and her black, waist-length hair, held in check by a thick braid with a pink elastic band at the end.

"Because I've made sure of it," Emerson said. "This bike right here"—he patted his handlebars as a different kind of rider might stroke a horse—"has all silver electrical wiring and fixtures. This baby costs sixteen hundred bucks, retail. Anybody want to buy it?"

"Stafford, you don't really believe in werewolves, do you?" Kathy asked.

He feigned surprise. "Don't you?"

"Of course not. If I did, I wouldn't be out here."

"Relax," he said. "I'm just covering all the bases. Because I'm superstitious, too. If I have thirteen dollars in my wallet, I take one out and put it in a pocket. You guys ready?"

"I can't believe there are so few people here," said Kathy. "It's a beautiful evening. Where's Erik, and Steve?"

"Erik's not coming," Kyle said. "I saw him this morning."

"What's he doing instead? Fighting with his wife?"

"Doubt it. She finally walked out on him. Went to Escondido, to stay with her mom."

"I still see her around," Kathy said. "With what's-his-name. The lame guy."

"What is this, *Peyton Place*?" said Emerson. "Let's go, already."

"What about Steve?" Kathy asked.

"He's more than half an hour late," Emerson said. "If he's coming at all, he can catch up."

"The lights are on at the school," said another member of the group. "There might be some kind of meeting or something."

"Let's go," said Emerson. And without waiting, he mounted his bike and pedaled off up Highway 79 toward Lake Cuyamaca.

The two high school boys in the group quickly caught up to him, and Kyle matched their pace. Farther back, Dennis, a painting contractor who sometimes traded work on Emerson's building for bicycling supplies, rode with Kathy, whose short legs put her at a disadvantage, but not much. She was strong, and the other cyclists enjoyed watching her legs work.

It was semidark before they crested the first ridge out of town, from which the view fell away toward the desert and the Salton Sea. And there it was, between the clouds—the full Moon, reddened by the path of its light through the atmosphere near the horizon. It would not get appreciably darker; the Moon would render their headlamps unnecessary for much of the ride.

They rode at a comfortable pace, staying in sight of one another and enjoying the cool of the evening. The road followed the ridge for a few more miles, then dipped around a series of descending curves, before cresting the rim of the bowl outlining the valley in which Lake Cuyamaca sat at the far end. The whole valley lay bathed in moonlight, and the group stopped to gather and admire the view before going on.

Engineers Road connects the little community around Lake Cuyamaca with the backside of the maze of roads on Cedar Mountain, behind the inn. Given the crow's-flight distance, it should be a shortcut, but it is not. The road traverses a hollow in the mountains, meandering around a series of sharp curves and several times reversing direction completely. Most of it is gravel, like the road to Moondog's house, and seems as remote. Only about a dozen people live along it once you get away from the lake; they have cellular phones because the phone company has never put a line through. Part of the road runs through a corner of Cuyamaca Rancho State Park. Car traffic is virtually nil, especially on a weekday night. The group of cyclists could count on having the road and its five-mile stretch of stupendous downhill, to themselves.

Engineers Road is a good place to pick up impressive patches of road rash as well, for it is easy to get carried away in the thrill of the ride, take a corner too fast, and have your wheels kick out from under you on the loose gravel. For this reason, and because his still-emerging reputation in town depended on his strict attention to safety, Emerson told the two kids to stop and wait for the rest of the group every mile or two before going on.

The two young men, only dimly aware that they might die someday, predictably tore out in front, bounding over the most hazardous patches of road surface as though they were moguls on a ski slope. Emerson and Kyle followed, with Dennis, trailed by Kathy, bringing up the rear. For the most part they did not use their lights, for the Moon more than adequately illuminated the way. Only when they stopped to reassemble did Emerson turn on his headlamp, so that the others could see him as they approached.

At the bottom of the five-mile downhill run, Engineers Road meets another dirt road, a truck trail that leads deep into the woods and meets another truck trail, which emerges somewhere near El Cajon, forty miles away. A wrong turn here was a sure way to get lost, and so they waited, Emerson and the boys, until first Kyle and then Dennis caught up with them. Kathy would be there in a couple of minutes, they figured, because despite her small size she was a good cyclist, though she didn't have the ballast to hit the turns as hard as the men did.

But a couple minutes passed, and there was no sign of her. "Think she might have fallen?" Emerson said. "Maybe I should go back and look."

"She wasn't too far behind me," Dennis said. "I saw her light on the straight stretches. She'll be along any minute now."

"If she fell, she'll just get up and keep riding," Kyle volunteered. "Kathy's tough."

Suddenly, the stillness of the night was rent by a scream—a naked cry of pure terror—followed immediately by another.

"Holy shit!" cried one of the teenagers.

"I'm going!" barked Emerson. "You all wait here!" His chain popped on the teeth of the gear wheels as he downshifted, and then he was standing, pumping with his full weight up the hill they had just descended. In seconds his headlamp disappeared around a curve. Kathy, not close to them, screamed again.

His heart pounding, Stafford Emerson drove the bicycle as hard as he could. Kathy was still screaming, and as he rounded a hairpin turn onto the stretch where she had fallen, he saw why.

His first thought hit him like a bullet: *My God, it's true!*

She was on the ground, underneath her bicycle. The bike was pinned on top of her by the huge forepaw of a hairy, thick-shouldered beast that looked like nothing he had ever seen in *National Geographic.* It was a werewolf, it had to be. Either that, or Stafford Emerson was losing his mind. The beast pawed at the bike's rear tire, which spun helplessly in midair. Emerson heard the tire pop and the whoosh of air as claws snared rubber. The beast growled in fury—it looked more like a bear than a wolf, although it really looked like no animal he had ever seen, even in nightmares—and Kathy found her vocal cords again and let out another piercing yell.

Stafford Emerson sprang into action. His conscious, reasoning mind had deserted him; instinct and adrenaline took over. He was running toward the monster, holding his bicycle at arm's length in front of him. The beast turned blindly in his direction, cocked its hideous head, and fixed him with one baleful eye. God, it was big! The animal bared its array of crooked, yellow-white, oversized canine teeth and growled. Emerson was dimly aware of a reeking, dead-fish smell as he crashed the bicycle into the creature's face.

The monster roared, rocked back on its hind legs, and staggered away from him. Emerson yelled something—and charged the beast again. The werewolf swiped at his bike, laying open the back of Emerson's hand, but Emerson held on. He jammed the bike sharply upward into the creature's chest, and thrust the handlebars at its hideous face, going for the eyes. The beast roared its distress, swayed, and fell to the ground on its side. Emerson prepared to charge again, but the werewolf raised its huge head, looked around as if in a daze, and let out a tremendous roar of unadulterated fury. Its teeth were horrible daggers, pointing in all different directions. Emerson recoiled from it, and the werewolf dragged itself awkwardly upright, and bounded jerkily into the woods.

Stafford Emerson lay on the ground beside his battered bike, panting, trying to regain his breath and slow the wild pounding of his heart. After a few moments he became aware of Kathy, still underneath her own bicycle, sobbing hysterically. He crawled over to her, lifted the bike, and wrapped his arms around her. She threw her arms around his neck and held on very tightly, sobs racking her body.

When at last he could speak, Emerson raised her head with his good hand, forcing her to look into his face. "Are you all right?" he managed to say.

She nodded and gulped. She was still terrified. So, for that matter, was he. He looked around at the moonlit road and the trees that lined both sides of it, looked for a long time before bringing his eyes back to hers.

"B-b-but you're not," she said, her voice trembling. She looked down at his other hand. "You're bleeding all over the place."

"He got me with his paw," Emerson said. "But you—you're not hurt?"

She shook her head. "Just scared," she said. She was crying now; streams ran down both cheeks. "Just really, really scared. Staff . . . it's true, isn't it? That thing . . ."

He nodded, and brushed away her tears with his unbloodied hand. "I think so," he said. "I've never seen anything like it."

"It . . . it came out of nowhere. It knocked me down—I didn't fall. It started to come at me, and then . . . I guess my light was in its eyes, and that confused it until you got here. Oh, Staff, you saved my life!" She encircled his neck with her arms again and kissed his chin, his cheeks, his ears, lips, forehead and throat in rapid-fire urgency.

She stopped abruptly, embarrassed. "I'm sorry," she said.

"No need to apologize," he murmured. And they held each other in silence for what seemed like many minutes.

"I think the silver in your lamp and in my bike drove it off," he said at last. "I think we're pretty damn lucky. I also think I'm going to have a talk with this Cyrus 'Moondog' Nygerski, who-ever he is."

They heard the sound of crunching gravel, followed by voices. A moment later, four headlamps appeared in the dark-ness. "Staff!" Kyle called. "Where are you?"

"Over here," he called back. "We're all right. Gonna need some help, though."

Indeed, Kathy's bike had a flat tire, and his prized, silver-wired machine was a wreck. It had cost him a lot of money, but it had probably saved his and Kathy's lives.

Gingerly he got to his feet, and helped Kathy to hers. She did not seem to want to let go of him. "Goddammit, Staff," she said softly into his ear, "I'm awfully glad you're superstitious."

They dispatched Kyle and the two boys back to the lake to get a vehicle. The boys did not ride out ahead. When they were gone, Kathy and Stafford told a disbelieving Dennis their story.

"I don't know what to say," the big man said in a small voice, when they were finished.

"I know what I saw," Emerson said.

"Staff?" asked Kathy.

"What?"

"That animal—there was something funny about the way it ran away, wasn't there?"

"I'm just glad it *did* run away," he said.

"I mean, it was . . . unbalanced, sort of. Wasn't it?"

"I don't know," Emerson said, still shaken. "I don't know."

When Kyle's pickup truck came around the curve, its headlights blasting away the darkness, it was greeted by three very relieved people.

# Chapter Twenty-eight

MOONDOG AND I sat up most of the night discussing what, if anything, to do. I suggested driving around, keeping our eyes and ears open, with the loaded pistol ready in case luck brought us face to face with the werewolf. But Moondog vetoed the idea. "More than likely we'd be stopped by the cops and hassled," he said. "Besides, people with any sense are gonna stay indoors. This is one scared town, even though nobody wants to admit it."

"But what if somebody gets killed?" I argued.

"Joe, we're just two people," he said. "We're not the Lone Ranger and Tonto. It may sound harsh, but it isn't our responsibility. What I'm most worried about is tomorrow."

"Because it's Halloween?"

He nodded. "It's getting dark before six now, with the time change. All those kids out trick-or-treating. It terrifies me to think what might happen."

"Most of the kids will be at the school," I pointed out.

Moondog nodded again. "I think we should be there, too," he said. "With the gun. Just in case."

We could hear the wind outside, whistling over the chimney and stirring the oak trees that surrounded us; around midnight, Moondog went outside to get some wood for the stove, and announced that the Moon was completely hidden by clouds. Perhaps an hour later it started to rain, in small, violent spurts that lasted no more than three minutes at a time. The stove crackled, and warmed the wooden interior of the house quite nicely.

Moondog went into the kitchen, opened a closet, and returned with a bottle of tequila and two small glasses. After pouring us each a generous shot, he set down his glass and the bottle, walked over to the roll-top desk, and from a drawer produced two small silver objects. Returning to his chair, he handed me what looked like a coin on a chain. "Here, take this," he said. "Put it around your neck."

Well, it wasn't a coin at all, I saw upon closer inspection, even though it was approximately the size of a quarter. It was a pentagram, a raised star inside a raised circle, the pattern duplicated on both sides. "Wear it," he said. "It could save your life."

I did as I was told. Moondog raised his glass to mine. "To a safe Halloween," he said. "And, if we're lucky, to the death of the Beast of Julian."

In spite of the tequila, we were both up early the next morning. The ground was wet, and long, gray fingers of fog draped themselves over the mountains. The wind shook droplets of water from the cupped leaves of the oaks; I could feel the moisture on my face as I stood on Moondog's porch, sipping the first cup of coffee of the day. The weather was as unsettled as I felt. Every few minutes the orb of the Sun would define itself behind the wispy clouds; to the north there were actual patches of open blue. I touched the silver pentagram that hung against my chest, and wished for the full force of the storm to arrive before nightfall and blot the Moon from the sky.

Neither of us spoke much on the way into Julian; we had no way of knowing what, if anything, had transpired under the light of the full Moon the night before. We were nervous with the thought that an attack had taken place somewhere in the area, and I think both of us feared in the backs of our minds that the latest victim might be someone one or both of us knew. And both of us wondered how long it would take the people of Julian to wake up to the truth.

Moondog drove slowly; we kept our eyes open for cop cars, dead cows, or any other sign of recent violence. All we saw, however, was one-legged Sven, about three miles past Santa Ysabel, on the side of the road with his thumb out. Moondog pulled over.

"Hiya, Sven," I said, as I slid over on the truck's front seat to give him room. "How's it going?"

"Don't ask," he groaned, adjusting himself and his walking stick in the seat.

He looked strung out—well, he always looked sort of strung out, but this morning he looked worse than usual. His eyes were bloodshot, and there was a scratch across one unshaven cheek. His blue jeans were torn at the knees, and the collar of his blue workshirt was ripped as well. His face was pale, and his hand shook as he rolled down the window. He gulped fresh air gratefully.

"Big night?" Moondog asked him.

"I don't even remember," Sven said. His breath stank, and I

marveled again at his teeth, which were spectacularly crooked.
"You goin' past Sleepy Hollow?"

"Sure," Moondog said.

"Just drop me off there, then," Sven instructed him. "I feel
like I could sleep for two days."

# Chapter Twenty-nine

STAFFORD EMERSON AND Kathy Boles went first not to the sheriff's office, where they did not expect to be believed, but to the *Julian Nugget*, where they knew they could at least find a discussion. They arrived at ten in the morning, to find Erik Gunn nursing a beer at his desk and reading the morning paper. Moondog and I arrived minutes later, and walked in on the middle of their argument.

Gunn looked as though he hadn't had much sleep. His eyes were red and sported large black bags underneath them. Since his wife had left him, he'd been drinking even more heavily than usual; the beer was probably a cure for this morning's hangover and a start on tomorrow's.

"I tell you, I know what I saw!" Stafford Emerson stood in front of Gunn's desk, his large hands gripping the edge, looking down at the editor, who slumped in his chair and stared back at him blankly. Kathy Boles stood close by his side.

"And I'm saying it was nighttime, the light wasn't too good, and you were agitated," Gunn said. "It could have been—"

"Damn right I was agitated!" Emerson railed. He waved his bandaged hand in front of Gunn's face. "The thing took a piece out of my hand. I'm lucky I'm even here to argue about it!"

"The light was fine," Kathy Boles said, quietly but firmly. "It was still clear then. I could see it as well as I can see you right now."

"See what?" Moondog said. All three of them turned toward the door; they hadn't seen us come in.

"Moondog, your timing is uncanny," Gunn said. He smiled thinly. "I think these people want to talk to you."

Stafford Emerson straightened his six-foot-two-inch frame. His eyes widened. "You're Moondog?" he asked.

"The one and only," Gunn said, and the relief in his voice was unmistakable. "In the flesh."

"What did you see?" Moondog said.

"Well, it was . . . it was incredible," Emerson stammered. "Even now I don't want to believe it. But on the bike ride last night, Kathy was attacked. We drove it off, but we both got a good look at it. I even got scratched. See?" He eagerly held up his bandaged hand.

"We saw the werewolf," Kathy said.

Moondog looked at Gunn. "And my guess is that you don't believe them," he said.

"Come on, Moondog! There aren't any—"

"What's Vern Whittier doing today?" Moondog asked the room at large. "Where can we find him?"

"Well, it's raining, so most likely he won't be working," Emerson said. "I bet he'll be at Quinn's pretty shortly after it opens."

"And that cop," Moondog said. "Blaisdell. I want him here too. We've got a lot to talk about, and not much time."

217

And thus it was that shortly after noon on October 31, while intermittent squalls blew through the Southern California mountains and the Earth turned its other cheek to the full Moon, an extraordinary summit meeting convened in the *Julian Nugget* office. Moondog was there, as were Gunn and I, and sheriff's deputy Frank Blaisdell, taking an unauthorized break from his shift. Also present were Stafford Emerson and Kathy Boles, as well as Vern Whittier, the only other person to have been attacked by the Beast of Julian and live. Gunn sat behind his desk; Frank Blaisdell leaned against one side of the doorway, walkie-talkie on his hip, arms folded across his chest. The rest of us sat in chairs in a loose semicircle; I had the swivel chair by the computer, while Moondog sat at Karen's squeaky-clean desk. The atmosphere was deadly serious. There were beers, but only Gunn, Vern Whittier, and I were drinking them. Whittier had taken a chair near Claudia Gaines's desk and the collection of knickknacks piled there, and had been periodically edging the chair away from it. He was the least comfortable person in the office, although Gunn looked a little nervous, too.

"All right," Gunn said, running a finger around the rim of his beer can as though it were a wine glass. "Let's get started." He looked at Stafford Emerson and Kathy Boles, seated close together in two chairs directly in front of him. "You claim to have seen this . . . ah . . . this . . ."

"Werewolf," Moondog said.

"If, in fact, it *is* a werewolf," Gunn reminded them sharply. "That's what we're trying to determine."

"I don't know what else it could be," said Stafford Emerson. "I got a good look at it. We both did." He looked over at Kathy, who nodded.

"Can you describe what it looked like?" Moondog asked.

"Like something from hell," Kathy said, and shuddered at the memory.

"Can you be more specific?"

"It looked like . . . well it looked sort of like an ape, except the head was different," said Emerson. "The head was more . . . more wolflike. Lots of teeth—huge, pointed teeth. Crooked teeth. And yellow—really discolored. And its breath stank, I remember that. Plus it had, well, haunches, I guess. You know, it really didn't look much like an ape, now that I think about it. Except for the fact that it was covered with fur."

"It didn't *move* like an ape," Kathy said.

"Did it stand upright?" asked Moondog.

"Sometimes it did," said Kathy. "It could."

"It was upright when I charged at it," Emerson recalled. "Because I had to lift the bike *up,* to hit it in the face."

"Thank God for that bike!" Kathy murmured.

"You mean my sixteen-hundred-dollar Silver Shadow?" Emerson's mouth twisted into a joyless grin.

"Why is it called a Silver Shadow?" Moondog asked.

"It isn't, really. That's just what I call it. The electrical wiring is all silver. Makes it more efficient, but it drives up the price like mad."

"And why did you take that particular bike that night? Because you were afraid you might meet up with a werewolf?"

"Until that night," Emerson replied, "I didn't believe in werewolves. I thought the whole thing was bullshit. But I'd read your article. We all had—everybody reads the *Muckraker.* None of us really knew how to take it. We joked about it before the ride, in fact. I guess my own feeling was that it was some kind of not very funny joke."

"That's what I thought, too," said Vern Whittier, looking up from his beer and straight at Moondog. "When I first saw that article, I wanted to put your head through a wall."

219

"I'm glad you didn't," Moondog said.

"If I could've found you, I would have. Vicki had just died, you know, and it seemed like you didn't give a damn, as long as you could write something stupid about it. But now . . . fuck, the whole thing's crazy, but you may be right."

"Why *did* you take that bike?" Gunn asked Emerson.

"Well, you know, it's a nice bike—*was* a nice bike," Emerson said. "It was the best bike in the shop. And yeah, I guess I was thinking a little bit about the silver. Like I said, we talked about how the Moon was full and all. Not that any of us *believed* it or anything. But you know we usually have about a dozen people. That night only six of us showed up. A few people who usually come stayed home. *You* didn't show up, as I recall."

"And a good thing, too, as it turned out," Gunn said uncomfortably.

"I dunno, Erik," Moondog said. "I think it's kind of a shame you didn't go. If you'd gone, you'd have your proof. You would have seen it with your own eyes. Seeing is believing, you said. That's why I want you to come to the Halloween carnival with us tonight. With your camera."

Gunn waved a hand at the chilly grayness outside the window. "It's totally socked in," he said. "What if it stays like this? Or what if your so-called werewolf turns up someplace else?"

"First of all, the clouds might make no difference," Moondog said. "No one knows. And while it's true that the werewolf might show up anywhere, or might not show up at all, isn't it your duty as a journalist to be on the alert? My God, Erik, this is the biggest story that's ever happened in Julian. If we get lucky, and the werewolf shows up, and you get a picture of it, you could be famous."

Gunn looked up at the door to the office, where Frank Blaisdell stood, listening impassively. "What do you think about all this, Frank?" he asked. "Does it strike you as a bunch of superstitious nonsense?"

"It's not nonsense when people die," Blaisdell said. "Whether or not it's a . . . a werewolf, as Mr. Nygerski here says, that I don't know. But I know it isn't something to joke about. I found the body of that teacher. I knew her; she and my wife were friends. It was . . . the worst thing I've ever seen."

"What killed her, if not a werewolf?" Moondog asked softly.

"I don't know," the deputy said. "I just don't know. A deranged person, a pack of dogs . . ."

"A pack of dogs?" Gunn repeated. "You never said anything to me about a pack of dogs."

"Erik, you know we talked to Mr. Jordan about his wolves. You know we asked around about dogs on the loose. Granted, it rarely happens, but—"

"It *never* happens," Moondog cut in. "And a pack of dogs would be seen all over the place. They wouldn't care if it was full Moon or not. They'd come around during the day, and if they were rabid, people would shoot them."

"It's just one of the possibilities we've looked into." Blaisdell turned his attention back to Gunn. "I'll admit it, since you're not taking notes. We're at a total loss. We've had four people die in what look to be vicious, animal-like attacks, and we don't have a single solid suspect."

Moondog and I looked at one another when he said this; we both smiled, ever so slightly, at the implied reprieve.

"And if I go to the investigators, or to my lieutenant, or even to my fellow deputies, and start pushing this werewolf shit, they'll probably have me committed, or retired because the stress of the job has gotten to me."

"But do you believe it, Frank?" Gunn asked.

The deputy sighed, and uncrossed his arms. One hand wandered instinctively in the direction of his pistol holster; he caught it and hooked his thumb in his belt instead. "No," he said. "I can't. I agree—it's weird. It's mighty fucking weird. But a bunch of mutilated bodies does not mean we have a werewolf on our hands. There's got to be another explanation for it. And a psychopath who's got a lot to answer for."

"Vern, you didn't see anything, is that right?" Gunn asked him. "Assuming that the same thing that attacked them attacked you. You don't have any idea what it looked like?"

"It hit me before I really saw it," Whittier said, unconsciously rubbing the side of his jaw with his short-fingered hand. "So I was pretty dazed. But I *did* see it. When it . . . when it was on top of Vicki."

"Did it look like a man or a beast?" asked Moondog.

"I didn't get a look at its face. And it was dark, you know. I thought it was a man. It was the *size* of a man. A big man. It was huge."

"And you had the preconception that it was a man," Moondog said. "You wouldn't expect an animal to come out of the bushes, slug you, and attack your woman. An animal wouldn't do that, but there are men who would. So in your mind, which influences what you see, you were predisposed to see a man. Right?"

"Yeah, I suppose that makes sense. Like I said, I didn't get a good look at it. I jumped on it, and it tossed me off and slugged me again. Whatever it was, it was goddamn strong. Threw me off like I was a shirt."

"So it stood upright?"

"Yeah. At least it must have been upright when it hit me, to hit me that hard. That fucker had a punch like George Foreman."

At that moment, the door to the office opened, and a head full of blond curls, at doorknob level, entered. "Hi, Daddy!" the little girl cried, and ran toward Gunn's desk. Gunn scooped his daughter onto his lap and kissed her forehead. "Hiya, sweetheart," he said, smiling at her. "Have you missed me?"

"Uh-huh." The little girl nodded her head vigorously.

Joyce Gunn stood in the doorway, her hands clutching the handles of a J.C. Penney shopping sack. "She picked out her own costume," she said to Gunn. "She's ready for you to take her to the carnival tonight."

Gunn looked at his daughter, then at Moondog, and finally at his wife. "I can't, Joyce," he said. "Something's come up."

Joyce's unsmiling expression did not change. "Don't tell me," she said. "You have to work."

"The person who's been doing these murders," Gunn said. "These people think he'll be around tonight. I have to be there."

"You said a week ago that you'd take her."

"I know, Joyce, I know. Look, I'll spend some time with her this afternoon." He looked at Diana, whose little face bore not disappointment but a here-we-go-again look that told everyone she was used to such squabbling. "We'll go out for lunch, and ice cream after, okay?" He bounced the girl on his lap and she giggled. "I'm sorry, Joyce," he said. "I didn't know that this was going to come up. I can't control when news is going to happen. It's the—"

"I know," his wife snapped at him. "It's the nature of your business." She looked at her watch. "I'll meet you back here at five. *I'll* take her to the carnival, if you won't." And without waiting for an answer, she spun around and walked out the door. "I hate your newspaper, and I hate you," she said from the hall.

This unexpected parting shot was so startling that for a moment there was complete silence in the office, as Joyce's footsteps descended the stairs. Gunn lifted his daughter off his lap. "Come on, honey," he said, attempting to be cheerful. "Let's get out of here."

"I have to go, too," said Frank Blaisdell. "Duty calls. Hang in there, Erik."

"We'll meet you here before the carnival," Moondog said to Gunn. "Look, I didn't mean to fuck things up between you and your wife."

"It's okay," Gunn muttered. "Things couldn't be any more fucked up than they already are." He looked apologetically at his daughter. "Excuse my language," he said.

"It didn't stand upright all the time," Kathy said suddenly. Everybody looked at her.

"It ran on all fours," she said. "At least, almost on all fours."

"What do you mean, almost?" Moondog asked.

"It was . . ." She looked at Emerson, beside her. "It was, well, gimpy. It didn't run right. I noticed that as it was running away. It ran like a dog, but it was sort of hobbled, like it was missing part of a leg."

"Missing . . . part of a leg." Moondog looked at me, his eyes intent.

"Goddamn," I said.

"Are you thinking what I'm thinking?"

"Mm-hmm."

"Is that significant?" Kathy asked hopefully, her eyes darting back and forth between Moondog and me. "You act like that means something to you."

"It might," Moondog said slowly. "Right now it means there's someone else we've got to talk to."

# Chapter Thirty

SVEN ANSWERED THE door on our first knock. It was about four in the afternoon, and though the last violent five-minute rain squall had left the area nearly two hours before, the wind still whipped the gray clouds against the faces of the mountains. It was cold, and completely overcast save for the occasional patch of cobalt blue that was quickly swallowed by the fast-moving cloud cover. Perhaps an hour and a half of gray daylight remained.

He looked a good deal better than he had when we'd seen him that morning. Although he hadn't shaved, he'd washed up and put on a different pair of ripped blue jeans and a clean flannel shirt. His feet—both the real one and the artificial one—were covered by the pair of timeworn cowboy boots he wore perpetually—even in his sleep, for all we knew. Again, I was struck by his eyes, which seemed almost otherworldly in their paleness.

"Hey, Joe," he said when he saw us. "What's up?"

"Hi, Sven. This is Cyrus 'Moondog' Nygerski."

"Yeah, we met this morning," Sven said, agreeably enough.

"You guys gave me a ride. And thanks a lot, by the way." He grinned sheepishly, showing his crooked teeth. "I was pretty messed up last night, I guess."

"If you don't mind, we'd like to talk to you about last night," Moondog said. "As well as a few other nights. May we come in? Won't take much time."

"Sure, sure, come in. Don't know how much of last night I remember, but what the hell. You guys want a beer?"

"No, thanks," Moondog said.

"How 'bout you, Joe?"

A beer might have calmed my nerves, but then again, the one I'd had during the meeting at the *Nugget* office and the two I'd consumed at lunch hadn't produced the desired effect. I declined also.

Moondog and I had spent the past few hours discussing our course of action and steeling ourselves for the confrontation. We had eaten a lengthy lunch at Quinn's—lasagna with several side orders of garlic bread—but Sven did not recoil from either the smell of our breath or the silver pentagrams hanging visibly around our necks. We had expected, however, that he would be alone. He was not; Joyce Gunn stood beside the gas stove in the small kitchen, cooking quesadillas in a cast-iron skillet.

Joyce glared at us as we entered. She was a pretty woman, with dark hair, fair skin, and blue eyes the color of sea rather than sky. Like the sea, a look from her could calm or kill.

Sven started to introduce us, but she cut him off. "I know who you guys are," she said. "You write for the newspaper. I just saw you there a couple of hours ago." It sounded like an accusation.

Sven had a grubby old green couch in the cabin's main room, and a couple of old overstuffed chairs that likewise looked as though they'd been passed from tenant to tenant. He lit a cigarette and flopped down on the couch. An ashtray overflowing with butts perched precariously on one of the armrests. Moondog and I seated ourselves in the chairs. A heavy metal band was writhing on MTV at the opposite end of the couch; Sven reached over and turned down the volume.

"Is this an interview?" he asked.

Moondog spread his hands out to his sides. "Do you see a notebook? Or a tape recorder? No, we're just trying to find out a few things, answer some questions for ourselves."

"Like what?" Sven asked.

Gunn's wife brought out a plate of quesadillas and a bowl of salsa and placed them on the small table in front of Sven. She flashed a severe look at Moondog and me, and went back into the kitchen. "Thanks, babe," Sven called after her.

"Where were you last night?" Moondog asked him.

Sven chuckled through a mouthful of food, and sucked a piece of salsa down off his mustache and into his mouth. "I told you, I don't remember too much about last night." he said. "You guys hungry? You want some of this?"

"No, thanks, we just ate," Moondog said. "Do you remember *anything* about last night at all?"

Gunn's wife had left the stove, and now stood in the open doorway between the main room and the kitchen, listening.

"Not too much," Sven said. "I was down on the reservation, drinking with some of my buddies, some of the Indians." He chuckled again. "Those guys are *serious* drinkers."

"Do you drink a lot?"

"Look, what is this?" Gunn's wife interjected. "It's none of your business how much he drinks. What do you guys want, anyway?"

Moondog turned in his chair to face her. "Mrs. Gunn, we're just trying to find out a few things about what's been—"

"My name is Joyce," she snapped.

"Sven here said it was okay if we came in and asked him a few questions. That's all we're doing."

"Well, *I* don't think it's okay," Joyce told him. "I think it's an invasion of privacy. You think that just because you work for the newspaper you can pry into people's lives, ask them how much they drink, who they sleep with, how much money they have, and whatever else you can think of that's none of your business. I think you should get the fuck out of here."

Moondog jerked a thumb in Sven's direction. "*He* invited us in."

"Don't answer any more questions, Sven," she said. "He's trying to accuse you of something."

"Joyce, do you ever read the *Manzanita Muckraker?*" Moondog asked her.

"I don't read newspapers," she said. "I don't have time for newspapers. I watch television. But I know who you are, Cyrus 'Moondog' Nygerski. I know all about your fucked-up columns and your weirdo theories. I think you're an asshole, stirring people up the way you do, accusing them of things—people you don't even know. I don't think your writing's funny at all. I think it sucks. I think your whole profession sucks."

"Jeez, are you always so friendly?" Moondog asked her.

"If this were my house, I'd kick you the fuck out of here," she replied. "Sven, I'd advise you to do the same. I have some things to do in town before I pick up Diana."

"I wouldn't take her to the carnival," Moondog said.

"And why not?" Joyce snapped at him.

"If you've read my column, you know why not," Moondog said quietly.

"Fuck you!" Joyce practically screamed at him. "I'm taking her to the carnival, because she wants to go, and her asshole father won't take her." She let a whoosh of air out of her lungs, and picked up her coat from the kitchen table. "Sven, maybe I'll see you there, huh?"

"Yeah, maybe," Sven said from the couch. "I might pop over there for a while. Depends on how I feel."

"Kick these guys out of here, will you? They're not cops—they're not even real reporters. They don't have any right to sit here and accuse you of anything."

"I'll take care of it, babe," Sven said. "Thanks for making me lunch."

" 'Bye." Gunn's wife slammed the door behind her.

"Now, then," Moondog said, moving forward in his chair, "where were we?"

"I think I was about to kick you out of here," Sven said, shoveling another piece of quesadilla into his mouth.

"Last night," I prompted.

"Right," said Moondog. "So you don't remember anything?"

"Not much," Sven said. "So what?"

"Where were you on the first of October, or on Labor Day?"

"How the hell should I know? I was around. What's your fucking point, man?"

Moondog looked at him for a long time before answering. Sven stared right back. Finally Moondog said, in the same quiet tone in which he'd been speaking all along, "I think *you* are the werewolf."

Sven coughed abruptly; a piece of salsa flew across the room and stuck to the opposite wall. He reached for his beer and took an urgent gulp. "You know, I think I *should* kick you guys out of here. You're a nut case, you know that?"

Moondog showed no reaction. "Do you ever feel strange around the time of the full Moon?" he asked. "Do you feel a little strange right now, Sven?"

I couldn't believe Moondog was egging him on the way he

was. Anxiously, I looked out the window. It had been gloomy out all day, but now the gray was growing darker.

"The only thing that's going to feel strange," said Sven, baring his yellow teeth, "is your face when I get through smacking you around. Which I'm gonna do if you're not out that door in thirty seconds."

For answer, Moondog reached into the inside pocket of his leather jacket, pulled out the revolver, and pointed it at Sven's chest. I gasped.

"I don't think so," Moondog said. "I think we're just going to sit here until the Moon rises, and see what happens. It should be dark in about half an hour."

Sven, who had been ready to leap at Moondog's throat, sat frozen at the edge of the couch, staring at the gun.

Moondog's dark eyes never left Sven's azure ones. "You know that I and one or two other people believe that the murders around here these past few months have been committed by a werewolf, a person who becomes a beast when the Moon is full. Every killing has happened on the night of a full Moon. Last night, two people reported being attacked by a large and incredibly ferocious animal. One of them told me the animal was limping, like it had lost part of a leg. *You* are missing part of a leg, are you not?"

"Yeah," Sven said. "My left leg, below the knee. So what?"

"When we picked you up this morning, you looked like you could have spent the night in the woods. You also say you don't remember anything that happened last night. Werewolves typically don't remember what they did in the beast state when they return to normal. But wounds, especially serious ones, like amputations, often carry over from one state to the other. How *did* you lose your leg, by the way?"

"Hunting accident," Sven said, still looking at the gun. "Long time ago."

"And how long have you been in Julian?"

"Fifteen years or so, off and on."

"What do you mean, off and on?"

"I've traveled around," Sven said, his voice regaining some of its inflection. "It's not a crime."

"No, but several crimes *have* been committed around here these past few months. Serious crimes. And I think you're the one who did them, though whether you can be held responsible for something you did as a werewolf will be up to the courts to decide."

"I suppose you've got silver bullets in that gun."

"Yes," Moondog said.

Sven flopped back against the couch and laughed, ignoring the weapon. "Suppose I just got up and walked to the door right now. What would you do?"

"I'd shoot you," Moondog said. His expression did not change.

"Then who would be the murderer?"

"Oh, I wouldn't shoot to kill," Moondog said, matter-of-factly. "I'd take out your kneecap. On your good leg. Then I'd wait for the Moon to rise, and watch you turn into a werewolf. Then I'd put a bullet through your heart and free your soul."

Sven shook his head and laughed quietly to himself. "All right, asshole," he said. "I'll tell you what I'll do. I'll sit here until it gets dark, and finish these quesadillas. You can watch me. But when I don't turn into a werewolf, I want you to get the fuck out." And he bent down and scooped another chunk of lunch into his very human, if contorted, mouth.

I looked out the window and saw that it was nearly completely dark. Suddenly I remembered something. "Moondog, we don't have a camera," I said. "How are we going to prove he's a werewolf, if we don't document it?"

Moondog's eyes flashed in my direction. "Gunn's got the

231

camera," he said. "We'll have to call him." Moondog stood up. "Joe here needs to use your phone, Sven."

"Don't got no phone." Sven shrugged. "Who can afford one, with times the way they are?"

Moondog thought for only a couple of seconds. "Then you'll have to come with us," he said. "Get up."

Sven didn't move. "Where are we going?"

"To the newspaper office," Moondog told him. "Get up."

"And if I don't?"

"If you don't, I swear I'll shoot you where you sit." Moondog motioned toward the kitchen with the gun. Sven slowly put his hands palms-down on the table, and pushed himself to his feet.

"This is kidnapping," he mumbled.

"Tough shit," Moondog said. "Hurry up. It's going to be dark in a few minutes."

# Chapter Thirty-one

IT WAS ALREADY DARK.

But it was still cloudy, and the wind whisked a few drops of rain out of either the clouds or the trees and into our faces as we walked the few steps from Sven's front door to Moondog's truck. Moondog opened the passenger door, and motioned for Sven to get in. Then he closed the door, and turned to me. "Here," he said, holding the gun out, butt first. "As of now, you're in charge of this."

I took a step away from him. "Now just a minute, Moondog . . ."

He smiled at me crookedly. "I can't cover him and drive at the same time, Joe," he said. "I've only got two hands."

"But . . . but what do you expect me to do with it?"

"The same thing I would do," Moondog said. He reached for my hand, and placed the gun in it. It felt cold, heavy, and dangerous. Being within sniffing distance of a firearm was a strict violation of my probation. If any member of any law-enforcement organization found it in my possession, I wouldn't just be sent back to the honor camp. I'd be taking up residence in the Hotel Slammer.

"Put it in your jacket," Moondog said. "But be able to get it out quickly. He could change at any time."

"Moondog, you didn't tell me—"

"No time to argue about it," he said. "Let's go."

We got into the truck on opposite sides of Sven. "Don't try anything," Moondog said to him. "Joe's got the gun, and he's just as crazy as I am." Though my heart was going like a trip-hammer, I patted the bulge in my jacket where the gun lay in an inside pocket, and tried to look stern.

The outdoor lights were on at Sleepy Hollow as Moondog rolled the truck toward the highway. There were lights in Blind Ben's cabin, and in a few of the others, but the main house was dark. Derek and Cindy and their two boys had already left for the carnival.

"You know, it's dark, and I haven't changed," Sven said. "Don't you think this foolishness has gone far enough? Let me out now, and I won't tell the cops a thing about it."

Moondog aimed the truck up the hill toward Julian, where the lights of town reflected off the low cloud cover. The Moon was somewhere up there, too, behind the gray, its light diffuse but still visible as an overall silvery brightness in the eastern sky.

"Maybe the clouds are too thick," Moondog said. "If the clouds blow away, and the Moon comes out in a clear sky and you still don't change, then I'll be convinced it isn't you. Until then, I'm not taking any chances."

We drove through town in the failing light. Several of the storefronts displayed glowing jack-o'-lanterns, pulsing orange lights, and images of ghosts and spiders and bats and witches. The usual crowd of teenagers hung out in front of the liquor store; groups of smaller kids, decked out in sheets and face paint and green wigs, were already starting to make the rounds. We didn't see anyone dressed in a werewolf costume; given the real-life carnage that had been visited on the town that summer and fall, parents seemed to have opted for more benevolent apparitions: Madonna, Teenage Mutant Ninja Turtles, and innumerable relatives of Caspar the Friendly Ghost.

The old jail, a stone-cold relic of the town's dead past for 364 days of the year, had been completely transformed. Black lights illuminated the interior. Thick spiderwebs hung from the corners of the door, and inside, several shadowy figures cast monstrous silhouettes on the stone. A bloodied mannequin with an ax in its back leaned halfway out the one window, screaming silently into the night.

We parked in the lot between the Julian Motel and the building that housed the *Julian Nugget*, and walked up the stairs. But Gunn was not in the office. No one was, although the door was open and the lights were on. "Damn!" Moondog said. "He told me he would meet me here. Where the fuck did he go?"

Gunn's desk looked the way it always did. There were newspapers and magazines and memos and other papers scattered haphazardly over virtually its entire surface. The big chair was pushed back; one drawer was partially opened. Three empty beer bottles stood on the heating unit behind the desk. A tall can of Budweiser occupied the one bare spot on the desktop amid the papers.

"Where *is* he?" Moondog wondered aloud.

The computer, I noticed, was on. The words on the screen ended in mid-sentence. Gunn had been working on an editorial about maintenance problems at the school, how they endangered the students and reflected poorly on Steve Dakota's leadership. I walked over to the desk and picked up the beer can. It was half full.

"It looks like he's planning on coming back," I said.

As if on cue, the downstairs door opened, and footsteps

started up the stairs. "Here he comes!" Moondog whispered excitedly. "Want to know how to drive an editor crazy?" Keeping an eye on Sven, he moved over to Gunn's desk and picked up the phone.

"Mr. Turner?" he said, without dialing, as the footsteps drew nearer. "Yes, I think we've solved the mystery. I've got the werewolf right here. No, he hasn't changed yet, but . . . What's that? Yes, I've called all the major papers and television stations. This story is too big for the *Julian Nugget* . . ."

"Jesus Christ, you *are* crazy," Sven muttered.

"Yeah—get that camera crew here right away," Moondog said into the phone, ignoring Sven. "He's liable to change at any minute. The guy's half-werewolf already, if you ask me. He's *really* ugly."

Sven glared at him as the door to the office swung open.

"What's going on here?" said Stafford Emerson. Kathy Boles, looking small and frightened, stood beside him.

Moondog gently laid the phone back down in its cradle. "We thought it was Erik coming up the stairs," he said. "I was just trying to have a little fun, at his expense."

"Hell of a time to be playing jokes," Emerson remarked.

"He was supposed to meet us here," Moondog said. "Have you seen him?"

"Not since earlier today, when we were all here," Emerson replied. "We're looking for him ourselves. We've been kind of driving around, keeping our eyes open for anything unusual."

"Do you have any, uh, protection?" Moondog asked him. He nodded at Sven. "In case it isn't him?"

Kathy Boles reached into her purse; her hand emerged clutching a small shiny cross about three inches long. "I remembered I had this at home," she said. "It belonged to my mother. I *think* it's silver."

"In any case, a cross should keep us safe, right?" Emerson asked.

"It should," Moondog said. "Although information on all of this stuff is kind of sketchy. May I see it for a minute?"

Kathy handed him the small cross. Moondog walked over to Sven, and held the cross inches from his face.

"What do you think, Sven? This put the fear of God into you?"

Sven just stood there. "It's a cross. So what?"

Moondog leaned forward, and pressed the cross against Sven's forehead. I half-expected to see it burn the flesh and to hear Sven scream for mercy. Instead, after one or two seconds, Sven simply brushed Moondog's hand away.

"You are *really* out to lunch," Sven said.

"Hmm." Moondog handed the cross back to Kathy, who put it back into her purse. "It's conceivable that I'm wrong. What's the weather doing outside?"

"It's still spitting rain a little," Kathy informed him. "One minute it looks like it's going to clear, the next minute it's all socked in again. I haven't seen the Moon."

"What's our next move?" I asked.

"We'll go to the school," Moondog said. "That's where everything's happening."

"That's probably where Erik is, too," I said. "Remember, his wife was pissed at him when he said he couldn't go. Maybe she talked him into changing his mind."

"Can I go home now?" Sven asked.

Moondog turned to face him. "Like I said, I might be wrong. If I am, I apologize. But no one really knows about the cloud factor. For all I know, the clouds may be keeping you from changing. Or clouds might have no effect—which means that the real werewolf might have already transformed, and might be lurking around the school at this very moment, ready to rip apart a bunch of kids. I just don't know. And until I *do* know, I've got to keep you in my sight. Keep that gun handy, Joe."

Nervously, I patted the outside of my jacket.

He turned to Stafford Emerson and Kathy Boles. "Would you guys like to come?" he asked.

"We were thinking of heading over there anyway," Emerson said. "There's probably some food left." Kathy looked at him, and shuddered involuntarily.

Moondog sensed her trepidation. He reached inside the collar of his shirt. Unfastening the chain, he removed the pentagram trinket and handed it to her. "Here, wear this," he said. "No werewolf can harm you if you're wearing a silver pentagram. I *know* it's silver. It'll protect you a lot better than that cross."

She turned the medallion over in her hands. "What about you?"

"We've got the gun," Moondog said, and looked meaningfully at me. I swallowed dryly.

Kathy put the pentagram around her neck and we left the office, after Moondog scribbled a one-sentence note to Gunn and taped it onto the computer screen.

We stepped out into the windy, drizzly night—me, Emerson, Kathy Boles, Moondog, and Sven—never far from my concealed gun. Tiny waves, driven by the wind, crashed against the shores of numerous puddles in the parking lot and on the side of the street. Above Justin Zak's construction site, in the direction of the school, a blurry patch of brightness revealed where the Moon was, though we could not discern its shape behind the clouds. "Do we walk or drive?" I asked.

"We walk," Moondog answered. "We might miss something if we drive. Besides, there won't be any place to park over there."

We walked across the side street by the jail, where a group of straggling trick-or-treaters milled about, examining the ghoulish display. We crossed Main Street, climbed a steep driveway, passed in front of the darkened real estate office to which it led, and made our way onto a gravel pathway atop the embankment. The wind whipped at our clothing. Clouds scudded across the face of the Moon; at times it seemed almost ready to break through, at other times it was obliterated completely. In other parts of the sky, stars would occasionally peek out from temporary holes in the cloud cover, but they were always obscured within seconds. I fingered the gun inside my coat, praying that I would not have to use it, and kept a nervous eye on Sven.

The path was muddy in spots from the rain, and footing was tricky. To our left the trees closed in next to the path, and all of us stole glances into the darkness between them. To our right and about twenty feet below lay the street, and beyond that the post office and a rolling, open field kept cropped by the cattle that grazed there. The few trees in the field waved their leafless branches crazily in the wind against the silvery sky, their shadows fading in and out as the clouds rushed past the still-obscured face of the Moon.

The path came out behind the high school baseball field, which lay deserted. Only the day before, the Oakland Athletics had completed a World Series sweep of the San Francisco Giants following ten days off in the wake of an earthquake. No one in Julian had paid much attention to the second all-California Fall Classic in two years—the town had its own dramas to follow.

The parking lot at the school was filled with station wagons, Toyota Land Cruisers, and other family vehicles. Two matronly old witches, their costumes augmented by pillows inside oversized stretch pants, stood at the entrance to the school hawking tickets. Having the Halloween carnival at the school served the dual purpose of getting the kids off the streets and keeping the campus from being too badly vandalized. I thought back to the Halloweens of my youth, and reflected on how much things had changed. There had been an element of viciousness to those evenings back then, especially toward institutions of authority, of which the school was the most prominent in our lives. A certain amount of wanton destruction was to be expected; fire-crackers thrown through classroom windows in the dark and buckets of paint thrown splashing doorsteps, walls, and playground weren't unusual fare. Halloween was the night we got to practice being hoodlums, and if we knew where our teachers lived and could reach their residences on foot, we hoped that they trembled in fear.

The two hags grinned at us as we approached the ticket booth. "Welcome, welcome," one of them cackled. She had a long, taped-on nose, with a prominent red wart at the end; it bobbed up and down when she talked.

"Do we have to pay to get in?" I asked.

"You have to buy tickets for food, and to enter the contests," the first hag said.

"We're just here to look for somebody," I said. "Erik Gunn. Have you seen him?"

"I haven't," said the second witch. "His wife and his little girl were here, though. *We're* wondering where the superintendent is. He's hours late."

"Mind if we just look around?"

"Sure you don't want to buy some tickets? You ought to at least try the cakewalk. There's a bunch of good-looking cakes in there."

"We'll come back if we need any," I told her.

Emerson pulled several crumpled dollar bills from a pants pocket. "How many tickets to eat?" he asked.

"Depends," the witch told him. "They're four for a dollar. Six'll get you some nachos and a soda."

"Let me have five bucks' worth," he said. "We might play some games."

Emerson and Kathy headed for the gym, or the multipurpose room, as it was called, where the cakewalk was being held, food was being served, and tables had been laid out for eating. Moondog, Sven, and I made our way through the crowd of costumed children, some of whom were accompanied by costumed and uncostumed adults.

Each classroom had created its own game room or chamber of horrors; crowds in front of each spilled out onto the playground. The longest line was at the far end of the building, for the haunted house in the two connected kindergarten rooms. We could hear the screams and peals of delighted laughter from inside the papered-over windows, behind which we could see the strobe lights pulsing. "Oh, man, I can't wait to go in there!" one boy of about eight, dressed as a dinosaur, said excitedly to his friend, a Frankenstein monster of sorts. The dinosaur's tail was fully as long as the boy was tall; it dragged behind him and sported a generous coating of mud on the underside of the bright green material.

As we watched, the side door to the kindergarten building opened, and a stream of scared but laughing children in costume poured out into the night. The front of the line tensed and jittered in anticipation; the next group was about to be admitted into the chamber of horrors. But just then there was a ferocious gust of wind, and a moment later we stood in the middle of a torrential downpour—cold, slashing rain that stung the face of anyone who looked up into it.

Several people screamed, and almost everyone ran for cover, so sudden and violent was the onset of the storm. A few kids at the front of the line pushed their way into the haunted house, past the startled teacher at the door. The schoolhouse roof overhung the building by perhaps a foot, and several kids squeezed themselves up against the wall in a vain attempt to stay dry.

"Let's get out of here!" I yelled into Moondog's ear, as the rain beat down and chaos reigned all around us. People were pushing and shoving their way toward any open door available; those classrooms that faced the playground were soon filled with drenched adults and children, their muddied feet sliding over the linoleum. I pulled at Moondog's arm and pointed to the gym. "In there!" I cried, above the noise of the rain. He turned to me, nodded once, and followed.

By the time we got to shelter we were both soaked. Beads of water dripped off my hair and ran down my face and neck and into my shirt. Twin streams trailed off the ends of Moondog's mustache.

Inside the gym, out of the rain, the carnival continued as if nothing had happened. The room was packed; music and the din of scores of conversations kept the noise at a festive level. At the front corner, away from the door, fifteen or so costumed kids of varying heights paraded slowly around a roped-off circle as tinny big-band music blared from two small speakers connected to a tape player on a table. A young woman too old for elementary school but nonetheless dressed in a rabbit suit pressed a button. The music stopped, and so did the marchers. The rabbit-woman walked over to a large, homemade wheel of fortune, and gave it a spin. "Nine!" she called out, as the wheel came to a stop.

This was the cakewalk, and a small boy in a spacesuit, standing on square number nine, was the winner. His mother clapped her hands excitedly, and led him to the row of tables lined up against the far wall, where cakes of all sizes and colors were laid out for all to see. Every parent in Julian must have baked a cake, there were so many of them. Meanwhile the rabbit-woman handed out lollipops to the losers, and prepared to start the game again.

242

I spotted Stafford Emerson and Kathy Boles at one of the tables, giving their full attention to an order of nachos; looking around, I saw Joyce Gunn, holding her daughter's hand, in conversation with another mother. Derek and Cindy's two boys were running around in the middle of the room, dressed as—what else?—camouflage-clad guerrillas.

I felt Moondog's elbow in my ribs. "Where's Sven?" he growled.

Sudden panic. I whipped my head around, looking frantically in all directions. But he was gone. He'd ditched us. "Damn!" I cried. "I lost sight of him when it started raining!"

"It's not raining now," said a man beside me, tall, stout, and bearded, wearing a raincoat and a cowboy hat. "She stopped pretty quick after everybody ran inside. Like someone turned off a faucet." He laughed and removed his hat, shaking the water off of it.

"Come on!" Moondog grabbed my arm and pulled me roughly toward the door. "Excuse me. Excuse me," he called, pushing through the crowd. People stumbled to get out of the way.

The air temperature had dropped at least five degrees in five minutes, but the man was right—the storm had stopped as suddenly as it had begun. I felt the cold slap of the wind in my face as we escaped from the body heat of the gym. I looked into the sky and saw fast-moving gray clouds, stretched thin by the wind, breaking into wispy filaments and tearing apart like bedsheets, leaving gaps of clear sky between. And one of those gaps was opening up in the east, over the playground, in the bright part of the sky. Moondog and I hurried away from the crowd by the door, out from under the covered walkway, where we could see. At that moment the wind pushed the last gray cloud from in front of the Moon, and the playground was bathed in light.

"Hey! Asshole!"

We turned.

"Yeah! You! Moonbeam, whatever your name is! So I'm a werewolf, huh! So I'm a beast of the night! Ah, hahahaha!"

One-legged Sven, looking one hundred percent human, stood at the top of the jungle gym, swaying in the wind and waving his arms wildly in the air. "Ah, hahahaha!" Several people emerged from the gym and the nearby classrooms at the sound of his crazy laughter.

"Look at me!" he screamed. "I'm a werewolf! See my claws? See my fangs? The full Moon makes me wanna KILL! Ah, hahahaha! Ah-oooooooh!"

"What the fuck is wrong with *him?*" someone said, behind us.

"Must be drunk," said another onlooker.

"Or out of his gourd on crystal," said another.

"And the first person I'm gonna kill," Sven went on, pointing an accusing finger at Moondog, "is that fucker over there!" He lifted his head, and howled at the Moon again.

"Ah-oooooooh!" someone howled back.

Moondog and I looked at one another. *That* cry hadn't come from the playground.

Sven crouched, and leaped from the top of the jungle gym. He stumbled, fell to one knee, and righted himself. Pretty agile, I thought, for a guy with one leg. He was breathing hard. "Come on, motherfucker," he said to Moondog. "Gonna teach you not to fuck with me."

"Ah-oooooooh!"

This time, everybody near us looked around. The howl had come from somewhere in the woods behind the school.

Sven took a step toward Moondog and pushed him, not too hard, in the chest. For all his bluster, he plainly wanted Moondog to throw the first punch. A small crowd began to gather, anticipating the confrontation.

But those who wanted to see a fistfight would be disappointed. From the direction of the parking lot, a tall man, wearing a black western hat, Lone Ranger mask, and cowboy duds complete with spurs, pushed through the crowd. With him were sheriff's deputies Kevin Byars and Frank Blaisdell, and the two hags from the ticket booth.

"Oh, good," I heard one of the adults nearby say. "Dakota's here. He'll handle this."

"We were worried about you, Mr. Dakota," said one of the witches.

"There was an accident on the way up here," said the Lone Superintendent. "Down near Inaja. A coyote ran out in front of someone, and when he slammed on his brakes the next two cars rear-ended him. I was three cars back."

"Anybody hurt?"

"It looked like it. They brought LifeFlight in, and sent the rest of us around the long way. Now, what's all this about?"

"Werewolves, I think," someone said.

Dakota glared at Moondog. "I might have known you'd show up here tonight and try to cause trouble," he said.

"What I'm trying to do," Moondog said softly, "is *prevent* trouble. You're all in grave danger."

Joyce Gunn came up behind Sven and took him by the arm. "Come on, Sven, let's get out of here," she said. "He isn't worth it." Reluctantly, Sven allowed himself to be led away.

Dakota made a short speech, telling everyone to go back to their games and food and conversations, that the carnival still had an hour to run and he hoped people would enjoy themselves and drive home safely. A good number of people, deciding they'd had enough excitement for one Halloween, gathered their children and headed for their cars.

The Moon shone down on the school grounds through the ever-widening hole in the clouds; a few of the brighter stars were visible also. With a start, I realized that I was trembling. I felt very cold, and not because of the night air.

When order was restored, Steve Dakota turned back to Moondog. "I want you out of here," the superintendent said.

"What?" I cried, before I could stop myself.

"Joe, is this guy with you?"

"He's with me," Moondog said.

"I won't have you running around here frightening everyone," Dakota told Moondog. "You have one minute to get off the school grounds."

"All right, we're going," Moondog said. "What we're looking for doesn't seem to be here anyway. Come on, Joe."

"What now, Moondog?" I asked him as we walked across the parking lot, stepping around the puddles. The sky was rapidly clearing. The Moon now rode high in the east, and in its half of the sky there were practically no clouds at all.

"Back to the *Nugget* office, I guess," he said. "Probably Gunn's back there by now. Shit, he missed all the excitement."

But at that moment, from somewhere up on the wooded hill behind the school, there came a howl so guttural, so tortured and filled with bloodlust, and most of all so inhuman, that all who heard it, including Moondog and me, froze. Borne on the wind, it seemed to rend the very fabric of the night. The terrible cry hung in the air for many seconds, then ceased abruptly.

Parents in the parking lot hustled their children into their cars. I looked wildly at my friend. "Moondog, do you think—"

"Quiet!" he hissed. "Do you still have the gun?"

"Of course I still have it. But we can't—"

Another howl shrieked from the moonlit woods. I shuddered violently.

"He's somewhere on the hill behind the playground," Moondog whispered. "Come on!"

"Moondog, let's get out of here!" I urged.

"Joe, there are still a lot of kids here!" he said. He was walking rapidly now, toward the chain-link fence behind the school, pulling me along with him. "He's close! Come on!"

"Moondog, what if it's somebody playing a joke?"

A third howl, as terrifying as the first two, split the night.

"That's no joke," Moondog said grimly. And a moment later he was climbing the bank behind the fence, bushwhacking his way between the trees. I had no choice but to follow him.

After several minutes we came out on a muddy, narrow dirt road that ran along the crest of the hill. On the other side of the hill was an abandoned mine site to which the road eventually led. Directly ahead of us was a clear area at the top of the hill, with a bird's-eye view of the school grounds.

Moondog stopped, and cupped his hands around his mouth. Facing the top of the hill, and the Moon, he let out a long, melodious howl.

And a moment later, on the bare spot atop the hill, a large, dark creature emerged from the shadows into the glow of the moonlight!

Even from a distance, we could see its haunches and the profile of its powerful canine jaw. But it was bigger than any dog I had ever seen, and as it raised its huge head I thought I could see its muscles rippling.

"Holy shit!" I breathed. I reached inside my jacket for the gun.

But Moondog put his hand over mine. "He's too far away," he said. "We've got to distract him, get him away from the school."

Moondog lifted his head to the sky, and emitted a bloodcurdling howl that must have been heard from Inaja to Lake Cuyamaca. It echoed in the stillness of the night.

A moment later, another answering howl came from the beast on the top of the hill.

Moondog stepped out into the road, in full view, and howled again.

"Come on, Joe," he growled urgently. "Run!"

He didn't need to say it twice. I have never run so fast in my life. We sprinted downhill along the road, feet slipping in the mud but keeping our balance, and as I ran I looked over my shoulder to see that the large black thing was bounding down the road toward us!

The road twisted away from the school and into a no-man's-land behind the town site. I knew there was an old mine back here somewhere, but I did not know where the nearly forgotten road met the streets of town, or whether we would make it to safety before the monster closed the distance between us. We ran through a small hollow and up a rise, and suddenly we were out of the woods. Across a long, rolling field were the lights of several houses at the edge of the town.

"Come on!" Moondog said, and pulled me off the road. We ran across the field, at the edge of the trees, trying to stay in the shadows. But the lights were a long way away. If we could reach them, we would be three blocks behind Main Street—three blocks from the safety of Moondog's truck.

But the moonlight had played tricks with our depth perception. We were less than halfway across the field when the trees at its edge abruptly fell away into a steep ravine. We now had two choices: pick our way through the trees along the steep edge of the embankment, or risk a mad dash across the open field in the full glare of the full Moon.

We stopped to listen. For a moment the only sounds I could hear were my own breathing and the pounding of my heart. Gradually I became aware of the wind, and of a rushing sound in the trees below us that sounded like a small stream.

"Maybe we lost him," I panted.

"Don't bet on it," said Moondog. "He's around here some-

248

where. He's avoiding the lights." He lifted his head and howled again.

Suddenly I thought I saw movement in the trees. I wasn't sure whether I heard bushes rustling, saw the shadows change, or *smelled* something out of the ordinary, but I felt a presence near us. I thought I felt the touch of a warm breeze on the back of my neck. The taste of fear, in the back of my throat all evening, moved forward onto my tongue.

"Moondog!" I whispered hoarsely. "What was that?"

"What was what?" he whispered back.

We were near the edge of the embankment. He turned to face me.

"Did you hear something?"

He shook his head. I remember him standing there like that, alert and upright, bathed in moonlight. Though his face was half-shrouded in shadow, I could observe in the way he stood that he felt excitement rather than fear. He stood erect, his head tilted to one side, listening to the silence of the still-young Southern California mountains. The moonlight accented every branch of the pine trees on the hillsides that surrounded us; it caught the rocky outcroppings, the patches of bare ground, and the small open area near the creek down below. But it seemed to be shining most brilliantly on the figure of Cyrus "Moondog" Nygerski, standing there in a scene of his own creation, in a moment of his own making.

I sensed that he was about to say something, but he didn't have time.

For the hills shook with a roar that neither Moondog nor any other human could have manufactured, and a split second later Moondog was tumbling over the embankment, locked in a deadly embrace with a huge, fur-covered animal!

I think I heard him scream, once, before the creature roared again. I saw something fly through the air—and I remembered with sickening clarity that Moondog had given his pentagram to Kathy Boles. I saw Moondog land on his back in a bush, and I saw his attacker—blacker than I had imagined, with pronounced haunches and a head that was more ferocious, more demonically singleminded, than any wolf's—rear up on its hind legs and come toward him.

*"Shoot him!"* Moondog screamed, in pure panic.

But the hideous beast roared again, and leapt on top of him. Scrambling down the bank, the gun already in my hand, I could see the moonlight glinting off the werewolf's slavering jaws as they gaped wide and descended toward Moondog's throat. I aimed the gun and fired. The shot went several feet wide and might have hit a tree; the werewolf ignored it completely. Moondog screamed in raw terror as the beast's horrible teeth came down on him.

I landed heavily at the bottom of the bank, perhaps ten yards away from them. I felt my ankle twist sharply beneath my weight, and grimaced in pain. The werewolf's jaws were open and dripping a mixture of saliva and blood; its head wavered in the air above my prostrate friend. I rose to my knees, steadied myself as best I could, and fired into the creature's chest.

The werewolf reared backward with the impact of the blast, roaring in agony. I leveled the gun to fire again, but I saw that it was falling . . . falling off Moondog, falling backward with the momentum of the bullet, losing its footing. The roar became a screech, then a wheeze, and finally a gurgle. The beast thrashed at the air with its giant forepaws and collapsed onto its back. Its hind legs kicked reflexively two or three times, and then it was still.

Suddenly it was deathly quiet. The wind stirred the tops of the trees, but did not reach down into the ravine in which we had landed. The babbling of the small creek, now very close to us, seemed deafening. The stream was hours old, born in that day's rain after lying dry all summer.

"Joe . . ." Moondog called out weakly. "Joe, help me."

I dragged myself over to him, my ankle screaming in pain. One side of his leather jacket was covered with blood. "Help me get this off," he said.

It was hard, because he couldn't move one arm at all, and when I got him out of the jacket I saw why. There was a gaping wound just below the shoulder. Blood poured from it onto the ground. I took off his bloodstained shirt and wrapped it tightly around the wound, tying it off in back.

"Can you stand?" I asked him.

"I think so," he said.

"I'm not sure I can."

We helped each other struggle to our feet. I leaned on Moondog's uninjured shoulder as we struggled over to where the dead werewolf lay on the underbrush, a wet red hole in its furry chest.

"Nice shot, Joe," Moondog murmured.

"But who *is* it?" I asked. "Look, it's got two full legs."

"Wait a bit. It'll change."

And sure enough, over the next hour or so, the body on the ground, clad only in a pair of torn blue jeans, slowly began to lose its unnatural, horrific features. One minute a fingernail would be black and pointed, and the next time I looked it would be clear and curved. Ever so gradually the black fur began to lighten and disappear. The haunches became smooth, the canine jaw receded back into the face, the gnarled claws shrank back into fingers. We sat on opposite sides of the body, silent in the silent moonlight, watching and waiting. The muscles of the legs shrank, but the creature remained long-limbed. The teeth in the open mouth became duller and less pointed. The hair receded from shoulders, back, feet, hands, face—and from the top of the head. I gasped in recognition at the body of Erik Gunn.

We sat there for hours, staring at the corpse of our dead friend. Neither of us said a word. Apparently no one had heard the shots, or those who heard them had thought first of the preservation of their own skins, for at no time did we hear the presence of human or animal anywhere near us. The Moon reached the height of its arc and began its descent, its summer of horror for its slave at our feet finally over. Another reign of terror was perhaps soon to begin, but we would not speak of that tonight.

It was Moondog who finally broke the silence. "Joe, you're going to have to drive me home," he said. "I can't move my arm."

"Do you think it's safe?" I asked quietly.

"It doesn't matter," Moondog said. "It must be past midnight by now. We can't stay here."

"But what about him?" I said, nodding toward Gunn's body. A stupendous amount of blood had seeped onto the ground around the corpse, apparently from the exit wound in his back.

"Leave him," Moondog said. "There's nothing we can do for him now. But we ought to find the bullet."

"What?"

"You've got to get the bullet. It should be under his body somewhere. Or next to it."

"Moondog, what the—"

"We can't leave a silver bullet lying around," he said. "They'll find the body. They'll ask a lot of questions. A guy like Gunn, in a town like this, he makes a few enemies. To the cops, it'll look like a straight-ahead murder. But if they find a silver bullet, they'll know it had something to do with us."

It was hard to dispute his logic. And I did indeed find the bullet, after about half an hour's search, despite my revulsion at poking around a corpse, and my paranoia that someone would come wandering across the field in the dead of night. It had gone completely through the werewolf's body—Gunn's body—and landed about twenty feet from where he'd been standing when I shot him. I held out my hand and showed it to Moondog.

"Joe, did you fire two shots?" he asked.

I flashed back to the attack. I *had* fired twice. The first shot had been a clean miss when I was scrambling down the bank.

"It went into the trees," I told him. "They won't find that first bullet in fifty years."

"You better hope they don't," Moondog said. "Or we're both in big trouble."

It was a struggle to climb out of there with my injured ankle and most of Moondog's weight on my shoulder. I didn't know how much blood he'd lost, but he was weak and barely able to walk. We slunk undetected across the field and back into town. It was late, late, late—no one was on the streets at all. The truck was right where we had left it.

I helped him into the passenger side, and got in behind the wheel. "The keys are in my jacket," he said. "In the right-hand pocket." I fished them out, and laid the bloodied jacket on the seat between us. Moondog slumped against the back of the seat and closed his eyes.

"I sure hope," he said weakly, "they never find that second bullet."

"They won't," I said, and started the engine. Without another word, I aimed the truck toward the highway and drove out of Julian, down past Sleepy Hollow and Inaja Memorial Park, and on into the moonlit night.

# Chapter Thirty-two

"JOE, IF I were you, I'd get the fuck out of here."

We were sitting on Moondog's spacious back porch; the late-afternoon Sun accented the small dips and rises in the rolling cattle land that fell away toward a row of pine trees in the distance. His arm was dressed and bandaged—I'd done a fair job of it—and my sore ankle was propped up in front of me on a pillow. Moondog's supply of beer was good for another day or two, and then one or both of us would have to go into town.

"It was Gunn all along," I said. "Do you think he knew?"

Moondog leaned back in his chair, took a swig of beer, and pondered my question. "No," he said at length. "No, I think his skepticism was real. I don't think he was using it to hide behind. Most werewolves don't know they're werewolves until their behavior becomes so hard to explain or reconcile that they guess the truth. And he'd only been a werewolf since June."

"I wonder if his wife knew. I wonder if that's why she left him."

Moondog looked off into the distance and laughed quietly.

"And I thought it was Sven," he said. "What we forgot was that Gunn was lame, too. Remember that day he almost fell over in the office, walking to the refrigerator? But I kind of doubt his wife found out. She was never home, and he was always in the office. If they'd seen more of one another, she probably would've been the first person he killed. It's strange that she survived, and Patsy Kittredge died."

"Why?" I asked.

"Because he had a crush on Patsy. I think he imagined himself in love with her. Sometimes that's strong enough even to overcome the driving instinct to kill. There are stories of werewolves who spare their loved ones and then go out on a murderous rampage."

"Maybe he was really in love with his wife," I speculated, "but only his werewolf side knew it. He was a complicated man."

"I know it. He had a lot of internal conflict."

"But how do you suppose he became a werewolf in the first place?" I asked.

"Who knows?" Moondog said. "Maybe something happened during that trip he took in June. He went up and down the state, traveled all over California. And this state has a lot of strange people in it. Probably one or two of them are werewolves. Maybe one bit him."

At this Moondog grew silent, and stared off at the mountains to the east, in the direction of Julian. I knew what he was thinking, for I was thinking it too, though we had not yet discussed it. The question hung in the air between us.

"I wouldn't stick around if I were you," he said again, not looking at me. "You and I know that Erik Gunn was a werewolf, but to the people who count, he's another unsolved murder. And both of us are connected to him. I'm sure they've found the body by now. Soon, perhaps tomorrow or the next day, the cops will be out here, and they'll be asking a lot of questions. The ugliness is far from over. If I were you, I'd get as far away from Julian as possible."

"Moondog, what about you?" I asked.

"I'll be all right," he said. "I can take the heat. I took it before, when Patsy died. They may suspect me because of what I've written, but they have no evidence. Besides, *you* pulled the trigger."

"That's not what I meant," I said softly.

Moondog took a long pull on his beer, and said nothing.

"He bit you," I said.

He looked at me, his dark eyes hard and inscrutable. "I'll be all right," he repeated.

"How can you say that?" I cried. "With what you know?"

Moondog got to his feet. "How many houses do you see around here?" he asked me.

"Well . . . none."

"Exactly. In fact, my nearest neighbors live more than five miles away. And they can be warned. They can hang pentagrams and garlic wreaths. Probably some of them already do. Did I ever tell you about the wolf cult in Ranchita?"

"No."

"Strange bunch. But tuned in when it comes to occult stuff. Listen, I'll be safe here. So will the town. I'll be careful. The worst I'll do is tear apart a few cattle each month. No one will miss a bunch of dead cows."

I was aware that my jaw had dropped and that I was staring at him in incredulity. I doubt if anyone else I'd ever met would have taken the prospect of becoming a werewolf so calmly.

"And, like I said, if things don't work out here, there's always Alaska," he continued. "You wouldn't believe the wide open spaces up there, Joe. Maybe it's where I'm meant to be. Among the moose and the caribou . . . and the wolves."

256

He turned to go into the house. "But, Joe, I'm serious. This place is dead for you. You're still new here, and after all that's happened, you'll never be accepted. People will whisper behind your back if you live here another thirty years. And thirty years is too long to live anywhere. Besides"—he flashed me a toothy grin—"I know where you live. You want another beer?"

It is winter now, in this little village on the Sea of Cortez, near the southern tip of the Baja peninsula. It has taken me two months to learn to pronounce the town's name. My Spanish is improving little by little. The climate is wonderful in its never-ending sunny sameness, and many of the American tourists who come down to get away from the snow need a guide or a transla-tor, for which they are willing to pay. Many others leave objects of value lying around carelessly.

They are the only contact I've had with my native country since I shook hands with Moondog over the flimsy barbed-wire fence at Jacumba, and climbed into the dilapidated pickup truck driven by one of his Mexican friends. I don't even know whether or not I'm wanted for murder, nor do I dare risk a letter to my sister in Oregon, who disowned me when I went to the honor camp. But it's a pretty good life here, not too strenuous or serious; there is music at night, and food, drink, and people who have become my friends.

And yet part of me remains in Julian, that little California mountain town whose wealth was never realized, whose reck-lessness was never tamed, whose past collided with present and evil with good in jarring impacts that prevented complete mix-ing.

And part of me remains with Cyrus "Moondog" Nygerski, the most unforgettable character I've ever met, who now faces the greatest struggle of his life. The Moon is waxing again; in just a few days it will be full. I wonder what it feels like to have one's

257

blood boil with violence, under the pitiless eye of Artemis, Diana, and the other names we have given to our beautiful but cruel sister in the sky. Part of me wants to wander those austerely beautiful Southern California mountains again, to smell their pines and cedars, to leap from rock to rugged rock, to see their arid contours as they are seen best, in the black and white of shadow and moonlight.

For it is in black and white that the human soul is most clearly revealed. We are all of us creatures of light, and of darkness.